GIRLS WITH LONG SHADOWS

GIRLS WITH LONG SHADOWS

A NOVEL

TENNESSEE HILL

HARPER

An Imprint of HarperCollins*Publishers*

GIRLS WITH LONG SHADOWS. Copyright © 2025 by Tennessee Hill. All rights reserved. Printed in the United States of America. No part of this book may be used or reproduced in any manner whatsoever without written permission except in the case of brief quotations embodied in critical articles and reviews. For information, address HarperCollins Publishers, 195 Broadway, New York, NY 10007.

HarperCollins books may be purchased for educational, business, or sales promotional use. For information, please email the Special Markets Department at SPsales@harpercollins.com.

FIRST EDITION

Library of Congress Cataloging-in-Publication Data has been applied for.

ISBN 978-0-06-341201-9

25 26 27 28 29 LBC 5 4 3 2 1

To Mom & Dad

CONTENTS

GIRLS WITH LONG SHADOWS

PART I

[ENTER] FRONT PORCH CHORUS

There never was a gator killing around here, contrary to everlasting rumor, and there was only one real murder, but it seems each bad thing that happens is like an incantation invoking the Binderup family, its women and their dying. We talk about the group of them when we say *her*. We light their candles when the power goes out, and we find their golf balls washed up in our yards when the bayou swells with storms.

When she was gone, we searched the world over, and in those days without her, we didn't hardly know what to do.

BABY BABY BABY

Baby A diluted Coppertone sunscreen with lilac craft glitter and coconut oil; Baby C rubbed it over her shoulders and mine as Gram ribboned her breaststroke through the murky bayou water in an elaborate weave. We watched, my sisters' and my identical bodies sprawled in different ways along the dock, baking in the sun, kicking at the water surface.

I rolled a clementine across the dock to my sister. "Read my future, Baby C."

She rolled it back. "You've gotta eat the whole thing first."

I dug my nail into the rough skin and peeled, popping small wedges into my mouth.

There wasn't much orange to eat. Our trees seemed to only produce paltry fruit, even after we'd read up on how to tend them properly. Eventually we gave up and left the trees to do their natural business. The citric smell had always settled sourly to me anyway, like diesel fuel or sick puppy dog ears. "There." I dropped the peel rind-side down, a web of fibrous thins.

Baby C sat up, pulled her sunglasses off as she studied the spongey white pith, touching spots lightly, then looking at me as if she were connecting dots into an elusive picture. Her skin was reddening; the bridges of our noses always caught the most burn.

"You're going to live a long life," she began.

"I already know that."

She looked at me with a near-humorous affront. "How can you know that?"

I shrugged. "I just do."

"Don't be so sure." She pushed her sunglasses up to frame her forehead. "And don't interrupt me. So you're going to live a long life. You'll be happy most of the time, but trials will come. You'll have kids—two or maybe three if you have twins. I see two births but three babies. You'll marry someone, and they'll be good to you."

"Well, I'd demand that much."

"Shhhh. All else I can see is that you won't be a better swimmer than you are now, certainly never better than me."

I thudded my hand flatly against her upper arm and she laughed, placing the orange peel over my mouth like a muzzle, then loomed over me, pulled her sunglasses back to cover her eyes. "This life is yours, B. Don't screw it up."

I brought her hand to my face, holding it open as if I were looking deeply into it for clues about her impending life, fated babies and fated spouse. Then I gave her palm a long, quick lick. She pulled away and lay down beside me, both of us laughing, her sweat dissolving against my tongue. Our very own voice interrupted us.

"Which one of you is going to take on my shed painting so I can meet Rich on his lunch break?" Baby A was lying nearby on the dock but not playing with us, serious about her suntan. The water sloshed audibly, an algae-heavy brown edged with weeds and weighty twigs. I looked over at Baby A, betting she was trying to imagine Rich Goodson's hands, grimy with shrimp guts from shelling tails at the Shrimp Shack, on her thighs, her shoulders. Goose bumps constellated her chest like a painful rash.

"As for her . . . ," Baby C said with a grin.

"As for me, what?"

"Give me your hand."

Baby A stalled, holding her right hand still as if she were deciding whether or not to give it away forever.

"Go on," I urged.

Baby A flopped her hand over, limp at the wrist as Baby C dragged her fingernail along our sister's damp palm. The tickle from Baby C's nail against Baby A's skin sent a shiver through my own hand. I flexed my fingers in an effort to coax the surge away. A bead of sweat dripped from Baby C's nose and splashed against the dock, coloring the sun-bleached wood a delicious amber. "Just as I thought." Baby C sighed dramatically for effect. "Dead as a doornail by twenty-eight."

"Twenty-eight!" Baby A shrieked, withdrawing her hand.

"I just read 'em. Can't blame me. It's right there, darlin'."

"Darlin'?" I chuckled.

Baby A relished in her scowling. "Oh screw off."

I pulled her palm toward me, stretching it taut with my thumbs. The life line carved out her thumb like a trench, and as I blinked into it, I realized I'd never looked intently at it before. Baby C was right: Baby A's line stopped quite short, feathering out into nothingness after two inches. A lump formed in my throat that I swallowed. "No, no. This is at least thirty-five."

Baby A yanked herself back, eyebrows furled as she tried to discern the thin line beyond the blind of sunshine. "What if I ran my hand along the rusty side of the dock ladder? Would it change?" Her tone was even and her legs shone with the sheen of glittery sunscreen. She stood, walked to the dock ladder that hung just hardly to the wood like a loosened tooth, and hovered her palm above.

"Come on," I said. "We're too far away from the first aid kit."

"And blood is really difficult to get out of wood," Baby C added.

"You'll live to be just as old as me," I offered with a laugh. "Promise."

After moving her hand about, she settled above a sharp, browned fang of metal that folded behind the back of the ladder handle I'd spotted many seconds before and hoped she wouldn't see. "What if I don't want that?"

Baby C rolled her eyes, bored. "What *do* you want, crazy lady?" Baby A touched her skin to the sharp part and began to lightly press.

"Well? Tell us. Wanna live forever?" I propped myself up on both elbows. "We could make that happen, I'm sure. There's got to be a witch or two in this town."

"Few willful drunks, at least." Baby C cracked her neck with a deft snap.

Across the way, an egret balanced on the Kinners' bulkhead, dipping its ecru head in the water, emerging with a small fish. Baby A, beginning to press herself farther into the sharp edge, glanced between the two of us. "Paint the toolshed without me."

Predictable. I let my elbows wilt as I lowered myself back flat against the dock. "It's going to take hours as it is."

"Days," Baby C corrected.

"Days!" I echoed. "Instead, how about a solid salt-and-pepper fifty? Or like, sixty-five with a stylish cane?"

I could tell Baby C was participating in but not watching our sister's temper tantrum; the sun she stared into instead burned her eyes, and because it burned hers, it burned mine. We both sneezed. Baby A did not bless us. Instead, she began to drag her palm slowly against the metal with precision, like eyeliner along an eyelid. I flashed to phrases Baby C often muttered to herself: *Manifest YOU. Fulfillment IS.* I'd never known, even after she tried to tell me, what they were supposed to mean.

"God. Would you stop it?"

We knew she hadn't broken the skin yet but that she was preparing to. Sweat cascaded down her legs like beads of urine. "Shed."

"No way."

"Shed!"

"Why don't I go meet Rich, and you paint for *me*?" I hoped humor might coax her away from the manic temptation gripping her. "He can't tell the difference anyway."

"Oh honey—" She darted her eyes up at me, still hunched over the ladder. "You could never play-pretend me."

I scoffed. "Course I could. We both could. We do it every day. I could count the people who can tell us apart on one hand. And"—I angled my eyes to match hers, tinged with meanness—"*honey*. Your Rich is not on one of them."

Baby A stood upright as if shocked, glaring between Baby C and me. "My eyes have flecks of green in them, you assholes."

"He told you that?" Baby C laughed.

"You know what he's trying to do, right?" I added.

Baby A twisted her toe against the foam of her flip-flop, and before she could reply, I shouted, "You!"

Baby A's face washed with a blip of fury; she bent quickly back over the ladder and swiped her hand clean open against the metal edge, then outstretched her bleeding hand in our faces like a crossing guard. "I hope you two fucking fry." She grabbed the library copy of *Big Fish* I'd been cradling against my chest and stepped across the grass toward the clubhouse, cursing us.

Baby C and I had gripped the bases of our palms instinctively, hoping the pain that pulsed through her wouldn't reach us. Sometimes I thought we almost liked how quick Baby A was to anger, how easy it was to provoke her into unrest. But we were never quite satisfied with her reactions, too extreme to be funny or too privately held to be worth the silent treatments we'd endure for days. She'd ride out her anger for the sake of it, to avoid admitting she was wrong or had forgiven us. I watched her silhouette move farther and farther away until she neared the clubhouse where our little brother Gull was sitting on a lawn chair, lapping water from the hose like a pup. Baby A tossed my book through the stream of heavy water and walked inside. Poor Gull scrambled up, then hoisted the recovered book in the air, waving it at me from so far away. I didn't need to squint to know the pages were soaked and I'd have to go at it with a hair dryer.

"Your book is halfway to ruin now," Baby C said.

"The library will have another copy."

"It's true about the years. Twenty-eight at the latest." There was a look of shame on her face for making a joke of it before.

"Yeah, but that's light-years away."

"Nine years is light-years?"

"Yeah." I shrugged. "Like dog years for dogs."

"She's spinning her wheels on Rich. That weird boy."

"He's just . . . odd. Not weird. Weird is like, keeps a lock of your hair under his pillow. He's just, stares at you in the parking lot."

"No, he's like, deer blood on his face at a football game."

"That was only the one time. And it was the Deer Park game. Made sense."

"Once was enough for me to know he's batshit."

"But so is she. Maybe they're perfect for each other?"

Baby C smiled, remembering. "God, it was awful," she huffed. "Do you remember that smell?"

They'd been dating for months, and Rich had yet to come over to the clubhouse, even on the weekends that his buddies played a round with the tip money they pooled. Rich didn't address us when we saw him around town, cowering in confusion until Baby A—his Binderup triplet girl—emerged from our lineup to rush toward him. Even though she liked to play like she was, Baby A wasn't a fool; there was no quality in our eyes for distinction. If we walked toward Rich in a huddle and she didn't declare herself as the one that was his, he would let us walk right past, too unsure to take a guess.

"How long do you think they'll last?" I asked.

Baby C exhaled. "I try not to think about it."

It seemed just as soon as Baby C and I turned our heads at the sound of movement through the water, Gram was pulling herself wetly up the dock ladder. I handed her the towel I lay on, admiring the lazy wrap of her hips as she tucked the stray cloth edge into her swimsuit band. "Where's the other one?" she asked.

We were level at Gram's feet, red toenail polish glinting upward. I thought for a moment she might have stepped through a drop of Baby A's blood.

"She's in a rage." Baby C strummed at Gram's toes like they were harp strings.

"It'll pass." Gram stepped into flip-flops and paused, her fingers lingering against the pulse of her neck. I watched the bayou water rivulet down her throat. My body tensed as hers did, though Gram tried to be casual about catching her breath. "I'll put her to polishing those clubs instead of Gull," she said. After a few moments, she dropped her fingers and seemed to steady.

Gull would be hard pressed to trade off his favorite chore. He loved polishing clubs. Moreover, he loved helping Baby A, especially when she was transfixed with anger. He wanted nothing more than to please, toting around quarters in case anyone was short for the vending machine, engaging elderly men who retreated to the clubhouse after a half-round, listening to their old stories, asking questions about stick-poke war tattoos. He loved the word *Vietnam*. He soothed himself with it, "Vietnam. Vietnam," saying it over and over.

Baby C pawed at Gram's towel hem. "Gram, get this—'Shifts in tides are necessary to usher in the summer's end. Though these may seem like brief squalls, they are signs that your metamorphosis is beginning. Each moment submerged in stress, dullness, or frustration is a stepping stone in this journey toward *the new you*. The full moon will bring the truest glimpse of your inner self to the surface. Seize this opportunity. Transform.' "

Gram tilted her head to the side. "What does that even mean?"

"Well, I just said it: 'Your metamorphosis is beginning.' "

I imagined Gram unfolding her towel to hold it outward like wings, then spinning in a magical circle. Instead, she lingered above us, scrunching water from her hair.

At the same moment that I marveled, "You memorized it?" Gram said, "Waste of paper." Then she laughed with a bit of a curl. "What are you paying for postage on that thing?"

Baby C squirmed. She had secret dominion over one of the ball machines outside of the clubhouse in order to fund her various newspaper subscriptions so that she could sample horoscopes from across the country. The one she read from was her most coveted and cost a whopping forty dollars a year. I had never counted, but suspected she got at least seven different papers a week. Hers was the costliest indulgence in the family. Well, monetarily. Gram could never know the dollar amount; Baby C had made us swear to it. So as my sister continued to wriggle, I swooped in. "What, like sixteen dollars, yeah? For the year."

Baby C blinked kisses at me. "At most."

I wanted to say, *I know you spend hundreds more calling telepsy-chics on the West Coast when you think we're asleep.* And I wanted to add, *What do they tell you?* Instead, I stared into the crisscross pattern of the back of Gram's one-piece, which was surely burning into her skin.

We stepped from the dock directly onto the green of the golf course, then walked with Gram toward the clubhouse, barefoot, splitting grass blades beneath steps. The grass across the whole county was dead or waning, valiantly, toward its crispy death. Not unusually, it was a dry summer, bloated and distended around us, squeezing us like bugs in a vise. The sweat dripped from our hairlines like fat opals to sting our pores, scarred from bouts of violent acne. Baby C hooked her pinkie through the belt loop of my shorts and tugged me angularly by the hip up the carefully en-gineered downslope of hole six, where all the long drives stopped too short of the hole for a clean putt. If you wanted to watch a struggle, that was where it happened.

We walked around the sand traps, and in passing, I pushed a wayward flagstick further into the ground. Our golf course was called Bayou Bloom. I'd always thought that sounded like a men's cologne—a beautiful name for a run-down place. One hundred and twenty-five acres bordering Longshadow Bayou that Gramp had purchased for a pittance after World War II. The engineering was catered toward high handicappers so new players could feel successful after a round, but more than being a playable course, Bayou Bloom was revelatory in its beauty. The holes were routed around patches of marsh, stalks of cattails; often ducks and egrets seemed to float in the same spot for weeks. The land was entirely manipulated in many parts, cobbled together with buckets of sand

and imported Bermuda; other parts were entirely honored, fairways placed where those thirty to forty feet occurred naturally. When Gramp was alive, he tried to walk the length of the course each day. The place hadn't made any kind of money since the early nineties.

The myth of Gram was what kept the golf course alive. As often as they gawked at me and the girls, our one-two-three, which-is-she eye trick, the patrons lionized Gram. The leathery fold of her skin gathering atop itself like ribbon candy, blotched with carcinoma. The depth of her voice, almost masculine, and her unapologetic crop of gray hair just below the ears. She couldn't be bothered to entertain them. She could hardly stand to cook the minimal concessions we offered. She brooded. She fussed. She couldn't wait for those men to get the hell out of her clubhouse, and they loved her for it. They talked about her when we weaved through Seeglow's grocery on Sundays. They incanted to Gram with her first name, Isadora, or her nickname, the Manatee, which they'd branded her as a young woman because she swam with such impossible mosey that fish didn't scatter when she neared. And Gram swam every day, up and down the bayou, in autumn and winter and hurricane season. I never could figure how she was allowed to exist that way; openly unhappy and not ostracized for it. The girls and I did our best to be amenable, cordial, invisible as we could, and people still couldn't get away from us fast enough. It wasn't that I wanted to be like Gram, because I didn't. I just wanted it to be easier for me, for them to know my name among the three.

Sometimes the men who worshipped Gram brought younger, deeply tanned grandsons or stepsons or daughters from out of town to their weekend back-nine rounds. They looked at us as if we weren't real. *Whoa*, they'd say when they saw the group of us. *Weird*. They touched everything we owned as if it were about to spark them, fumbling ball markers, gripping club shafts as if they'd never held anything in their lives. When Gull floated into the room, they exhaled with relief as they wondered, *Which one of them was fucking that football player? Which one of them do they say predicts the future? Who would I choose if I had to?*

The course was a liminal space where patrons—mostly middle-class, middle-aged—folded the thirty dollars it cost to play all eighteen holes into our hands as they cupped the backs of our palms, knowing we'd keep their secrets, agreeing to ignore ours. We created a course that made them feel like winners in the middle of a marshland. We left them alone even as they crushed beer cans against their thighs and underhanded them into our woods. We didn't acknowledge them around town unless they called to us first—"Hey, you're the . . . "—when we'd smile enough to assuage their interest. On the golf course we weren't incredibly multiplied or illusive, we were side characters in their only reprieve from the five children they supported on a chemical-plant wage. Mostly, they didn't regard us at all. But their wives and children and mothers-in-law—they watched us move about in a swooping tercet as if we hadn't been born in the very same hospital, attended the same schools and churches. It wasn't the difference between men and women, it was the difference between golfers and porch sitters, people who came into our space and those who watched us from afar.

We were our mother's spitting image. We knew we walked her face around town, but people couldn't bear to say that anymore. Instead, they told us tangential things like how they still had her complicated breakfast order taped to the kitchen wall of the diner, or that they'd almost hit her with their car in 1982 when she rushed into the middle of the street to save a turtle. There was guilt enough in the girls and me looking exactly like each other. For us to be saddled with our radiant dead mother's face was often too much to stand. I suppose the only thing this relieved was that nobody bothered to guess about who our daddy was, because there didn't seem to be a hint of him in us. Harriet Shrub, the church altar guild chair, labored under the fear that it might have been her son who fathered us illegitimately with our raggedy mother-girl Murphy. The two had run around together in their youth. Murphy taught Harriet's son how to play blackjack with Monopoly money at a youth retreat and how to sneak out of the chapel during the sermon, and worst of all, she got him hooked on cigarettes, which the son apparently never kicked, and which Harriet never forgave our mother for, even in death.

When she got ahold of us, Harriet would tilt our chins up, bringing the brink of our cheekbones near a light. Then she'd drop our faces and turn away. It was no big secret she'd always wanted a girl.

As we neared the clubhouse, following behind Gram, I saw Gull had wound up the water hose so sloppily that I'd have to unspool it. Inside, he was sitting cross-legged on top of my book in the wooden swivel chair behind the desk, trying to flatten the water-warped pages. Baby A was leaning on her elbows over the register, snapping a tank top strap against her collarbone. The first group of morning regulars had just trailed onto the course with their Styrofoam cups of black coffee and their wheelie bags. They were older, retired, and liked to mess with us because it made them feel connected. *What's your name, young lady? Which one are you? You can't be her!* Baby A had bandaged the cut on her hand with a scrap of rag and duct tape. It looked like a beauty queen's sash.

Gram unspooled the towel from her waist and tossed it to Gull, touching his face and then his forehead. He swaddled himself in it best he could, struggling to tuck the corner. Arms strapped to his sides, he huffed a one-note sound that was Baby A's cue to push the corner into an open fold near his chin so that when he wished, he could fish it out with his teeth, metamorphosize just as Baby C's horoscope predicted.

It puzzled me that he enjoyed this, though I'd heard of babies or nervous dogs who craved constriction. Our Gull was deaf in his left ear; the hearing in the right had been fading since he was born, for bodily reasons. Last the doctors had said back then, the slowly fading hearing in his right—I remember which by picturing the way he turned his head toward sound—was at thirty percent. By the time he turned eighteen, it would be gone completely.

"I've got an errand to run, Gram," Baby A said as firmly as she could.

"No, you certainly do not."

"But Gram, I can get that communion wine for Aunt Rachel on the way." Baby A had lip gloss on her cheekbones, patted down to diffuse the texture. She was grinding her teeth, wishing for bubblegum.

Gram thought a moment. "All you girls go, then. If little miss has an *errand*."

It had been months since Baby A had gotten caught with Rich in the church cemetery, knocking back green apple Jim Beam, and Gram still hadn't forgiven her. She'd told Gram she was going to drop off the altar linens we'd helped mend. It was Harriet Shrub who found them, called Gram to let her know she was thirty seconds from summoning the sheriff. Gram made Baby A swear off Rich Goodson and drinking and lying; she had done none of it, and Gram knew. She charged Baby C and me with her so at least our sister wouldn't stumble into trouble alone. Gram couldn't be bothered to watch her, or any of us, closely enough. That extent of maternal effort had died with our mother nineteen years before.

Baby A rolled her eyes. Gull waggled in his towel cocoon, nodding toward the chalkboard with tee times, then rattled off their names, practicing the subtleties of enunciation he struggled with: *Micheletti, Cottingham, Crowder, Bell-Benitez*. He nodded his head to demarcate each syllable, delighting in sound the way we'd forgotten how to. As Gull sounded out the town's names, Baby A darted her cherry tongue in my direction, an agreement to come with us embedded within that warm motion as she moved heavily toward the door. When Gram's footsteps descended the hallway connecting our house to the clubhouse, Baby A snatched the truck keys off the counter. "Off to Aunt Mama's."

"Would you stop with that shit." All I could picture was Aunt Rachel's head on our mother's body, their morphing dawdling around, unbalanced, about to tip over.

Baby C poked Baby A real hard in the side as we crunched the parking lot gravel and slid across the truck bench seat. "She only says it 'cause we hate it."

Baby A flapped the driver's side visor down to shield her eyes, grinning into the sun.

We could usually be united, or soothed, by music. The twangy, low-toned young women of the late nineties and early aughts nourished our need to feel like we'd been talking, all that life-time, to people other than each other. We wanted to be a chorus. We wanted crooning and fiddles, knuckle-thumping against the nearest metal. Baby C fed a Dixie Chicks CD into the slim stereo mouth.

We'd taken to hiding our contraband CDs; the Dixie Chicks discography lived inside the car manual. The Eagles were beneath Baby A's nightstand, the Shins in a spare copy of *Ben Hogan's Five Lessons*, and—worst of all—Elliott Smith was at the bottom of a wire basket stacked with Tampax boxes. Gram didn't have tolerance for anybody that sang unsure of God, or unsure of themselves. Truthfully, I think it hurt her to hear us sing, all three vocal strands braiding to resurrect her daughter's gone voice. We didn't push Gram on it, and anyway it was more rewarding to listen to the music after having hid it. Baby A jabbed the stereo key with her finger to find "Cold Day in July." We liked Natalie and Emily and Martie. We decided once, under Baby A's fierce influence, that if we'd had proper names, we'd have liked them to be those. *The moon is full*, we sang. *And my arms are empty.*

Aunt Rachel answered her front door promptly after I'd knocked with the toe of my shoe, our arms heavy with generations of altar-anxious sweat. She called Jason over to help relieve us, flopping the tufts in a heap inside the foyer.

"I'll deal with these later." Aunt Rachel smiled. "Now come on in, it's a barn burner. I mean really"—she guided Baby C by the arm toward the kitchen, which smelled of warm spices and house cleaner—"which Greek god do you have to blow around here to get a breeze?"

Jason made a retching sound. "Goddamn, Mom."

"Jason Roger Upchurch, don't you talk like that in my house." It'd taken an entire breath for her to say his full name. We laughed. We were jealous.

"But you can talk about—ugh, never mind." Jason bounced a ratty tennis ball against the terrazzo tile, barefoot and bare-chested, wearing only swim trunks and jewelry made of shells. "I'm going back with them to Gram's."

"We're just painting the shed. Won't be any fun."

"Fine. Then do y'all girls want to watch a football scrimmage at the old stadium later tonight? Dolbie's B team is playing ours."

"What position are you again?" Baby C asked, sinking her hand into the chip bag Aunt Rachel had unrolled and set in front of us. She loved to ask people what position they played in sports because as they explained it, even our cousin Jason, they twisted their limbs in an attempt to charades-convey exactly what they were exceptional at making their bodies do, and how they did it. I liked the indulgence of watching instead of being watched. Jason, stoked by the question, was standing upright and shaking his arms out, preparing to tackle an invisible body, forgetting to answer the question.

Aunt Rachel pulled the chip bag away from us and pushed in its place a stack of carrot sticks and mozzarella balls atop a paper napkin, leaking through. The mozzarella was the expensive kind that bobbed in its own juices in small orbs. We savored them. Jason, looking a bit wounded that we'd blown off going to his scrimmage, tossed the tennis ball against the tile so hard that it rebounded powerfully into his chest, making us all laugh. He then rolled the yellow shedding ball across the counter to me, and I rolled it back. This for a while: rolling the world back and forth.

"Oh," Aunt Rachel said with the jolt of memory, "I have something for you girls." She retreated down the hall and pushed around the inside of a wooden drawer, returning with a handful of small glass bottles. "There's a story, too." She arranged nail polishes in a row beside the carrot sticks: two were neon, three were soft pastels, and one was jet black. The paint had separated after years in Aunt Rachel's drawer, a thin slick of oil floating on top. She picked them up, one by one, and shook them back into harmony as she told us how our mother had stolen these polishes from the drugstore and made her harbor them. "When your mama went home with all black fingernails save for a single neon-pink pinkie, she wasn't allowed over at my house for a whole two weeks. That's why she grabbed those pastels."

"For backups," Baby C interrupted with a soft smile. Aunt Rachel nodded, the black polish bottle in her hand, jostling it lightly. She unscrewed the top. "Wanna try something?" she asked, already laughing. We stretched our fingers out and apart, holding real still on the countertop as Aunt Rachel brushed the black onto our every nail, no paper towel beneath our hands to catch the spray of haphazard strokes. Eventually, I was blowing on Baby A's nails while hers dried and Baby C was blowing on mine. As she painted, Aunt Rachel told us about the time our mother hemmed her homecoming dress nearest she could to her actual ass cheek with a stapler. Coach Keith hadn't let her in the gym at first, holding her back as he circled her like an animal about to sit down, until she suddenly screeched, moved away from him, and said, "Now *Coach*." He'd been so flustered that he let her in without another word. "Never told your gram, neither," Aunt Rachel said. "Or she'd have set your mama right. On the drive back to your house, she yanked each staple out with the edge of a cuticle pusher. Floor of my car was absolutely littered in wire."

Baby C asked what the dress looked like, and Aunt Rachel lit up. She waved her back to the primary bedroom—our nails were dry by then—and after a while our sister emerged in a puff-sleeved floral frock, its hem brushing the tops of her feet. We howled. Baby A swooped behind her, ducking under the skirt to gather the fabric upward to the same ass-grazing height. Baby

C pushed her away, knocking into her head with a knee. Aunt Rachel had retreated behind the kitchen counter with me to get a better look at the two squabbling in a tornado of faded, treasured material. Aunt Rachel hung her arm around my neck and pulled me into a tight hug so brief that it was as if I'd been shocked by a single, reviving pulse to the chest; our mother's arm, at once, heavy around me, too.

"Oh," Baby C murmured with excitement. "Can we keep it?" She swung the bottom of the dress in an arc as if she were a proper southern belle. Baby A put the back of her hand to her forehead, draped herself dramatically over the back of the living room couch in a swoon.

"Lord knows I couldn't fit it." Aunt Rachel moved to touch the sleeves protruding from Baby C's arms like diseased lumps. "You look just like her," she breathed. "I wonder if she'd want you to have it?" Her back stiffened, grip still on a raised sleeve, knowing she shouldn't have said that out loud, and adding quickly, "Certainly, you can."

"No, we know." Baby A rose from her slope on the couch. "It's gotta be weird to give away someone else's stuff. Especially . . ." Both Baby A and Aunt Rachel looked at each other, confused, trying to speak to something they had yet to fully parse. I felt embarrassed to watch them stumble but was heartened at my sister's willingness. When Aunt Rachel looked at us, sometimes she said "Mur—" before catching herself. Sometimes she stared at us for long periods of time when she thought we weren't looking. And sometimes, at Christmas or on Murphy's birthday, she cried. They'd been best friends since they were little, unrelated by blood, though she called our gram "Gram" as did Jason, and they'd raised him to call us "cousin" and us to say the same. She'd been our second emergency contact when we were in school.

She'd taught us about our periods and icing angry pimples with Colgate. I hoped we were enough for her, in the absence of her friend, but I was never sure.

Baby A forced a giggle. "Sometimes when she thinks of our mother, Gram mutters, 'Selfish thing.' "

Aunt Rachel laughed with her belly, her full throat, neck moving like a seagull's when it gulps. "She was a red-hot poker. You'd have run her ragged."

I knew what she meant. *She'd have ruined you.*

We knew we'd have to sit around and chat a bit before Baby C would be ready to take the dress off. "Aunt Rachel," Baby A began, her elbows on the counter. "Why don't you tell us the real stories?"

"What do you mean?" Aunt Rachel shook her head.

"You know like, tell us about smoking behind the laundromat or sneaking around, sneaking out. Where'd y'all go at night? Who'd you see?"

"Smoking behind the laundromat? I don't know who told you that, girl."

"Yes, you do." Baby A raised her eyebrows, and we snickered.

"Well, we certainly didn't sneak out at night."

"Now that's not true, either. Why won't anybody tell us about her?"

"You're just gonna go and copy her, that's why."

"What's so wrong with that?"

The room quieted. Aunt Rachel looked at the ceiling and then her hands, picking at the skin around her coffin-shaped nails. "Your mama got in a lot of trouble. And I ran around with her, that's true, but we had some close calls. Some bad nights."

Baby A resisted rolling her eyes, though she slapped the edge of the countertop. "It's not like sneaking out at night is what killed her during childbirth."

I stilled, as did Baby C, who was twirling a swatch of lace in her puffy dress sleeve.

"No," Aunt Rachel said, sobered. "It didn't."

But it put her in that room, pregnant with you, I imagined her thinking. *Left me with a big mess of babies to clean up.*

We picked at the food on the counter quietly. Baby C slipped into the bathroom and reemerged with our mother's dress draped across her arm like a waiter with a napkin, her T-shirt cut just the right way, so it revealed the freckled top of her left shoulder. Her shorts' fly was down, but I didn't tell her just then. We handed over the communion wine I'd fetched from the truck, and Aunt Rachel gave us tinfoil packages of food to carry back to Gram and Gull. The packages smelled damp with meal, corn, and peppers. "Give that sweet boy a kiss for me," she hollered as we climbed into the truck.

"Why'd you have to say that stuff?" I reached across Baby C's lap to fasten the belt, touched briefly the exposed zipper flap of her jean shorts, which she instantly tugged upward.

"Oh, stop it." Baby A turned the wheel of the truck carefully. "You want to know."

"But I don't want to hurt her feelings."

"Yeah," Baby C added softly. "After giving us such nice gifts, too."

"She's a big strong girl." Baby A exhaled. "She can deal."

"It makes her sad, though. Thinking about our mother that way."

Baby A peered at us briefly over the top of her sunglasses. "You know, I think she likes having a tragic thing to mope about. Gives her nuclear suburban life a little intrigue."

"That's an awful thing to say." Baby C was petting our mother's dress like it was an animal.

"And not true," I added.

"Look. Just because you two don't understand, doesn't mean it's not true. She likes being a dead woman's best friend. Who wouldn't?"

"Well, I don't like being a dead woman's daughter."

"Me neither," I said.

Baby A cackled, tugging the hot-to-the-touch steering wheel in an opposite direction. "I don't believe that for a second. There's nothing more dramatic than being left. And drama *by default* makes you interesting."

"Wow," I said sarcastically. "You should write a book."

Then we laughed, all of us, as we rattled around in our furnace on wheels.

The air through the rolled-down window smelled of metal and wet rags. The whir of construction was ambient as if worlds away when really it was only the next town over, a loud and forceful widening of their narrow roads. It was clear where the border between Longshadow and Texas City began because all the grass and trees in Texas City deadened and slumped over. There was something very unfinished about Longshadow, too; abandoned silos on overgrown farms, miles of three-foot grass between the chemical plants—the BP explosion had happened years before, and it felt like we were always talking around it. And when we talked directly about it, older folks like Gram couldn't help bringing us further back to the Disaster, they called it, in the forties. "Hundreds died," they would say, "including my [cousin/ brother/daddy/friend], and it's like we haven't learned a dang thing." They called it other names, too: Monsanto, Carbide, Grandcamp, as if whoever they'd known that'd died, wherever they'd been, was where the disaster had *really* happened. There was a film of dread floating above our heads that *that* was our future, working at plants or waiting on someone who did to come home. I thought of Gull in a hard hat, sacrificing the hearing he had left, and winced into the breeze.

"Aw hell," Baby C shouted as she turned to me for backup. I was not surprised to see where we were headed, or keen to argue about it. "She's serious. You're really serious?" Baby C angled her head toward Baby A, who had steered us into the Shrimp Shack drive-through line, one rusty car away from the window.

"I'm just going to tell him when I'll be home."

"Never," Baby C mumbled. "We're dumping you at the boat launch before we get there."

Rich stood at the window with a paper hat on his head, microphone curved around his ear. He blinked wildly when he looked into the car at our sunburned, same faces. He rested his gaze on the one grinning dizzily at him. How it must've felt to not be able to place affection; a sexually tense three-card monte. Baby A leaned out the window, still buckled in, right foot on the brake. "I'll be back later. You're off at three thirty? I could meet you in the parking lot? Or you could come over? Paint the shed? We're painting the shed today." She spoke rapid-fire. Rich's face flustered.

"Parking lot? Yeah, three thirty." He'd moved the microphone away from his mouth, said past Baby A, "Hi, girls."

Baby C and I sat stoic as he ogled, mouth opened a bit, transfixed by our multiplication or our disdain, or both. Rich passed Baby A a greasy paper bag, and I hated that she was touching what he touched, that she let him touch her. I pictured his face streaked in dried deer blood.

"Three thirty it is. I'll probably show up sweaty and dirty with paint," Baby A said, her tone lingering, eyes narrow. "I hope you won't mind."

Baby C popped a fried shrimp from the greasy bag into her mouth and just as quickly spit it back in her hand, passing the bag to me. She slung the chewed bits onto the pavement through the rolled-down window. Rich was stunned. As Baby A shifted the truck into drive, she pumped the brakes to jostle us around, then sped purposefully over a speed bump. My head whipped violently, no headrest to catch it.

"You two are truly embarrassing," Baby A said as she shook her hair out, rolling up the crank window. "I really—God, I just . . . screw you guys."

Baby C forced a fried shrimp into our sister's mouth, her black nails against the clear sky behind us like a jump-scare. "Ugh." Baby A smacked her lips as she chewed. "It's so good."

We laughed, high-pitched and out the window, having turned the radio up to combat the wind, hair blown sticky into the Vaseline on our lips. Then Baby A slammed on the brakes. "We forgot the dry cleaning."

MISSUS DEER

Mr. Mitchum had already drunk a few warm beers by the time we returned to the clubhouse. He was stumbling around the lobby to catch Gram's attention. She was focused on cutting up onion at the desk so she could keep an eye out for groups with approaching tee times while Mr. Mitchum pretended to be interested in whatever Gull was reading. He edged toward Gram, biting to ask her tender questions like, "Gee Manatee, whatcha put in that soup?" In his mind, Gram would say, "It's not soup, you buffoon, it's gumbo." Though Mr. Mitchum knew full well it was gumbo, he'd lean on his fists and ask, "What makes it gumbo, not soup?" And there Gram would go, spouting off about soup in a way that manifested love or promise, at least in Mr. Mitchum's head.

The white cast of Gram's sunscreen dulled her face as if she were a ghost. It was all I could focus on as Mr. Mitchum rattled on, even though this was Gram's usual state. Gull often mocked her for this, pulling at his chest like a jellyfish for *white*, then rubbing the skin of his face dramatically as his eyes rolled back, *lotion*.

Mr. Mitchum announced to no one, his buddies still circling the seventeenth hole, "Isadora, I could get you tarps for that shed."

She pulled her head up from the cutting board. "That'd be helpful, Curtis."

"I'd have to gather them up, of course. But I could."

Gram's eyes found me and Baby C, slouched on the couch, Baby A already gone down the hallway to change shirts. "That is, if these girls don't finish it today," Gram said.

Mr. Mitchum looked at us through a fog as if at those words, we'd materialized in the room. "I simply can't . . . darlins', you ought to wear initial necklaces, you know, the rhinestone ones? The print shop on Houghton does rhinestone stuff. I know the owner, Mrs. Newton, and—"

"That's quite enough, Curtis," Gram interjected. "I'll let you know about the tarps."

"I really could. I'll see if the guys will take me. We carpooled, you know."

"Of course you did, Curtis." Gram began to sweat over the onion, pushing chopped thins farther toward the corner of the cutting board. "Girls. Where is your sister? You better get on with it."

I sat up, pushing Baby C's slack shoulders off my chest, neither of us particularly moved by Mr. Mitchum's bewitched confusion. "She's changing tops."

I had asked Baby A to grab me a new top, too, knowing we'd tear them off within the hour, painting in our swimsuit tops and shorts we cut from thrift-store Wranglers. My shorts were tied with hair elastics at the waist so they didn't slip. Boys from towns over liked to flip around on wakeboards and motorboats on those thick, humid days, passing our property at least twice, once on the way out and once on the way back. We knew these boys enjoyed the shine they created, upright in boats with expensive sunglasses and neon swim trunks as if they were slicked gods. From the bayou, at the speed they went, if they cared enough to crane their necks they could catch a coherent glimpse of us, our lace, our haphazard painting.

The toolshed was not but seven feet tall, a couple extra feet wide, took up a square or so of land between the driving range and the first hole. Gram set us to painting it a sage shade of green because its original white had soured. She said, after debating in the color swatch aisle, that we could paint the inside however we wanted, so without much faff between the three of us we settled on a beet pink called Magenta Chirp. I lugged the boom box down the hallway, piled it into a Racer Wagon with brushes, paint, and mason jars of lemon water screwed closed. Gram promised she'd send Gull out with sweet tea if we made it past lunchtime without complaining.

Baby C fetched a Sara Evans CD from under the truck bench where we'd hidden it, cracked plastic cover. We didn't turn the volume up too loud because the guests were likely to holler at us that it distracted their backswings, short putts, long putts. "Like it could get any better," Baby A should have said under her breath, mock-swinging an invisible stick, grabbing her spine, keeling over. Instead, she leaned on a ladder anchored below the roof wing, holding a plastic cup of light-green paint.

While the Sara Evans CD ran through, Baby A and C matched pitch as I contributed a pin-sharp hum. Then my hums began to vibrate, then my mouth, then the ground, and the three of us perked up at the familiar thrum of motor mingling water. We each stepped away from the shed, hoping to see a pack of shirtless boys idling by the dock, but it was only the sheriff's department on water patrol. They'd made regular rounds in the summer ever since the Deer girl died years back. The whole tragedy caught us all by the lip and yanked us out of a reckless, communal happy-go-luckiness. Rumors swarmed that her skin had festered into scales in her time at the bayou bottom, her hair had fallen out, and she'd come up bald. The lore surrounding her eventually eroded any real memories, until she was an exotic, eerie idea that we loved to be afraid of.

The Deer family was known for their cascade of redheaded children. They were useful people with skills and time, pleasant, always grinning with a hand outstretched. Ansley had just married into the Richardses, their youngest son so awkward we were shocked he managed to woo the symmetrical likes of Ansley, who worked mornings at the Starbucks inside the Kroger before her community college classes. The couple had been sputtering up the bayou on a boat with another Richards boy and his wife. Ansley leaned back, her timber-wolf hair pirouetting in the breeze. I say timber wolf because it was stick straight and sharp. I say timber wolf because this story stalked us, and just when the town had moved beyond it, someone would burst into tears having felt its presence. Ansley breathed in engine fumes with her head arched back, admiring the huff of clouds waning gray above. Fumes fogged those clouds into spotty vision, ringing ears. She reached toward her new husband before passing out and falling off the back of the boat.

Ansley hit her head on the way down. Her new husband jumped in instantly. The water muddled itself a cruel murky brown; he said he couldn't see his hand in front of his face, much less either of Ansley's. He dove as far down as he could go, which wasn't so far in the end. The sheriff's department riled up their boats immediately. Coast Guard rushed up from their usual patrol on the bay, speeding through deep, blind curves. Neighbors dug up wetsuits and snorkels that'd been unused since college trips to Cozumel. When people talked about it, they recounted the image of Gram flopping across the course in flippers, the best swimmer in town—of course they'd called her. I remember hearing it. "*Isadora, Isadora,*" ricocheting off the grass. Just as Gram sucked her teeth around the jelly curve of a snorkel, the Coast Guard siren sounded.

Ansley was found exactly where she fell. Not a thing aimed to move her, no nudging creatures or wayward sunken tires. What it must have been like to watch them pull her up, everyone in their backyards peering out, all the golfers on the course standing waist-deep in water, loafers soaked, feeling around the shallow end as if she'd have drifted there. Gram made Gramp corral us around the TV. Gull wasn't even crawling then, so we couldn't have been but ten.

Ansley was twenty-two, beautiful, permanently paled. When we talked about her, the girls and I struggled to say her name. And when I thought about her at the bottom of the bayou, I pictured my face on her body. Really, it was our face, so I suppose I could've been picturing any one of us. The bayou had a grip about it. I'd felt it before, holding us hostage on our swims. Yet we gave ourselves to it every morning, not fearing enough that it could steal us away.

There was a benefit barbecue for Ansley held at the peacock farm on Oleander Road by the high school. The pasture was littered with blow-up slides and plates of brisket, slices of purple onion big as a bracelet, Mrs. Taft's special tang sauce in squeeze bottles. I remember it being bliss, the girls and I tugging at each other's arms to get ahead for the slide, the bouncy house, running through the legs of our townspeople, who swept our hair with hands meaning to pet us or slow us down. Wild, inappropriate fun. Even though Ansley's face was plastered on a poster by the serving tables, it didn't dawn on us entirely why we were there. The peacocks caused occasional traffic jams as people drove in and out, birds moseying across the gravel road and then stopping to fan their feathers in protest. Then, the birds began to scream.

The peacock screams sounded real, like a woman in absolute terror. It must have been the commotion of the benefit that set them off, but like a row of cars that'd been slammed into, the screams carried and echoed as if encouraging each other. Mrs.

Deer couldn't take it—she dropped to the ground, clutching her ears closed, screaming herself. People who didn't know better tried to shush the birds, lunged at them with outstretched palms for making Mrs. Deer so upset, but the birds were huge, fearless, and they lunged back. By then I'd scurried over to Gram, as had Baby C. We hid behind her legs and watched the town lose its communal mind, unsure where our other sister was until the bubble of people sheltering Mrs. Deer burst. It was then that we saw Mrs. Deer huddled on the ground, face in the dirt, with Baby A lying atop her arched back, screaming to high heaven at the peacocks. Baby A clutched behind herself as if she were Mrs. Deer's backpack, roaring at the commotion of people and screeching birds. She was sonic. I could almost see the sound rings leave her mouth and move to lasso the birds. Baby A's voice thundered with anger, purpose. Looking back, it was like seeing a mother lift a car off her pinned child; we believed it, just barely, the miracle of carnal instinct we were witnessing.

Baby A didn't stop the peacocks, but she did urge them away. The flock retreated to the back of the farm to keep on screaming, but at least away from Mrs. Deer's face. The pair stayed in that limby, abstract huddle for a few moments—Baby A lying across Mrs. Deer's back, clutching at her ribs, and Mrs. Deer with her face to the ground, palms pressed to her ears, sobbing.

Nobody tried to rustle them up or pry my sister off. People politely feigned going back to whatever they'd been doing, watching the tender heap out of the corners of their eyes.

Eventually, Mrs. Deer reached her hand around to find Baby A's, and they got up. Mrs. Deer scooped up my sister and carried her around for hours as Baby A held silently to the woman's neck, resting her weary head. It meant we had to stay most of the sweltering day and that our sister couldn't play with us, but even then we knew it was important for Mrs. Deer to do this, so Baby C and I toddled off as an uncomfortable pair to play in the sand and spy on the screaming birds.

When the blow-up slides were deflated and the sun was setting orange, Gram walked gently up to Mrs. Deer, who reluctantly handed my sister over, asleep. The women looked at each other, having both lost daughters, and spoke in hushed tones. Mrs. Deer summoned Baby C and me over, gathered us into a hug, and did nothing but stroke the collective of our hair for a long time. She mumbled, maybe a prayer, maybe an incantation to whatever glow infected us.

That was the only time my sister ever did a selfless thing like that.

Baby A slept on the car ride home and for the next few days, as if she'd purged all of her energy with those screams. I understood even as a little girl that my sister had saved that woman's life. I was astounded that she had that in her, and that I hadn't known it.

Even more, I was ashamed that she could give something I never could, strong in a way Baby C and I were not predestined to be. Mrs. Deer and Baby A had a bond after that, as much as anybody could have with just one of us. I envied Baby A for this hugely until one Easter Sunday, Mrs. Deer walked up to me in my Easter dress as I crouched over a flower bed, poking at the doodlebugs, and kissed my forehead, saying into my hair, "My girl." Except I wasn't.

For her sake I leaned into the sad kiss.

We'd each done this for each other, pretending valiantly to be the sister these people thought they were holding. Unspoken between us was that when these things happened, we never told each other. As Mrs. Deer went on hugging me, I watched Baby A over yonder pluck a plastic egg out of a bush and drop it into the basket Baby C held, trailing after her. Our dresses had been the same salmon color. All three of us had frayed bows clipped in our hair.

This flood of tender memory made me consider volunteering for Baby A's painting, but I hesitated, trying to figure out the impulse. Just then, Baby C peeked her head around the shed corner and called to me, "Hello. Earth to you. Gull's been trying to get your attention."

I turned, and there Gull was, hoisting up a glass of tea. He asked if he could use the cowbells to drive away the stray chickens pecking at the parking lot as he signed *chickens* with tea-sticky hands. Gram wasn't in view, so I said yes, because Gull liked the tinny vibration of the bells. If the patrons complained, Gram would deal with them.

"I'm gone," Baby A announced, down from her ladder. "I'll be back in an hour."

Baby C plucked the brush from her hand. "That's all it takes."

"That's not counting the fooling around part at the beginning." Baby A smirked.

"Here's hoping he doesn't get *nervous* again," I said with a wave of my brush. Baby A slapped my ankle as she walked off. So we released her to her fooling, without envy. Then Baby C and I took a break. We sat cross-legged outside the shed, drinking our tea, tugging grass blades up like lashes from a giant eye, eavesdropping on a group of young fathers talking about a neighborhood get-together. We'd always been invited to neighborhood things by extension of the Upchurches, but I wondered whether the men would think to invite us anyway as they walked by, which they did, tipping their baseball caps with clubs strapped to their backs. "Hear that, girls? Block party on

Casa Grande this weekend. Pool hopping from yard to yard."
Another man cut that guy off, adding, "Not the Mendozas' of
course."

I nodded. "We know she likes her privacy."

"It's the medicine they've got her on. Sucks the life out of her."

"Well, hopefully, sir"—Baby C squinted her eyes up—"it
sucks the cancer out, too."

He shifted in his wingtips. "I don't mean to be indelicate, darlin'. Not often do we have such tragedy in our neighborhoods."

Baby C and I sat, quiet, living, breathing iterations of tragedy.
How easily they seemed to forget about the awful things around
them as soon as it was no longer fodder for gossip. The men stood
over us, uncomfortable. "Your mama . . . ," one of them began to
venture before Gram walked up, slapping the shoulder of a man
on the cluster's outskirts. "I've got lunch in the clubhouse. Come
on now. Let my girls work."

The men churned out smiles in Gram's company, walking
ahead while she lingered with us. "Which one of you sent Gull
hog wild with those bells?"

I raised my hand, and Gram began to laugh. "He drove the
Amatos so nuts, they sent their mess of grandchildren over to
wrestle the bell from him, brought sweet Gull by the collar to tat-
tle. Sometimes I wish you could whup other peoples' children."
She motioned us to follow her.

We balanced the wet brushes across our water jars, holding
hands as we walked. "Gram," Baby C began, "it's the grandpar-
ents' fault. Those kids don't know better."

"If I sent you on that kind of errand, you kids would scoff in
my face." Gram grasped my hand as she turned to me. "Where is
your sister, speaking of?"

Baby C and I exchanged a look, offering only, "Out."

"Fine." Gram opened the clubhouse door for us and lowered her voice, knowing full well what our girl was up to. "If that goddamned boy gets her into any more trouble, I'll call the sheriff myself."

"Gram," I said quickly. "You can't say goddamn."

As we sat at the clubhouse table, eating lunch with patrons milling about, my gut began to shimmer with an ache; I could feel Baby A's turning stomach, burning ears, the wet hot air. Baby C, who was crumpling a sopped piece of biscuit into her mouth, put a hand to her clammy neck where Rich's lips were on our sister. I felt it, too. We'd have phantom hickeys as echoes of Baby A's forming bruise. I reached to put my hand over Baby C's, still clamped to her own neck, sallow green paint dried to my knuckles. I motioned to Gull with a nod toward the cowbells Gram had faux-confiscated for the sake of the Amato grandchildren. He lifted one in each hand, clattering away.

Gram reentered the kitchen with empty bowls.

"The Casa Grande pool hop is this weekend," I said.

Gram scrubbed out the bowls, setting them on a drying rack. "Take Gull."

Baby C was oblivious. "Can I join you tomorrow morning on your swim?"

"Can you keep up?"

"No."

Gram wiped a wooden spoon with a paper towel, then put it back in the gumbo pot on the stove. "Course you can. If I pass too far ahead, you'll have to trust your way."

"It's just up and down."

I pictured Ansley Deer's body, up and down, at the bayou bottom.

"If you say so." Gram leaned against the counter, took a generous drink of water.

That night it poured rain. Our instinct was to dance in defeat of the ongoing dry spell, but Gull pointed past us to the shed weeping green streaks. Thankfully, we'd primed it. Phone calls echoed inside the clubhouse to cancel tee times as the rain continued longer than its usual fifteen-minute flash. Gram was connected to the desk phone, crossing names off the chalkboard. Baby C and I dashed through the thick, humid rain, collecting flagsticks, Gull in tow, stopping every so often to lean his head back and lap at the air. Baby A was still gone.

We brought the flagsticks back, soaking, and stripped down to our skivvies before walking into the clubhouse for towels. After putting on dry clothes, we ate TV dinners on the couch. Gull picked the peas out of his vegetable medley and carefully transported them to my tray via fork. I reached to steady his hand, and he gasped, grabbing one of my fingers. He held the black nails to his face, giggling at such defiance. Gram looked over briefly, noticed my nails painted darkly, and turned back to her episode of *Jeopardy!* I'd expected it to feel like a victory, but when Gull released me and I leaned into Baby C beside me, we put our hands next to each other, gazing at them and thinking of Gram. It was a small devastation we felt between us, knowing Gram had spent all the maternal hotheadedness she'd had on Murphy, leaving none for us. We'd have liked a little fuss, a little concern, but Gull kept on gathering up the peas, and even though we'd known a few answers in the Patent Pending and Funny Hats categories, Baby C and I refrained from shouting them out.

Baby A showed up half past ten, sneaking through the side door. We heard her bare feet patter frantically down the hallway and up the stairs. She flopped herself onto my bed, hair frizzed from the rain. "Miles from nervous," she said matter-of-factly. Her black polish was already chipped off in spots, which saddened me hugely, as if I'd realized she was balding prematurely.

There was a red ring on her shoulder blade edged with small marks. "He bit you?" My voice cracked.

She rolled to face me, tennis shoe sliding off her foot to thud against the floor. I winced. It'd wake up Gram.

"*We* bit." She sat up, took off her remaining shoe, and slid out the door quietly, down the stairs to microwave the TV dinner we'd left on the counter to thaw for her. She ate in our room as Baby C fluttered through her horoscopes and I tried to read myself to sleep, the stench of singed Salisbury steak polluting all breathable air. Finally, I shut *Big Fish*. "Choke it down already."

"Would you take a pill," she chided with a full mouth.

Baby C crawled over her newspaper pages, organized in some pattern I didn't understand. "Let me see that cut."

Baby A handed herself over as she shoved a piled-high fork into her mouth with the other hand. Baby C gingerly unwound the already tattered cloth as I peered over her shoulder. The cut was thin but long, still reddened and angry looking. Baby A hadn't quite managed to place the incision along her life line, as she'd hoped; it had become a lengthy detour to the side.

"Looks okay." Baby C lightly ran her finger over the new line. Baby A didn't flinch. Just kept on shoveling Salisbury steak into her mouth, eyes lingering on our closed cell phone as if she expected it to ring. I could tell Baby C was fretting over the cut. I wanted her to hear my thoughts without having to say them: *Is it too far apart? Does it hurt you, too? Will it change her fate at all?*

As if she could sense our deep thinking, Baby A said casually, "Did I do good?"

I looked to Baby C to answer. She was still running her thumb lightly over the cut. *Twenty-eight*, I thought on loop. *Twenty-eight*. She tilted her head like a puppy that'd heard a faraway ringing. "You did perfectly alright."

"At what?" I blurted.

"Yeah." Baby A looked down at us, crowded around her palm. "At what?"

"You did fine at trying to hurt yourself for attention."

Baby A rolled her eyes and laughed. "Well, sure, but did it work?"

I nodded along, wanting to know, too.

"We're supposed to be mastering tenderness, right now," said Baby C. "Our horoscope said, 'The little things are the big you are meant to conquer.' "

"Well, gee, if only you'd told me we were supposed to be 'conquering tenderness'—"

" 'Mastering.' "

"Whatever." Baby A squirmed. "Everything is a big thing. That's not news."

Baby C let our sister's hand fall away from hers, shrugging. I'd later come to regret how ashamed she felt about her interest in the future and how deeply she needed to be comforted, told that it'd be alright. We trampled her hope a bit. Acted like she was no better than the rest of us, when we all knew she was.

"What is it you said? Twenty-eight?"

"Round about." Baby C's face appeared sallow to me, like she could use a little blush.

"I'll be long gone by then."

I poked Baby A's cut with my finger quickly, hand still splayed for us to gaze at. "That's what we're afraid of, you freak."

"No, no, no. Like San Diego or Des Moines. Hundreds and

hundreds of miles." She shoved the last bit of food into her mouth.

"We'll find you wherever you go."

At this, she shivered. "That's such a creepy thought." Which hurt my feelings then, thinking she wanted to rid herself of us so fiercely that she'd just as likely avoid us forever, and hurt worse later when I considered maybe it was the thought of her own face finding her that made her shiver like that and made her want to be hundreds of miles away.

Baby A wrapped her hand again with the same scrap of rag and peeked downstairs to make sure Gram's bedroom light was off before pulling a bottle of green apple whiskey from beneath the bed. We talked about what we'd wear the next day and about getting all the polishes next time we returned to Aunt Rachel's. We talked about how bad poor Jason was at football.

Then we recounted together the time he broke his toe kicking a frozen soccer ball, each of us arguing over details, swearing one of the others had gotten the most important part wrong.

[ENTER] FRONT PORCH CHORUS

Isadora's better days were brilliant. Late sixties summers, Isadora showed up at the dance hall with Craig and the two twirled about the room, smiling. She'd drink beers with us as we compared the wear on our boot soles. That was when she pin-curled her blond hair, which she'd secure a cap tightly over before her triumphs. They came from all over to watch her—the Manatee—swim, that was true.

Gaggles of us saw her off at the boat launch and then drove the miles toward Galveston Bay to meet her at the finish. We rowed beside her in canoes or paddle boats as she arched and breathed, striving. Then she'd pull herself out of the water with a gasping grin, thin arms carved with muscle, and curl into the towel Craig held outstretched. They'd whoop and cuss and laugh, her and Craig. Like two old buddies. It was like that even after their girl was born. And like that until he passed, really, which was about the time she stopped with the curls and the skirts on Sunday, let gray eat up her blond and stomped around Seeglow's in Bermuda shorts, scrap T-shirts. Sadness tugged at her lip like a fishhook. Nothing but sad. Things only got worse with those babies and that boy. All of 'em, just poor things.

GATOR KILLINGS

The story went that when our mom found out she was pregnant, she was eighteen and she wasn't much scared. She wore brunette curls and mid-length linen dresses better than any girl in town. Aunt Rachel drove her to a CVS a town over so word wouldn't get back that Isadora's daughter was buying pregnancy tests. Our mother bought two, peed on them with her skirt hiked up behind a dumpster, then placed them on the car dashboard to bake as both girls gritted their teeth. Murphy waved her hands and chanted over the tests, laughing, and laughing still when the screens blossomed plus signs. "That was her way," Aunt Rachel said. "Never could take a thing seriously. Not even having babies. She ate all the stuff you aren't supposed to. Fooled with cigarettes and pot and beer. It was all I could do not to tell your gram, if only so I could have someone else to help argue your mother straight." But she didn't tell Gram and neither did Murphy. It wasn't until our mother fainted on the back nine that the truth of us emerged, right there in dazed slurs on the golf course. "Your gram," Aunt Rachel said, "wasn't surprised. What she was—well, was concerned."

They booked an appointment with the only gynecologist within fifteen miles, Gram thumbing through *Good Housekeeping* in the waiting room. Dr. Perez called Gram back for support when he told our mother she was indeed pregnant—with triplets. Everybody sobbed. Dr. Perez, our own gynecologist by then, laughed when he told us the story. "A marvel you girls are," he said. "People would kill for three."

Murphy's pregnancy became the town's gossipy preoccupation, because even well into her third trimester, Murphy was mowing the course lawn and tinkering with the carts. "She relished the attention," Aunt Rachel said. "Rubbing her belly like a crystal ball and smirking just to watch people squirm. I remember they said, 'For a girl that young, triplets are plain unnatural.'"

When I pictured it in my head, I pictured the discomfort on townspeople's faces, the way they must have rebuked her. And when I keep my mind there, I can almost see our mother's face.

Dr. Perez said when he delivered us, C-section of course, that our mother's tears were angry and fat like the gummy raindrops beetles carry on their backs. And there is where the story stopped when Dr. Perez or Gram told it. Aunt Rachel carried on a little further to our bluish feet, our alien underweight bodies wriggling in NICU pods. She'd linger on the NICU pods, how they were our crystal-clear homes until Gram toted us back to the course, leaping weeks forward, leaving behind our mother, dead on our birthday, the emergency embedded beneath it all.

Only once had we gotten her to talk about that day. She'd been drunk at their Fourth of July party when the girls and I cornered her by the hot dogs, handed her another Shiner, and asked Aunt Rachel soft questions until she finally admitted to seeing it. "She just died. Right there, quick as light before anybody could do a thing to stop it. Pushed me and your gram out of the room, but didn't close the damn window. We saw everything. And your gram was the one holding me! Can you believe that? It was horrible. A horror I couldn't hardly accept. Took me days. Days and days and days." She looked as though she were about to vomit. And after we got what we wanted, we left Aunt Rachel there beside the hot dogs, stuck in that memory like boots in mud. I remember she looked shocked, then. Like she was telling us about it, a thing that'd happened half a lifetime ago, and she still couldn't understand.

"We're damn awful to make her tell us that," I'd said as the girls and I settled by the hot tub.

Baby A bristled. "Don't say *damn* just because she did."

"She's right." Baby C clutched her stomach as we swung our legs over the steamed water's edge. "That wasn't nice."

"We're not awful." Baby A tightened the strap of the bikini top she was practically bulging out of. "It's our right to know." Then she searched the crowd of the party as if for a face.

It wasn't until we were six months old, Gram finally comfortable enough to take us to Seeglow's for grocery Sunday, that people around town could confirm what we looked like. It's no wonder they saw us as having just happened one day, appeared in a stacked stroller on the canned goods aisle. Our sharply same eyes were looming in Longshadow, our loose blond curls dispositioned toward brunette. Our baby teeth emerged and fell out in sync, one after the other. We left the tooth trio in a pill tin on the clubhouse mantel, ran barefoot the next morning down the cold tile hallway to a stack of six quarters, fifty cents each. Of course, this didn't matter because we shared a piggy bank, though Baby A seemed to amass money in secret that I never cared enough to inspect. All of our sets: eyes, hands, feet, teeth, ears, glowed and transformed in unison to identical avail.

Gram, hard as she tried, had trouble telling us apart, too, thought to paint our fingernails different colors or pierce our virgin earlobes with unique gemstones. Baby A was disappointed when this did not happen because she'd called dibs on CZ diamonds. We joked about this stuff often, but it twinged. Rarely was there a break in our feeling like we were different to anyone but each other. Then Gull came along. Gull, who could sense the shades of a sunset and smell rain washing up the coast, who never wavered in calling us by our full, correct names. We aged and our inclinations blossomed, but by then the effort made by others to distinguish us had evaporated, and we remained "Hey Babies" or "the Manatee's girls" or "Baby One, Two, Three." Our quiet arrival into the world seemed the logical genesis for our mythic aura, the reason people could not remember why our names were not funny but unfinished, or that our looking exactly alike was eighty percent our mother hanging on for dear life, twenty percent the ghost of a man we were never sure of.

Gramp told us that it wasn't until we were about a year old that Gram would let him sing our mother's songs. He sang them while giving us baths in the kitchen's farmhouse sink. We were too small to remember with any degree of truth, but when I imagined it, the scene was this: Gramp would say with a coo, "Your mama's favorite was 'Down to the River,'" and then he'd sing, our baby noises almost carrying his melody. If the bath took long enough or if Gramp didn't have chores to do after, he'd sing "Tennessee, 1949." Then he'd tell a sink full of babies how their mama sang at the town's Bluegrass Festival each August and that two years in a row, she'd won, singing the same four songs. I pictured Gram bristling in the corner, Gram who never sang and hardly spoke of our mother. In my fantasy, our little brains took Gramp's singing and made it stone fact in our subconsciouses. That way we'd have always known our mother, even if just through her songs and Gramp recounting the same few stories about her stealing baby chicks from the local farm or making a mythic hole in one that nobody else saw.

"Your mama was like that," Gramp would say, though of course we didn't know what he meant. The way our mother was, was strictly theirs. We had her body, and that was having quite enough. Sometimes I'd wonder how the people in town would've treated us had Murphy raised us instead of Gram, had her loss not created a gigantic rip in the thrill that should've been identical triplet girls in such a small place. I tried to picture Murphy's face all the time. I'd catch my profile in the mirror out of my periphery and pretend it was her, walking in the room to throw her arms around me.

In the next few days we finished painting the shed, and the elements nestled back into dryness. The trees seemed to scream when squirrels bent their branches. The bayou was almost declared unswimmable due to the pH, but the announcement was never made, though Gram had it on good authority that it should've been. Still, she and Baby C started swimming that long stretch, though we told Baby C it would turn her hair sour if she made it a habit. Gram hollered over us, said when *she* was swimming the Rio Grande, the Red, the Brazos, she'd surface thick and blond as ever, without fail.

Most mornings I watched from a bunker with a coffee cup in hand as Baby C and Gram slipped into the water like wishes and pushed off the dock with their feet. Gram soared ahead as Baby C pawed with great effort, which was no use; Gram was the best there had ever been.

In south, north, east, and all of Texas, from 1968 until she had our mother, nobody swam long-distance like Gram. She'd started her swimming young, said she did it because she wanted to go somewhere but not really leave, then discovered she had endurance and skill. Gram joined junior leagues until she outswam them, moved to the high school groups, then started training with local college athletes. Eventually Gram—the Manatee— had outswum them all so she trained on her own, swimming from Longshadow Bayou into the mouth of the bay, mornings and evenings, sometimes midday if the water was cool enough. She swam marathons across the county, across the state. She had a way that couldn't be emulated. Gram grasped the water like a child reaching for a cloud, only Gram could grab it and make it move her forward. The bayou whittled her body, not to thinness but to tranquility. Gram was thin but not frail, her hair still soft even though it was graying toward white. Her clothes didn't fit her, but the swimsuits did, which is why the men tended to fish as long into the afternoon as they did, to catch her figure in the distance. She simply *was* beautiful, she didn't have to be told. She embodied it, commanded it, and seemed to hate thinking about it.

"My, my, Miss Manatee," a man in the clubhouse said, an unfortunate blossom of sunburn reddening his temples and ears. "Goodlookin' girls you've got here. So much like—"

"Yes. Girls that oughta be back by ten if they know what's good for them."

I hugged my towel tighter while Baby A negotiated. "What if we send Gull back early?"

"How? On the collar of a hunting dog? I do not think so."

"Across the water, I mean." This was Baby A's way, pushing issues she already knew the answer to.

"Not while I'm alive, young lady. That is your brother. Selfish thing. If Gull gets water in his good ear, I'll have your hides." Gram traded the nice bath towels we held for tattered beach towels splashed with bleach stains, stacking them in our open arms. One more thing to give the town evidence that we weren't worth them. "I'll be by Rachel's later. I've gotta pick up shipments at the warehouse, so I'm taking your truck."

I pushed Gull's orange plugs tightly into his ears, holding his narrow chin steady as he rolled eyes the shade of weak coffee when I asked if he needed floaties. We fluttered across the water into the soft mouth of the Upchurches' boat cover, keeping Gull at the center of our formation. Jason was waiting on the dock. He plucked Gull up by the shoulder like a daisy and laughed as Gull darted toward the house as soon as his feet hit the ground. Jason lingered to give us each his hand, which Baby C and I took. Baby A used the ladder grip to vault herself up instead, then bounded toward a cluster of boys she'd probably seen Rich hidden within.

"The team has been asking about you," Jason said. Baby C and I looked at him until he finished. "All of you."

Because of Baby A's tryst with Rich and her fling with Wendell the autumn before, boys thought we were easy, all of us, because we must have shared everything, right? That was why the team was asking after us. We'd graduated the year before, smack in the middle of the pack, near-identical grade point averages. No extracurriculars. No senior ad taken out in the back pages of the yearbook with baby pictures and grown pictures. Just left to mill about as our peers went off to college and returned for summers with Greek letters on their chests and new hobbies like pickleball and macramé. Jason was headed for college that fall, and I was trying not to hold it against him or envy him too hard.

I found Aunt Rachel in her kitchen, pulling Gull's plugs gently from both ears. He winced as she wiggled the pieces out. She knew very few signs except for his name, but he read her lips especially well, eyes fixed at her mouth, head angled to catch ambient sound. "When are they going to get you hearing aids?" Gull's face blushed with shame. *They* was us, and *we* didn't have thousands of dollars stashed in a covert hearing-aid reserve. The elementary school had once offered to pay for the hearing aids, but they never followed through. Best they could do was clip a microphone to the teacher's collar that blasted the instruction through a pair of foam headphones, but it's not like they loaned us the gear over the summer. We noticed that Gull struggled more and more when he was outside of school, inching closer to mouths in conversation, eyes straining.

She reminded Gull to stay in the bounds of the connecting yards, to which he agreed, toddling off to tangle himself in a pool noodle. Then she tugged at my shorts and sighed. "My girl. These are asking for trouble. Put your hands to your side." I did, a bit proud that the shorts ended well above my fingertips. "Two inches more, at least," she decided.

"Why? Nobody cares."

"You don't want to send the wrong message."

I decided to embody Baby A, to say the thing she'd say. "I don't think it'd be so wrong."

Aunt Rachel looked at me with exhaustion. She saw that I was trying the idea on and that I hadn't quite believed it myself, so she walked a tray of raw hamburger meat out to Uncle Henry at the grill. I imagined her telling him I was turning into trouble like my sister or our mother, and my face reddened, though I watched Aunt Rachel out the window, idling beside my uncle, her lips not moving at all. I pulled my shorts down and walked out the sliding glass door toward my sisters, who stood in a huddle of shirtless boys. Poor Jason, his exposed back scattered in acne we'd promised him charcoal scrubs would fix. He held steadfast to the idea that special soaps were for girls, even when we begged him. The acne patches looked painful. Cystic and ripe.

He propped a sweaty elbow on my shoulder. "Get us a tee time this week." It was this confidence, which only emerged when we were around others, combined with his last name, that kept us from complete social exile, so I didn't mind when he turned it on us, though he seldom did. Along with the Italians from Galveston, the Upchurch family had settled the town of Longshadow, and they had their name on everything: Upchurch Road, Upchurch Funeral Home, Upchurch Memorial Park, hyphenated with other last names so people that married into the family didn't lose their tethers. Even though we weren't blood to Aunt Rachel, Uncle Henry, or Jason, they allowed us the shelter of saying so. Jason couldn't sense how his arm on my shoulder made the nearby boys' guts roil. How they looked at my sisters and me square in the sternums. I pushed his arm off me, still trying to embody Baby A, wherever she was. "Take that up with Gram."

He rolled his eyes, which I followed only to land on Q Johnson, standing with a Sprite can. "She'll make me wait."

"Then wait."

"Or . . . ," he lulled, trying to lead me where I knew this was going.

I buckled at the knees to avoid bending over as I sifted through the nearby icebox, popping open the frosty tab of a Dr Pepper as I spoke. "The last time you night-golfed, Gram about switched us on the driving range. You broke the planter for her sago palm and chipped a clubhouse window."

"That means *no fuckin' way*, Jason," Wendell piped up.

I nodded, noticing a fresh scratch on Wendell's cheek. He had a track record, not just from Baby A but from other girls we trusted, of being too forward. He'd corner you, grab you, expect you. I imagined in the moment, soda can numbing my grip, that the scratch on Wendell's face had chips of nail polish blistered inside it, baking in the sun. That he'd soon get a bulbous, painful infection. I couldn't decide if I thought the scratch was made defensively or deliciously. I'd have had to ask her to be sure, whoever she was, but I knew he wouldn't sport a mark like that at a community event if he wasn't chomping at the bit to brag about it. I imagined she was perfectly pleased with him and herself, and that no innocent woman had been injured in the making of this wound. Knowing what Wendell had been back then, and the man he would become, I was glad Baby A had tried to steer clear of him after their fling ended.

"Too bad," Q said, gaze stuck on the ground. His olive skin oiled in the heat.

Q Johnson was supposed to be my fixation that summer, my attempt at the romance Baby C found in her horoscopes and Baby A found in boys like Rich. I wanted to be somewhere in between, to wrestle with desire because it—desire—seemed to occupy my sisters' time in a way I hadn't much known. I'd just floated all that while in their wake, toward whatever Gram demanded. And besides, Q was the only sweet boy there was, had ever been really, in Longshadow. He was asks-about-your-day sweet. The cartilage in his nose was uniquely bent, eyes rounded out like simplified equations. Bulky glasses covered all of this, though I wasn't entirely sure he didn't prefer it that way. I wanted Q to look at me. Bright eyes. Familiar eyes. My tan, smooth chest. I wanted to be wanted, maybe more than I wanted to want.

I brought two fingers to my jutted hipbone above the elastic of my shorts as I stood in the cluster of boys. There was a large brunette freckle where I touched. I tapped around it. "I guess, if you came late enough. And swear you won't break anything."

"After the football scrimmage?" Wendell asked.

"I mean, like midnight. You'd have to bring your own clubs. If we banged around the closet, Gram would hear." Q was nodding rhythmically, watching a dog in the distance circle around a tree trunk before it sat. I knew I'd revealed myself to Jason with the fingers at my waist. Baby C padded up, feet slapping against the wet ground. "And you'd have to park in the alley. She can hear an engine minutes away."

Baby C touched the fingers by my hip, curious. "She who?"

"Gram," answered Jason.

"What are we hiding from her?"

Q gave his attention like a wish, favorable between Baby C and me. "Night golfing." Baby C squeezed my pinkie. "Steer clear of windows."

Q laughed, but hadn't I said that? I breathed deeply, feeling faint with surfaced embarrassment as I shimmied away from her hand. She pulled my arm back as if in a dance and said, "Girls are waiting for us at the Shuggarts'. Julie Martelli says her brother is back."

As we weaved through bustling yards toward Bailee Shuggart's, I let my sister walk ahead while I watched. Everything— the mood of our presence, our hip-to-leg ratio, the plumpness of our lips—was the same. My sister said there was a pair of boys pissing over a fence, and I heard our sole distinction: her voice a higher, grassy falsetto. I said "Yeah" and was disgusted that my voice was nothing but agreeable, engineered for harmonies, for yes-ma'ams and certainly-sirs.

We sat on the roof outside Bailee's bedroom, watching our classmates create a whirlpool at the shallow end of the pool, holding hands and spinning in a circle. They spun in unison to conduct a strong enough current to let go and get cast about in the swirl. Their bodies clanged together while they laughed, every touch inescapably sensual, so stripped down and damp. When the whirlpool broke, the illusion shattered as if it had never happened. They did not marvel at their creation. They didn't dizzy with the whiplash of motion. They bobbed languidly toward corners of the pool, dove to retrieve plastic toys, touching each other in small ways under the distorted surface. I wished I'd been in the middle of it.

Julie burst onto the roof with a beer bottle in hand. "Geez, you guys stink."

Baby C and I craned our necks, discreetly sniffing our pits. Everybody stank. It was summer. Julie sloshed beer onto my thigh as she sat in a jumble next to me. "It's so much nicer in Ann Arbor. God, I wish I was in Ann Arbor."

Bailee reached for Julie's beer and took a sip. "Why were you in Maine?"

"Michigan, you idiot."

"Ouch," I said, as if I'd been pinched.

"Well then, she shouldn't be dumb." Julie lifted the hair up off her neck to cool down. "Anyway, we have family there. A house on the lake, you know."

"Which lake?" Baby C asked. I grinned covertly, knowing Julie would say some variation of *Ugh, I don't know*, which she did.

"Anyway," Julie began again like a bad habit, "we picked up Pete on the way back. The college guys are so hot at A&M. It's ridiculous. And Petey's friends are all older, which makes them way hotter. I wish I were going there." She said this to remind us she was headed for Middlebury next month, where she would have opportunity and possibility, and we—the girls and me—would be stuck here, digging golf balls out of bayou muck.

"How is A&M on the way *back* from Michigan?" Bailee asked.

Julie narrowed her eyes hatefully at the side of Bailee's face. She'd always resented Bailee for being beautiful and kind and wanting nothing from her. "You wouldn't know, would you? When have you ever been anywhere?"

Bailee wasn't fazed. Just tilted her head a bit. "We go to San Antonio sometimes."

Baby C knocked my knee with hers, both of us with laughter biting at our lips. Julie scoffed, got up, and left her half-empty beer behind as she crawled back through the window.

Bailee exhaled. "Do you think college has made her brother less weird?"

This time, Baby C and I laughed. "He wasn't weird," I said. "Just . . . reserved."

"And for an objectively hot guy, that's weird."

"I don't know." I picked up Julie's beer and swirled it around. "I've always thought there was something sweet about him."

"That's because he hardly says anything."

"True!" Baby C nearly shouted, then recoiled as it reverberated through the yards. We had to talk this way about the Martellis. Their dad had been, and was still somehow, the safety manager at BP. Most everybody blamed him in part for the explosion, wanted to slash his tires when they saw the emblem of his midlife crisis—a burnt orange Ford Charger that he treated like a Porsche—double-parked in the Seeglow's lot. I'd only known one of the fifteen men that'd died, Rich and Cart Goodson's dad, which garnered the only smudge of empathy I reserved for them. Julie seemed to ignore the whole thing, choosing to feel persecuted, which I'd have thought would unite her with the girls and me, peel back her fierce veneer, but it only seemed to embolden her meanness. So we had to talk critical; it was the only power against them we had.

Bailee motioned for the beer. "One of you should date him?"

Baby C and I looked between each other, scrunch-faced. "Which one?"

"Does it matter? Oh!" Bailee fluttered spastically like a caught butterfly. "There he is." I followed her finger to see only a collective of floppy-haired heads, shirtless bodies.

"Where?"

She pushed into my shoulder with hers. "In the green trunks. With the close cut."

Pete had always had a closer haircut than other boys, sheared to the ears even when the football team got mullets and the baseball boys grew rattails. Everyone assumed he'd go into the armed forces mostly because of how seriously he treated hunting, like a sport, but word got around his second year of undergrad that he'd scored so highly on the MCAT that Texas A&M was going to admit him to the veterinary medicine grad school program early, without finishing his undergraduate degree. It made sense to me. He always seemed to look at the girls and me as if we were wounded dogs, although I wasn't sure that he didn't look at everyone that way. He was nice enough. Quiet and odd, like Bailee said. He had helped tame the disdain for his father by carrying our football team to a 4A state championship, which we came a couple yards from winning. I saw grown men cry after we lost that game, the whole town gathered in the Rice University stadium, a bunch of boys keeled over on the field sobbing into their helmets as the team from Lake Travis whooped and hollered around them. It was the same feeling, looking at him from the roof, as it was watching him on the field; expecting brilliance of him, someone I didn't know at all. Pete squirmed in his flip-flops, shifting weight between his legs, until, as if he could feel himself being watched, he looked suddenly behind him and up toward the roof. I cowered, and the girls laughed with their backs straight. His eyes in the difficult night were like a coyote's caught behind a garbage can, uncanny and nearly neon.

Bailee rattled on, even while we watched Pete, eventually arriving at her agenda: to bleed us for information about Jason, whose shell necklace clutched his neck like a string of baby teeth. It made me think of Gull and the tray of sand dollars that he coveted, shoved under his bed, his direct line to an underbelly water world. Sometimes we'd pass his room to see him crouched, sandwiching his head between two shells over his ears, trying to hear the ocean or existence, angels mumbling.

Baby C shouted Jason's name from the roof, and Bailee swatted at me as I sat silently beside them. Bailee sneered, "Oh my God guys. Shut up. You bitch." All the while she grinned, face pinking in July halogen, and I thought about Q Johnson, who'd been standing in the cluster with Pete and Jason. I tried to feel something for him, even something as simple as want, but I was all thought, no feeling, and only felt ashamed.

"What do you like about Jason?" I asked Bailee.

"He's so funny. And"—she popped up, as if having a revelation—"he treats you girls just like anyone else. That comforts me. Like I could trust him, you know? He wouldn't go talking about us. Other boys can't help themselves. They've got diarrhea of the mouth."

We laughed in reflex, though Baby C and I wilted a bit again. It wasn't Bailee's fault—they all acted that way, like kindness toward us was a charity. She was right about Jason, though; he could keep a secret. He made it look easy, like you could forget things you didn't want to know or remember. I wished I had that, and I felt encouraged that the quality of privacy could breed connection and desire. I told myself I was ready to step into sex and love and crushing and stupidity. Julie and Baby A, even Bailee, made it look like the only thing to do, like such fun.

Somebody raced up from the boat dock to say there was a gator, which caused people to funnel away from the party and toward the dock he'd run from, pointing and leaning over the edge, snapping pictures with flip phones. Baby C rested her body against mine. She asked if there'd ever been a gator killing.

"Of course," I said. "Surely."

She asked where. I said between here and the bay. "Bullshit," Bailee said. I told her to ask her dad, who managed a marina on Galveston Island. She yelled down, "Hey Daddy, has there ever been a gator killing?"

He looked up at us. "Not in the last five years."

The answer contented Baby C, who'd shifted to picking at dead skin on her heel. Bailee left to immerse herself in the huddle of mop-headed boys, looking silly on the lawn with both hands on her hips, loitering obviously near Jason. I cringed, thinking of myself moments earlier near Q, fingers at my hips. The pangs in my stomach hadn't subsided; both Baby C and I had been squirming covertly on the roof. I hoped that, wherever Baby A was stashed with Rich, it wasn't in some bush or brush. I was always oddly anxious she'd get poison ivy in an awful place. I was jealous that Baby A didn't have to wonder about boys. She just knew. Knew what she wanted, who had it, and how to get it. I looked over at Baby C on the roof and wondered if she wanted boys that way, if she sweated sometimes in her dreams, too.

A snap of fireworks broke out in a cluster of boys in the Crack-hauers' yard, shirtless with Zippos and beer cans. Some dad snatched the lighter and walloped his hand against each of their necks, saying, "Boy, it ain't dark enough yet." I laughed so hard I had to get off the roof. Baby C didn't care to follow.

Mr. Shuggart, who was standing near the pool covered in a milky film of sunscreen and salt, waved a chicken kebab in my face when I emerged onto the porch. I nibbled around the wooden skewer as I spotted Uncle Henry entering the yard to pawn off Aunt Rachel's extra tamales. He asked me about the benefit

tournament the next weekend, and I told him that if he offered
Gram those tamales and donated a whole wad of cash to the children's hospital we put the tournament on for, he could probably
shoot a spot. He got quiet in a way that could only mean he was
thinking about his work at the funeral home. It was a given that
Gram would weasel him onto the tournament roster, knowing
full well she'd have to deal with the other men when they pitched
a fit. "Isadora, that's plumb nepotism," they'd say, and she'd turn
her back in response.

An hour later, after the sunset, those boys popped off fireworks,
disregarding the burn ban. An off-duty sheriff flicked at a lighter
alongside them. "Just aim well above the trees."

Firework trash littered four backyards and dangled from trees
like streamers. The dim night was forgiving, casting our silhou-
ettes in ways that made us straighten up, remembering that we
were still in a masquerade. I'd left Baby C on the roof, alone.
Baby A was off somewhere dark, hiding with Rich. I felt breath
against one of their chests. I felt wincing in our shared stomach.
She was about to get sick again, Baby C. She had been throwing
up, for no discernible reason, since we were thirteen. Sometimes
Gram called it a bug, dehydration, heat exhaustion, or said Baby
C was "upset." Nothing she ate seemed to settle her. We didn't
talk about it.

I hadn't dipped in anybody's pool that day. It felt weakening,
stripping in front of the town, splashing around with their kids
like we were the same. Though they were cordial to the girls and
me in front of Gram, there was always a sense that we were un-
welcome, a bother. Murphy's bastard triplet girls, with eyes that
brought her back from the grave. Harriet Shrub had bothered to
show up, to everybody's surprise, and she grasped my face again

while I stood in the grass, tilted it toward the skittish neon bursts. I was happy not to be her granddaughter. If I'd wanted to stop her compulsion, I could've reminded her that there was a fifty-fifty chance the girls and I'd be blinking her son's brown eyes right back at her, or that our hair would likely have a defined curl as hers did. Anyway, I kind of liked being touched.

Jason and the boys—Wendell, Q Johnson, and the Goodson twins, Rich and Cart—snuck over to play night golf, and it went off without a hitch. Cart was back just for the weekend; he'd been gone for the bulk of that summer, leading Boy Scout trips through parks across the state. The boys yammered about the itch to get out, never saying where they'd go. They ate beef jerky and corn nuts, chewed with their mouths open, cackled. Their tummies jutted out above their jeans, forming beer guts, save for Jason and Q. They scratched and ate and laughed, pointing their fingers at each other. They feared nothing, and we couldn't relate. We'd thought they were pathetic, those boys, though we weren't sure if we were entirely different.

I was too focused on Baby C and Q Johnson to make the easy short putts later that night. They were standing close to each other, their shadows fused. Jason and Cart put their foreheads against the golf club grips and spun around with their heads hung, golf clubs as their axle, then tried to walk in straight lines until they fell over. They rested where they landed, dizzied by ricocheting stars.

Baby A had said Julie was going to show after she helped her parents clean up the pool-hop trash in their yard. I looked into the shine of every headlight for Julie's car, but she never appeared, which was just as well. I didn't really want to hear more about who she'd thought had dressed like a slut at the pool hop, or which parents she'd heard were stepping out.

My gut turned over like an engine again. I figured it was Baby A behind the toolshed with Rich, but I looked up to see Baby C standing behind Q, her hands over his, clasping him correctly to the grip of a putter. I could sense their sweaty warmth. It seemed clinical; on its face there was no cause for worry. I tried to feel for her stomach, her mind, the swirling. I could see on Q's face that he was aiming outside the hole on purpose.

Baby C seemed to take Q's easy missed putts as sincere mistakes, showing him different ways to grip the club, better stance, better posture, until she couldn't bear to watch the ball so short of the hole. She exhaled deeply as she released her hands from atop his—just another untalented boy.

Baby C lay down next to Wendell, splayed across the lawn. Q lingered, looked over at me as I stood, hovering my palms over tall monkey grass to feel the sharp blades. With Q's eyes on me, I began to mimic the distant bullfrog song and waited for him to cackle the way he did with the boys. Instead, he walked toward the hole and fished a golf ball out, sat near my sister, and pointed behind the toolshed where Rich and Baby A were.

"Go inside," Wendell shouted at Rich and Baby A. "It's cold." But it wasn't. It was so hot that sweat pooled in the folds of my elbows. I lifted them into the inky evening sky to air-dry like I was a mystic who could make the water rise; I felt ridiculous. Desire for Q bucked around in my chest. The southern night sounds mocked me.

The boys trickled away that night around two o'clock in the morning. Rich had driven and made them all wait until he was done sucking at Baby A's neck in painful patches, his eyes shut so hard. I could feel the suction at my own jugular as I watched the desperation on his face. I twitched beneath the tightness as if bugs were biting me, slapping at the air for effect, afraid the boys in the truck were watching. Cart nearly honked, but Wendell swatted his hand away from the wheel before it landed. The boys clattered their untrimmed nails lightly against the metal body of the vehicle, arms dangling from windows. It sounded like a miracle of tin bells.

If Rich had opened his shut eyes, he would've been pummeled with the boulder of Baby A's body doubles, just as chiseled, just as beautiful, but not nearly as willing, which is why he clung to her. When I watched Rich kiss my sister and pull away, he seemed stupefied, walking off as if he'd just conquered something, shoved his dingy flagpole into the cheekbone of a new planet. Then the boys idled down the drive, following their weak headlight cast. Flagsticks scattered across the course were limp. It was a breezeless night.

"He just about sucked out your thorax," Baby C said as she reached to touch Baby A's forming bruises.

"Felt nice, huh?" Baby A smirked.

"No." I winced. "Felt like being vacuum sealed from the outside in."

"A sexy vacuum."

We laughed, getting our loudest sounds out before going inside. Gram was hellfire when we woke her up with hollering. Baby C's fingers swept over Baby A's skin. "Maybe they'll look like Cassiopeia in the morning."

"That's a planet?"

"No, a constellation."

"Will you predict my future by staring into it?"

"I can only do that with pumpkin seeds while they're drying."

"And the orange peels."

"Yes, the orange peel. But you've gotta eat the whole orange first."

"Relax," Baby A said. "I'm too tired for the future. We need to creep down the hall single file."

Together we stepped only on the sturdiest edges of the hardwood panels. We moved toward the bedroom that held our dreams and waited to hear the rustle of Gram in the other room. Clothes slipped off our lithe bodies like butter. We left them on the floor, admiring the stray ways the linen and denim settled. It was no use putting them in the hamper, knowing we'd step into a different combination of them when we woke: my shorts on Baby A, her tank top perfumed to death and hanging off Baby C's shoulders.

The girls seemed to drift into sleep easily. Baby C muttered a bit as she cozied up to her pillow, *Manifest YOU. Fulfillment IS* on quiet refrain until she'd muttered herself to sleep. I tossed on my twin mattress, overwhelmed by the thick wall of heat that seemed to be pushing down on me as I lay in bed, the raucous bug buzz. Eventually I retreated down the hallway to drape myself across the clubhouse couch. Curled fetally, I set my face on the armrest like a dog waiting for someone to get home. Sometime midmorning, Gull gathered inside the shell of my legs when he followed Gram downstairs to preheat the oven. She woke us a while later with a dripping whisk in one hand, other hand beneath it to catch the frothy drops. "You two want to help me ice these sweet rolls?"

Slouching beneath the blanket hanging across his wingspan like a cape, Gull followed her to climb onto the counter and drag a lazy butter knife coated in powdered sugar frosting. The girls slogged into the kitchen. "I told you she'd be down here," Baby A said as she pointed at me. "Why'd you get up so early?"

"Bugs were too loud outside the window."

Gram slapped a hand against her exposed leg, swimsuit cutting just at her hipbone. "Makes me wonder why we even bought you a bed." She kissed my forehead. "Our very own lookout." Baby C shrugged, and Baby A walked around the kitchen island, stuck her finger into a glob of cinnamon roll icing, and licked it off.

While Gram and Baby C swam, Gull and I retraced words on the concession signs, scrubbing the fairway chalkboard to write down the pairs for the benefit tournament the next day. I lifted Gull to scratch away the congealed dirt in the chalkboard corners. He tapped his finger below each letter I wrote, glancing from the board to the scrap of paper with the lineup, checking my spelling. It was a list of clergy, physicians, athletic coaches, and friends-of-friends who qualified just barely.

As we set up, I considered Q and Baby C the night before. If my hands had been the ones he'd held against the golf club, maybe I'd understand what, if anything, I wanted from him. You know how when you touch someone, you learn? It was that I wanted someone else to know me, to tell me who I was, that I was a good person, to be my own enough for them to single me out beside my sisters. Not enough to be easy, the way Baby A was with Rich. But I wanted touch—I needed it to learn. Who the hell could I convince to touch me?

People filtered into the clubhouse in pastel shorts and pageboy hats as if our livelihood was immersive theater. They chattered and practiced their swings, turned golf balls over nervously in their hands. After a while I spotted Q beside his father, with Jason and Uncle Henry. Baby C brisked absently by with a tray of downturned lemonade glasses, and I watched uncomfortably as Q looked her up and down. I wondered if he was trying to riddle out which she was or if—as we all craved—he knew it was her.

There was a quiet conviction about Q. He didn't need other boys to tell him what to do.

Most players had pulled fistfuls of oranges from our trees, which we had always encouraged because there was only so much orange juice a family could drink, and the citrus reminded them to hydrate. Still, men swooned themselves silly in the heat, refusing to sit for a second as warmth overwhelmed their veiny necks. I'd learned when we were younger that putting ice cubes inside an ear cools the body near-instant. The patrons managed to wrangle one man toward a cooler as he swayed on his ankles. Before they sat him atop it, I reached in, not announcing myself before pressing the cold into his reddened ears. He turned his face to see me—sweating angel number two—and I recognized the patron as Mr. Shrub, Harriet's husband. It seemed when I saw her, she was always alone and lonely, so when Mr. Shrub turned up it always took me a stride extra to place him. His eyes were bloodshot, skin flaking, pulsing. He let out a small laugh as he kept an empty gaze on me. "Thanks, sugar," he said, reaching for the ice cubes I held in the other hand. I spilled them into his palm and let him take hold of the melted fraction against his ear.

"A smart one, this one. You tell the others I said that. You—the smart one." He blinked, and the purposeful flutter of his lids struck through me. The *others*. I would not tell my sisters that I was the smart one.

I wanted a bottle of water from the cooler he sat on, but I stuck my head under the spigot behind the toolshed instead. I looked out toward hole nine, what we called Pine Needle Walkway, where Mr. Shrub was back on his feet, attempting an off-balance three putt.

Q was caddying for his father, as Jason was doing for Uncle Henry. Gram had paired them up to be kind. I slipped inside the toolshed, dragged fingers beneath my arms, and smelled them; a sweet tinge clung to overwhelming musk. I darted inside the clubhouse for a magazine, flipped through *Better Homes and Gardens* until I found an untorn, most likely rancid DKNY Be Delicious sample to rub along my contours. Then I waited for Gram to send me on an errand. My stomach wrenched with a familiar, shared sensation. I wondered if it was nerves, or if one of the girls was getting sick from the heat. I thought it might be that Rich had snuck over and stolen Baby A away for a quick tryst, but as I considered this, Baby A burst into the clubhouse for some air, hand at her stomach, too, catching my scent. "You smell like bug guts and peach juice." She pressed her sweaty nose to my neck. "Who's it for?" She caught a slab of my side between her fingers and twisted. "Tell me, you tart."

"It's nothing. We just smell so bad. I thought—"

Baby A dusted her sight across the room, dodging old men and furniture, then dragged me by a piece of arm fat to the window. "Should we take a guess, then?"

"Oh, please. Jesus. Really. I'm a sweaty gross mess, that's all."

"No, no, no. The only people here are old men and us. Why would you give a rat's ass how you smell? Unless it's . . ." She peered beyond the spotty condensation on the window. Gull was sitting by a ball bucket, knocking a tee around between his ankles. Gram and Baby C were off screen, doing as they should have. Baby A drew in a deep breath. "We don't know him, or him. That guy is grayed. That guy is married, but he does look young. So it's Q or Pete Martelli. Or it's Jonah Kwiatkowsky, but I like to think you have taste."

I wanted to evaporate. I wanted to slap her, bite her smooth skin, rip at her hair. As she tried to zone in on my desires, I wanted to scream at her that I wasn't even sure I had any, okay? The way my stomach turned when Rich kissed her, the way my skin burned when he touched her; it didn't feel, through her, like something I wanted. But what was wrong with me? Well, what was *wrong* was that I could never be sure it was me that they stared at, and how could she be sure? I wanted to poke my finger hard into her chest. *Huh? How can you be so sure?*

I looked away from her desperately, for Gull or Gram. They'd tell her to pound sand. To leave me be. I looked back, and her finger was against the window, in line with Q's body, wading through the vibrations of heat. He looked thirsty. "I need to get them drinks."

Baby A gripped my upper arm. "It's him?"

"Let go." I yanked away from her with an out-of-character ferocity. Her expression faded as if she'd had a realization; the bells behind her eyes seemed to toll. "Oh, I'm sorry. I'm so sorry." As she chased me into the kitchen, where I submerged my hands in an icebox on the counter, she kept her voice low. "I didn't know. Which of us is it?" I plunged my hands farther into the ice. "Who does he think you are?"

The ice and her questions had stunned me. "What?"

"That's it, isn't it?" Her hand was on my arm again, gentled. "He thinks you're me. Or her. Or he thinks she is you."

"He doesn't think of me," I said into the cold of the cooler. "If anything, he thinks of her. I've seen it." Ice popped out as I wriggled around. She kicked it toward the fridge like a puck. I gripped two cold colas, expecting her to argue: *How can you tell? You know these dumb boys, their brains begin in their britches. You wouldn't know.* Instead, she wiped my wrists with a dishrag.

"It happens every time," she said. "It's a whole thing, really. The *talk*. Before, you know. When they flirt or touch my knee or some shit. They just need convincing."

"I don't want to convince anyone—"

She touched my face lovingly, in a way she hardly did, the way a mother might when her baby cries. "It doesn't matter, in the end, which of us it is."

This compounded my confusion. "How can it not matter?"

"Sometimes"—her gaze flickered between me and the window—"it's better."

She told me about the game they played, she and Rich. How in his ear, she rattled off our names as they kissed, while his hand surveyed her skin, toppled over slopes and delved into her trenches. The hot-and-cold game where you tell a person *you're getting warmer* or *you're freezing, oh, you're ice cold* as they circle around a prize. It wasn't temperature she taunted Rich with—it was us. He neared her hipbone, and she cried my name; he kissed her collar, and she whined about Baby C. She stayed silent in the areas that had her written all over them; the soft bit of underarm as it met the side of breast, her inner thigh, her outer lip, biting down like it was honeysuckle, about to spill a sweet drop. This was how she kept Rich coming back for more, bottle-feeding this deep confusion. And what part of it was his fault? Growing up in a town that paid no mind to our differences? Other things were his fault, but not that. Other things. Bigger things.

Baby A touched my jawline and said that was my spot, too. How had she decided this?

"Your stomach turns deepest here, and here, and there." She moved her hand across my body clinically, as if she held a stethoscope. I was horrified. Shocked she was using the idea of us as sex bait. Confused that she was bringing me in on it, urging me toward the same. This was why Rich looked at us that way, why he seemed so gross and sly. But who else had she done this to? What other boys were walking around as if they'd been with all three of the Manatee's girls?

I wanted to shout: *Our bodies aren't yours to fool with. This isn't fair. Take it back.* But all that came out was, "Don't you *ever* tell Baby C."

"Never."

"What does this mean?"

She seemed to glow as she stood. Maybe it was the heat or my raucous heartbeat, but something was closing in on me, her hands on my hands, trying to convince me of such a carnal thing, a thing she'd not offered to me until I was so desperate she couldn't stand it anymore. The whole while, she'd been kind of smiling. "You can be whoever they want."

WANT

Being who they want. Being wanted. Wanting. Being. She didn't say I could be who I wanted. She said *they*. They wanted revivals of Gram, mini-Manatees. Reincarnations of our mother. They wanted Gull to be blood. The course to be less dead. They wanted it to come naturally for us—everything. As I mulled this over, I plucked at my eyebrows and blew the coarse feathered hair away. I toiled for so long with fingers at my forehead that I expected to have picked myself bald. I thought about our mother and Gram, where their tender spots sparked, so much of their bodies I'd never learned.

When we were fourteen, the girls and I had talked the presence of our mother over as seriously as we ever had, standing nearly naked and comparing parts. Someone had stopped us that morning in Seeglow's, blinked psychotically into our three faces, then burst into tears. Gram had coddled the woman long enough for her to blubber that she'd returned from out of town to visit her parents and had only heard Murphy was dead, not that she'd had three girls. "How do they look just like her?" she had gasped almost angrily at Gram. "How?" Gram shook her head, held the woman by the shoulders, waiting for her to realize she ought to be embarrassed which she shortly became, wincing away from us as if we were feral hogs she'd almost hit with her car, ashamed but still threatened. We'd shattered her reality. We lived, we breathed, we looked just like someone who was gone. I held Baby C's hand on the car ride home as she cried quietly, Gram fussing about how uncouth and ridiculous the woman had been until she finally said, "There's nothing to do but feel pity for the woman, running around these years, not knowing a thing like that."

We retreated immediately to our room and taped photographs of our mother, slipped from scrapbooks, to the vanity mirror, Baby A and I occasionally moving to our upset sister to rub her back. The grain of the photos made it impossible to see beyond the bead of Murphy's eyes, much less the marks on her body. Still, we measured ourselves against the idea of her, and each other.

"My hipbone ends just here."

"Mine too."

"My second toe is longer than the first."

"Mine is."

"Same."

"Our hair, let's sway it in the light."

We bent our necks back and rustled, gazing from side to side. It could've been anyone's hair. There was no telling. It came down to counting freckles.

"If we'd known how many she'd had . . ."

We said this to Gram as we loomed over her in the recliner in our skivvies. Gram tilted her head at this like a pup with a question. She toyed with a flap of skin on her neck. "Girls . . . ," she began, then paused to gaze through us and back through the years. "I never lived a day thinkin' my baby would be gone. That I'd have to keep her around somehow." She drew her attention back, admiring our faces. "Look what she left me, in just her way. Perfect reminders."

Thinking our mother had died "in just her way" seemed to make the whole idea easier on Gram, because then there never had to be a reason. Like a dream, she could let it go.

The girls and I ran back up the stairs and continued to pore over our skin, tallying marks on a notepad in an impossible merry-go-round. We tapped our fingers along, each slight shade of brown blurring into the next until the room, our breath, the day, was one giant unconquerable freckle.

We'd wanted to be different from our mother and each other, but not too different. We didn't say this. Sixty-four freckles each, exactly. One hundred ninety-two together. We could've cried. Gull had been waiting patiently outside our door to ask the number—he'd been learning to count—and Baby A could hardly stand to tell him.

I put this moment and Baby A's admission in the clubhouse side by side, trying to reconcile how she could feel such a need for individuality that she'd stand naked with us as we counted our marks with her complete compromise of any personhood just to play a game with Rich Goodson, to screw with his mind. Part of me was convinced I was making too big a deal out of what she'd told me. I'd give anything to go back, to tell myself that I wasn't.

The night of the freckle-counting those years ago, Baby C insisted, flustered, that we pile into a cart with her and drive out to the thirteenth hole, the farthest from the clubhouse we could get. Bayou water sloshed against itself in melodramatic measure; the creatures of the course croaked and trilled. Baby C huddled us onto the green with cutout cards, a flashlight, and a handful of beads. It felt like we were in a film, the feeling that what you're living in, you will return to forever, so I straightened my back and fluffed my hair a bit. Among Baby C's materials were the pictures of our mother from the mirror as well as newspaper clippings I hadn't seen before. When I zoomed in on them, I realized that they were our mother's obituary and our subsequent birth announcement, from entirely separate sections of the same day's paper. "God, what are you going to make us do?" Baby A said with a tinge of judgment. "Pray over it?"

Baby C pulled a headband made of colored braces bands from her pile and stretched it across her forehead. Then she distributed bracelets of the same to us. Baby A launched hers with a sting at my skin. To my sister's question, Baby C nodded once and grabbed our hands, bowed her head. "Dear Mother. We come to you not knowing what to do. And we come to you, um, trying to find you and, uh, wanting some answers. So, we pray, please give us the guidance to find you but also to feel better with, um, our, uh . . . bodies. It is hard that we look like you and each other. It makes us sad, and other people sad, so please show us what to do and touch our hearts and everything. Yes, um . . . Amen."

While she prayed with her eyes closed, Baby A and I looked at each other in periphery, unsure if we should poke fun or if this was something Baby C needed to be serious. Our sister lifted her head, released our hands, which she'd squeezed red, and exhaled. "I found something." She shuffled around clippings from that week's paper. "This says: 'Gemini, the domestic cycle clashes with external endeavors. Take leave and listen to the hoofbeat. The artist who paints the pasture yearns for deeper greens. Escape the house to learn the world. Dream yourself untangled.' "

She gazed at us with neon hope, pointing. "It means something. It means, uh, well—"

The sheen of tolerance Baby A maintained had burst, and she threw her hands up. "I'm sorry. I really am, but are you trying to resurrect her from the dead? I mean, are you worshipping Satan now? I just—"

"Stop it," I said sharply. "It's just the paper."

Baby A's eyes narrowed; she'd expected me to join her. "Look, I know we're all feeling lumped together and very weird about it, but I'm sorry, C, I'm not praying to Satan or our dead mother for you. I'm just not."

"Don't be mean," Baby C said with an outstretched hand. "Please."

The dark wrapped around Baby A as she stepped into the golf cart and drove off, leaving us a nine-minute walk from the house. Baby C began to cry again. We carried her scraps back in our hands, the beads clattering around inside the cups of our bras. "Don't let her hurt your feelings. Oh please, don't. She's just being mean for the sake of it. You know she doesn't think you worship Satan." As we walked, Baby C stopped every few steps to wipe her eyes, not once saying a word against our sister but vowing in silence to never share our horoscope with her again, even when she told me Baby A could *really* use it. We left our ability to talk openly about our mother on the thirteenth hole that night, and an anger toward Baby A hardened in my sister that wouldn't erupt until years later, that summer of nineteen, when we pulled and stretched away from each other.

The benefit tournament lasted the next few days. Each morning we made sure to wear the same color we had the day before, which seemed a betrayal, making it easier on them. By the second day a barbecue food truck was parked in our gravel lot, hocking sandwiches, making the air smell of pepper sausage when we'd worked so hard to make it smell like grass.

As we got dressed, Baby C threaded a bow like her own through my hair, working her fingers gently as she whispered our horoscope from one of her papers into my ear. " 'This month will end practically, with your sensibility prevailing against temptation and self-doubt. Push feelings of unworthiness and shame out of July's door and welcome the new bloom of August, bringing with it rest and bright moments of belief in yourself. August welcomes you to bloom anew, too.' "

Having not heard her, Baby A let out a great sigh. "It's nearly August."

"Almost school time for the others."

"I need to make tips today," Baby A said. "Our gas guzzler is killing me."

"We're supposed to be getting tips?" Baby C asked.

"Almost school time," I repeated mostly to myself.

"Julie was supposed to bring me her cute skirt. Dammit."

Baby C kept on in my ear, flipping through her stack of papers to reread a section she'd marked. " 'We have allowed contentment to muddle the telescope. Surprise, symmetry, and the fruits of hard labors are already taking seed in your future. Sharpen focus and steady both feet! It is time to begin the voyage toward joy. The time is ripe.' "

Her hands returned to my hair, curling the ends around a finger. "Isn't that just great? *The time is ripe.*"

Baby A rolled the cuffs of her shorts, moving across the carpet to do the same to mine. Then she walked out of the room. Baby C kissed the top of my head where the sun had burned my scalp. "It's a great way to put it," I said, to show her I was listening. "The time is ripe."

She tugged on my hair a bit, then tugged my ear around. "Can I tell you something, B?" Her voice lilted with a flight that rattled me. I nodded, my back still to her. "The other day, I brought Jason's group some cold water. Q said he was dehydrated, so I drove him back to the clubhouse—you were dealing with Mr.

Shrub, remember?—and Q said he'd like to text me sometime, so I said 'No, call.' Then he said he'd call, and before they left, he pulled me behind the toolshed and kissed me on the cheek. On the cheek! Like a real gentleman." Her head was rested against my back. "It just feels true, now. *The time is ripe.* I'm so excited. I could die."

My throat contorted with tears. I was grateful to have my back to her, as it afforded me a precious moment to collect myself; if she knew I'd even thought about Q, she'd never take him. That was the kind of person she was. I turned slowly on top of the comforter to face her, her cheeks pinked beyond belief with glee, and what I thought I'd felt for Q was instantly dwarfed by how much I needed to see my sister fulfilled. I hadn't expected that. The deep ache in the pit of my stomach the day before, in the toolshed, had to have been the heat of their movements, their stowing away behind a few trees, that cheek kiss. Still, selfish thing I was, I tried to poke a few holes. "You seemed annoyed with him at night golfing, though."

Baby C waved her hand. "Oh, I was just distracted. It was a full moon. I was feeling all sorts of uncanny things."

"Well, do you think anybody saw?"

"Him kiss me?"

I nodded.

"What does that matter? They wouldn't know the difference. Besides, it was the cheek. Sweet as can be." She'd moved from fidgeting with my hair to squeezing the circulation out of her bare feet. I covered her hands with mine, unfurling her grip, and exhaled as I decided to let Q go. Even in this world—my world, in which everything was supposed to be about me—I was fine to let them be. In part, I was relieved. Many times I'd envisioned Q pulling me behind the toolshed for a kiss, and in each imagining,

I'd felt like a fool, like a stand-in for a movie scene that was embarrassing to watch.

"I'm happy for you," I said.

The girls and I milled about the grounds, tending where we could to the wayward needs of the tournament on its final day. Baby A pulled me aside frequently to check her makeup, or for help rolling the cuffs of her shorts. Baby C was riding around most of the day in a golf cart stacked with water bottles, ball markers, and plastic cups of cubed fruit. My avoidance of them was otherwise successful; I had something of Baby C's to keep, and something of Baby A's, which was only difficult to deal with when we were all together. Q was there, watching the players who'd made the cut finish their last rounds. I tried to dampen my awareness of him so that I could be better at letting the short-lived possibility of him go.

I was exhausted by the tournament and relieved it was nearly over.

Even the animals stalking about the marshy spots seemed tired. All the egrets had fallen asleep standing up. The fairway was browning, chunks missing from its face where there'd been big swings followed by mostly misses. Everyone's short games were perplexingly off; the putts were lined up, their grips on the clubs were fine, and somehow the ball would curve just about the cusp of the hole, or halt—out of nowhere—a few inches short. The golfers looked at us, half skeptical, as if we were standing behind the trees, cursing the trajectories of their shots, wanting this disappointment for them. Bayou Bloom had always been, if nothing else, a playable course. That weekend something gurgled beneath, rattled us where we stood. Though the golfers walked about staggered, they'd racked up a bunch of donations for the hospital, enough for Gull to stay in their good graces for a few off-the-books ENT appointments.

Julie Martelli appeared, driving a cart around with Baby A in the passenger seat, the two of them cackling, pointing at the men hunched over to putt, the frump of their pants against their flat behinds. Julie's laugh cratered the tranquility of our safe space, for me and the patrons. She was only on this earth to judge, we all knew. I hoped she and my sister wouldn't spot me as they bopped around. That they'd drive on by.

As the last two groups played through the seventeenth and eighteenth holes. Dr. Dotson maintained a steady two-stroke lead throughout the weekend, scoring an eleven-foot eagle on his first hole of the day, ushering the wind out of the sails of the men trailing close behind. I made my way back to the clubhouse to catalog the current scores before adjusting the board to reflect the doc's inevitable win. The heat had wrung me out. I trudged along the grass with my head hung, watching my feet as each step sent a tense ache up both calves. I prayed Baby C and Q were stashed away in the woods so I wouldn't have to look at them, and the awful, vengeful part of me that resented her for having done nothing wrong, for being perfect and secure and wanted, hoped they'd never return. The metal *thwack* of clubs striking golf balls resounded, a morphic sound that could create the same blood-stilling boom as gunfire, could engage the stagnant air and tree branches in ways that landed on our ears like music. I'd been hurrying so wildly through the course in an attempt to rush away from my thoughts that I didn't realize I'd cut the corner toward the clubhouse too quickly, pushing through the back door, where I toppled over Gull, who was carrying broken bottle glass. Instinctively, his grip tightened around the shards in his hand as we collided. The squawking tears were immediate. Then the blood.

I scooped Gull up, barged past the patrons sitting in the club-house den toward the kitchen, and set him, curled with pain, on the island top, covered with sticky wet rings of lemonade and pea-nut shells, the only concessions we offered besides the gumbo.

Gull shrieked louder. He'd stuck his hand down on the counter to brace and got stray lemon juice in the cut. I made sure to keep a hand on him as I scanned the room. "Where is the fucking first aid kit?" When I turned back, gripping the only medicinal-looking tube I could find in our drawers, Gull had leaned away and was being wrapped in a towel, tightly, hands above his head as Pete Martelli secured the tail end beneath his armpit. Pete was pressing the hem of the towel to Gull's palms. "Peroxide," he said, not looking at me but smiling into Gull's flushed face. "Bandages and antibiotic ointment."

I looked at him, daft. He nodded at my hand. "That's Neosporin."

"I know, I—"

I went back to digging through drawers, flabbergasted by Pete's suddenness and the fear of what Gram would think, until I finally found the plastic first aid kit beneath the sink behind a curvy pipe and opened it like a treasure chest at Gull's side. I mus-cled Pete to the side as politely as I could and took Gull's palms into mine, leaned him over the gap between the island and sink that we could barely close, and poured the peroxide over his mo-saic of cuts. Gull winced, then relaxed when the peroxide didn't sting like he'd anticipated, distracted by the bubbles erupting from his skin. I remembered tensing, too, anytime Gram doused my wounds. Baby A always insisted that it hurt, but that was her way. Cold water washed over Gull, and he unwound at the rib cage, letting his belly bulge out with a full breath.

For good measure, I splashed some water on his face, signing to him as I said the word *heal*, pulling the symbolic pain from both my shoulders into fists. I did it over and over: *heal heal heal*. Gull nodded, his small hands throbbing, and didn't move to mock my gestures. I grazed both of his palms with my thumbs. He yanked away. I pulled him back in and brushed the hurt spots with more pressure until I could feel the poke of a bottle shard.

Pete was still there, watching, moving too familiarly toward the drawer beside the stove, where he pawed around until, miraculously, he pulled out rusted tweezers. He was duller than I'd remembered; pale in the face, the whites of his eyes soured. Still, he was undeniably handsome, blond in all the right places, with a sharp, all-knowing bend. He was clearly unsure how to handle being in a handsome body, which made me feel a twinge of pity, quickly squashed by the realization that it was entitlement that guided him comfortably about the clubhouse kitchen. He didn't respect our space or, by extension, me. My back stiffened as he poured peroxide over the metal ends of the tweezers and wiped them clean, making quite a show of it as my little brother cried. Pete stepped in front of me and took Gull's hand from mine. "May I?" he asked Gull.

"No." Gull shook his head. "Not you." He looked pleadingly at me. Pete handed over the utensils as I poked poor Gull repeatedly, trying to grasp the glass, both our faces spotted with tears. Finally I implored Gull to let Pete try, to which he agreed with a solemn nod.

Just then Gram swung open the clubhouse door, talking about something utterly trivial with Mr. Mitchum. She severed the conversation mid-sentence and followed the undercurrent of commotion she intuited toward the kitchen. I clenched my teeth—she was going to chew me out or smack me or both.

"What in the hell is going on here?" Gram stood in the doorway beneath a stained-glass mobile she'd been given the day she decided to take Gull in. With its staggered panes swirled with different hues of orange and yellow and pink, as if flowers had been ground up and blown in a fuse, melding the indescribable vibrance of summer into sheets of glass, it circled her head like a crown. Pete didn't look up or answer; he seemed to hardly notice Gram's booming voice.

I slumped further over the island, making a point to wipe the tears from my face. "I knocked into Gull, and he had bottle glass in his hands. The scare cut him."

Gram put two fingers against her neck at her pulse. "The scare cut him," she echoed, eyes roaming about the kitchen, not yet decided on how to react. The room stilled as I focused on the fingers at her neck twitching with her heart rate, as Pete Martelli picked around Gull's fleshy skin, as it was entirely my fault. "What I would like to know is, who on this side of somewhere thought it was a good idea to leave glass on a golf course?" She sent her voice flaring into the clubhouse, knowing the jagged walls would amplify the sound. "That's what y'all fools want? Children getting cut up? Just let me find out who did it."

The men in the clubhouse tensed with guilt. Being yelled at by a woman seemed to surface all the other stuff in them, making their muddy eyes bulge; the wives and the children and the money, you know. Before marching in there to fetch the intercom system and yell at the whole roster of patrons on the course, Gram soaked a hand towel, wrung it out, and molded it to Gull's head like a bandanna. He mewled and laid his head in all he could find of her—an elbow crook, billowy with the scars of removed cancerous moles. Gram let him rest there for a moment as she peered at Pete. "You're studying medicine. Is that right?"

"Veterinary medicine." He didn't lift his eyes, still focused on the shard. He looked like an overgrown child playing a game of

Operation. Gram seemed to see him fully, the way she saw us all. She reached to straighten the crease in his collar; it bothered her, as crooked things did.

"Well." Gram patted Gull's back, withdrawing her grip from Pete's shirt. "That'll work, won't it?" She looked at me, and I nodded, heartsunk.

Gram pressed the two fingers that'd taken her pulse against Gull's vibrating chest—to tell him she loved him or that she'd be back, I couldn't figure which. She stared at the scene a moment longer, then breezed past. I heard her voice over the loudspeaker not a minute later: "This is a no-glass golf course." The bottles had been San Pellegrinos from the barbecue food truck in the parking lot. Gram shooed the truck away and sent the other girls on a rake across all eighteen holes, looking for the glint of green.

"Ah." Pete dropped a mite-tiny piece into his palm, held it up to catch the kitchen fluorescence. He pushed the towel up from Gull's eyes to show him, saying, "See how it blends in?" Pete probed the glass so it'd flop on its opposite side. "Sharp little guy."

"Can I have it?" Gull asked.

"No." I pinched my thumb, pointer, and middle fingers together to sign *no*. Then I drew my pointer finger sharply to my own palm and screwed into it harshly: *pain*. "It could hurt you again." I dove the nose of my entire bent hand into my flat palm: *again*. Gull slumped and began to wriggle out of the towel, shimmying the tightened edge free of his armpit. I held him at the shoulders while Pete pulled a spool of bandage out of the plastic kit. Gull was annoyed; he'd been held up longer than he'd wanted. He flicked his eyes around like they were marbles, amusing him, while Pete layered the beige fabric across Gull's wound so it would adhere to itself. When Pete pulled the fabric taut, Gull perked up. His eyes were puffy and red, crusted with tear gunk. God, I felt guilty. "Yes, it's tight," I said, turning the grip on Gull's shoulders into a soft rub. His blue T-shirt was spotted with blood that would tarnish to a green-brown tint in the wash. "I should go get him a new shirt."

Before I turned down the hallway, I saw that Gull was leaning as far away from Pete as he could get.

I returned with a fresh shirt, faded yellow with a print of Tiger Woods in his iconic 1997 Masters victory stance. In the kitchen, Gull was still marveling at the glass splinter, situated a safe distance from him on the countertop. When he saw the shirt I'd picked, he cheered.

"He's a Tiger fan?" Pete asked as I tossed the bloodstained shirt on top of the dishrag pile in the corner.

"Huge."

Gull scurried away toward the clubhouse couch, the guests stepping away from him as he waved his bandaged palms, wiggling stiff fingers. With the pain gone, he would enjoy his gauze gloves. Later Gram hoisted him up on the scoreboard ledge to let him shift the numbers around, and he gummed his grip around the oversize number cards, shuffling the deck. It was the last day, the last round, and Dr. Dotson had won, seven under, with Mr. Palmer in second at under five, and Uncle Henry at the very bottom of the board at two under, smiling hugely beneath his Titleist visor. Pete took a step across the kitchen tile toward me.

"Thank you," I said, obligated. Both of my hands death-gripped the cuffs of my linen shorts.

Pete smiled at my feet. "Only a year of vet school so far," he boasted, "but I've learned a lot about humans and animals."

"Humans?"

"Oh yeah. So much of what's inside us is the same. Like your arm. The bone structure is real close to bats, cats, and whales."

"What about my arm is similar to a bat?"

Without touching me, he pointed to my shoulder and bicep. "Mostly the upper stuff."

I wanted to laugh, but instead was struck by how indecipherable he was, stoic one moment and then exuberant about bats and cats the next. The tweezers were still in his hand. He hadn't been a bit nervous probing poor Gull's flesh. I couldn't understand how doctors could give babies and puppies and the elderly shots, or surgeries, or do the things the world needs them to do, altogether violent things, and be wholly calm, precise even. Did they squirm in operating rooms? Did they feel grief or doom when they saw the unseeable things? Far beyond me to understand.

"How do you do that?" My voice cracked. I blushed, getting a cup of water from the tap.

"What?"

"Dig around in someone's body, like it's nothing?"

He grinned flatly, revealing the little boy he'd been, catching frogs in rain gutters and standing over wounded bugs, nudging at their broken parts with stubby fingers. I'd avoided little boys like that, ones that hoisted critters in your face and screamed "Look!" and rattled off facts like it was conversation. Little boys like that acted as if they knew everything about bodies and inner workings, but I knew, even as a little girl, those boys didn't think that hard about the real inner workings, melancholy or confusion or discomfort. They only knew happiness and anger, and I'd never liked that, how they exploded into small rages, and when they'd gotten over it, moments later, they expected you to be over it, too. Maybe this was what I was trying to read in Pete's face: Was he an angry boy, or could he really be as calm as he seemed? Gramp had described Gram as stoic when we were young, and Baby C asked what that meant. He said, "Stoic means steady." But later in our bedroom, Baby C, who'd clearly wrestled with it quietly all day, said, "You know, I think stoic is sadness. Just faked." I'd agreed.

Pete twisted his toe into the tile. "You get used to it. They train the nerves out of you with lots of fetal pigs, fish, a fair few snakes, if you can believe it. Watch a lot of videos of the animals they can't, you know, ethically bring in. Makes undergrad look like cake, you know?"

Blood droplets hardened against the tile. I stared into them, ashamed: no, I didn't know. Pete cleared his throat. "I guess, I just mean that it's more difficult than I thought."

"They said you got in early. So it must not have been that difficult."

"Getting in isn't hard. Just a test. It's the memorizing and studying and making sure you know exactly what is where, and . . ." He seemed to struggle, eyes fixed at the right corner of the universe, wondering upward.

I interrupted, hoping to spark a thought with an easy question. "Is it hard because they have eyes that look back at you?" Surely, I thought, this must've been it.

"You'd think, wouldn't you?" He tilted his head. "But no. That's not why."

We fell into silence, nudging our feet around the tile, chewing at the insides of our mouths.

"I should really get back." I moved slowly out the kitchen door toward the heat of outside that would realign the reality of my day; there was trash to pick up, golf carts to hitch together and drive back.

Pete stayed behind in the kitchen for a bit, mopping up water from the marble-top island with paper towels. Mr. Mitchum told Gram later, "I thought y'all'd got yourselves a cleaning boy."

[ENTER] FRONT PORCH CHORUS

Pete Martelli wasn't but twelve years old the first time he was in the papers: "Local Boy Bags Monster Doe." The boy was pictured in a puffy camo coat, knelt beside an elongated body, holding it up by the antlers, its face slackened, the boy smiling. "The gun was almost as heavy as her," he said in the article, with a note that he made that remark sarcastically, giggling, as the doe weighed 160 pounds. When asked for his secrets, which was what we read for, the boy said, "Just spot the one that looks like it'll stay still the longest," as his father spoke up to add, "Having a nice section of woods don't hurt." We knew the Martellis had one of the nicer deer leases in the county, which Mr. Martelli ran away to after the explosion. We saw them each fall, proudly driving their Jeep Wranglers along the highway, bodies roped atop. And we were proud, too. We owned the meat market they dropped the deer by to be butchered, and we owned the taxidermists where they took the skins to get stuffed. We ate venison fajitas they brought to the Casa Grande pool hop and indulged their stories about the deer blind where they peed in coffee cans and ate beef jerky. "Got her clean between the shoulders, heart and lungs, to best put her out of her misery," the boy remarked. The journalist noted that he was already a Pee Wee football name to know; that gun was surely hoisted on future running-back shoulders. We cut out the article to save in case his mama hadn't. We thought about it often when we drove past the football field after hearing, on the radio, that he'd won us another game.

THE VERY BEST ONE

Pete was winning football games when my sisters and I finally grew into our legs, at fourteen. The three of us slept over at the Martellis' the Friday night our high school's team tackled their way to the state quarterfinals. I'd expected Pete to stay out that night, crash at Wendell's or the Goodsons', but he went home after they raised enough hell at the Dairy Queen. We were upstairs in Julie's room, flipping through the yearbook with a pen, connecting the dots of who we thought would marry each other like mapping stars. A CD twitched circles inside Julie's stereo. It was so loud that Baby A was the one who said "Someone's clomping up the stairs" as she sat with her back to the doorjamb.

Pete shouldered the door open, leaned boozily against the chipping white wood. His letterman jacket was molded to his body with sweat. Why they wore those monstrosities in the Texas heat, I never understood. Julie had whispered through the grapevine of the bleachers to get her hands on some weed, and when Pete entered the room, she slipped the baggie of clumpy green from beneath the rug. Baby A looked at the bag and laughed. "Where are the rolling papers?"

Julie deflated. "Vidalia didn't say we needed rolling papers. She just . . ."

"Then you should've bought a joint."

The two fiddled awhile with a torn paper plate, a page from a magazine, and two index cards, shuffling the green around until Pete, peering from the doorway, had had enough. He went to his room down the hall, then returned, sat between Baby A and Julie, stacked an anatomy and physiology textbook on top of an ottoman, then smoothed out a thin brownish paper and rolled the cleanest, tightest joint.

"Um," Julie rumbled. "Where the hell did you get *that?*"

"I've had it."

"Duh. Why?"

Pete shrugged. "Same as anyone else."

My sisters and I exchanged looks, excited that weird good boy Pete was a sometime stoner. He extended his hand to Baby A. "Lighter?" I swear, I thought Julie's brain was going to explode out of her ears. It was magical to witness. Baby A put her scratched Zippo into Pete's palm, and Julie opened her bay windows, letting the rank night in. All I ever envied of Julie's was those windows. When we slept on her floor, I pictured Peter Pan's shadow slinking up the wall, its hand finding me, whisking me away just for the night. We took our hits with wrists rested against the windowsill, directing the smoke outward. Pete blew a few rings, and Baby C laughed so suddenly she blew flecks of snot across the arm of Julie, who screeched instantly, yelling that Baby C was disgusting. Then the rest of us were laughing just as hard. Baby C's laugh turned into a nasty cough she was desperate to muffle. Pete told her to pound on her chest to get the air out, so she sat in Julie's desk chair and pounded on her sternum, which sounded like another person ascending the stairs. I bowed out after two half-assed hits. Julie and Baby A did maybe three, then let the paper burn against the windowsill as they whispered. And strangely, Pete stayed, sitting on the bed, his sneakered feet touching the ground. I could feel him in the room, picking at the hole in his blue jeans.

I splayed across Julie's shag carpet and laced my fingers between the strands, listening to Baby A and Julie cackle about how ugly Margaret Wheeler was with braces, jutting their teeth out as they made chittering noises by sucking on their tongues. Baby C said, "No, no, no. Margaret is a Capricorn. She jus—just uh, um. She just can't dress her face." And we laughed harder at the idea of Margaret dressing her face.

Julie tossed me a pink gel pen and slid the last *Cosmopolitan* quiz to me across the floor, everyone else's markings for "Are You a Hot Challenge?" penned in the margin of the page.

The conversation swirled around me as I read the questions. The first was: "How hard must guys work to get you to go out with them?" I was torn between *You tell them you're busy the first time, knowing you'll say yes the next* and *Always say yes! Why miss out on Mr. Right?* Slowly, looking drearily as the high turned my insides into delicious putty, I circled the latter. On to the second: "At a party, you're not sure if a guy is into you or another chick. You: *Flirt brilliantly for a few minutes, then go to get a drink and force him to come after you* or *Stick by his side when your rival is around, hoping he'll realize you're the better catch.*" I burst out laughing, reading the last option aloud as my sisters giggled, too. "What?" Julie balked, twisting the hem of her coordinated pajama set into the ball of her fist.

Baby A rolled her limbs like water across the carpet until she was sprawled completely, looking up at me with adoration. "*We* are each other's rivals," she said with a glint, reaching for one of my hands and one of Baby C's. "None of us is"—she paused, blinking, smiling—"better. Duh."

"Surely that can't be true." Pete's tone was stone-sober, almost analytical.

Baby A blinked at him, hard. "What the hell would you know about it?"

"I'm just saying. Numbers wise, if there's three of you, surely one is . . . better."

"Not to us. No, no, no." Surprisingly, this came from Baby C, who shook her head with eyes closed, wagging her finger at the ground.

It went quiet, Pete's eyes still on us, each of our heads spinning like dueling tops. Julie scoffed, releasing her pajamas to wave her hand in the air. "Pete. Jesus Christ, go away. You're making it weird." Then she grabbed the quiz from me, pointing dramatically at her circled number in the margin. She'd written "Too-Tough Tease" beside it, the highest score on the quiz.

Baby A and C had circled "Savvy Siren" with their pens, marking their initials next to it. I totaled the hypothetical points I'd scored in my head, knowing I should've been at the bottom, a "Desperate Dater." As if wiping my chin on my shirt sleeve, I looked over my shoulder and made eye contact with Pete as he stood to leave. He had totaled the numbers, too, watching me take the quiz. His eyes flickered with pity, or an odd hue of shame, and I felt even less adequate than before: the desperate one. Gathering my legs, I sat upright and marked my initials beside Baby A's and C's, even though it was a lie, then tossed the magazine back at Julie, the pages ruffling loudly in static air. Each of us girls were somewhere between pained laughter and confusion. Pete announced he was "leaving alright, gosh," and as soon as he cleared the room, Baby A grasped the magazine and smiled proudly at me. "See, Julie?" she jeered. "Told you."

Julie's face said *I know you're lying*. And with her mouth: "So?"

"Goes to show. Any of these boys would be lucky for a chance with us. Sirens, at that."

Julie sighed. "Well, I wouldn't waste my breath on these boys, much less my body. No way am I going to fuck someone until college. Because then you can at least compartmentalize them. Like, do you want a frat boy, or a guy that rock-climbs at the gym?

Here, they're all a big hick mess." Her body flopped against the floor as she loosened her limbs. My sisters and I were left, sitting upright, to look at each other and discuss, silently, what she'd said. Calling us trashy. Calling the boys in town the same.

Baby A tried to save a little face. "Who said anything about fucking, Julie? It's a magazine quiz, for crying out loud."

Julie laughed at the ceiling. Kicked a foot up at my sister. "Oh please. You know what they say about you."

The buzz had worn off on all except Julie, who sipped at a glass of water, chipped the polish off her purple toenails, then stripped to her skivvies with the windows wide open. "It's too hot to sleep in clothes," she'd said, right before ordering Baby C to Dutch-braid her hair so she could wake up with waves. Not only had the opened bay windows let the tyrannical humidity in, but Julie refused to turn her ceiling fan on because she didn't like the rickety noise. As Baby C sat behind Julie, Baby A rifled through her bag and pulled out a miniature bottle of bourbon. "That weed wasn't enough to help me sleep. Little nip, any-body?"

I shot her a look of disapproval, which she shot right back. She thought I killed the fun, and she said it often. I'd already exposed myself as the desperate one of the bunch; I didn't want to stoop any lower. So as my sister knocked back half the small bottle and Julie drank the rest, I excused myself to the bathroom and slathered some of Julie's expensive Clinique moisturizer along my neck. Studying my face in the mirror, I thought about color. Honey and olive hued my skin; rich auburn, my eyebrows, eyelashes, the fuzz above my lip; blue, inherited from my mother, the eyes through which I saw the world. All this was duplicated in Baby A and Baby C, near exact, I knew. But I couldn't fathom, as

I looked at my face, how people who are and feel and believe so differently could *really* appear the same.

Back in Julie's room, she and Baby A were nestled too close for a queen-size bed—Baby A was the only one she'd let sleep there, claiming Baby C and I were too big. Julie Martelli had always been able to tell us apart. It was nothing she admitted because she didn't have to; she spoke to us with consistently different levels of disdain, only tolerating Baby C and me because it was Baby A that she wanted. They were both willful and wolfish, and that united them.

Baby C curled on the pallet of pillows at the foot of the bed, both arms gathered lazily across her chest. I settled next to her, watching fireflies nibble at the screen. The bugs trilled, trying to waft inside the room.

Sometime in the night I was shaken out of a dream. Pete stood in a towering shadow, jostling my shoulder. "Your sister," he whispered. Beyond him, light spilled from the hallway into the room through a small crack of opened door. I stood and moved sloppily toward the bathroom, where I found Baby A kneeling over the toilet. Pete lingered beside her, spectating. "Do you think the weed made her sick?" he asked in a low voice. "Should I get some Advil?"

"No," I said immediately, rubbing my sister's back as she lifted her head weakly to say, "Advil. Yes. My head. It's killing me."

"No."

Pete was fumbling, had taken a few steps back. "I could grab it. It's just in the—"

"No." I caught his eye and held us there, so he might understand me. "No, please."

There was silence, which Baby A broke by gagging into the

toilet bowl. Pete looked between us as if he could hardly understand what was going on. Then, in the same flash, he seemed to tire of us, retreating toward his bedroom without a word.

With my hand still on Baby A's back, I craned my head to see if I could tell whether the commotion had woken Baby C. A heavy, dazing pain was piercing Baby A's head and mine, and surely, even in sleep, Baby C's head, too. We'd slept through this often, Baby A's torturing of her own body, and by extension ours. I was grateful for those times as I clutched my temples and swallowed the lump in my throat.

"God, it's making me nauseated. What did you get into?" I asked softly, sensing the motionless house, knowing we were alone.

Baby A shook her head, stray hair already mingling in the toilet bowl. I pulled what I could back into my grip and repeated the question. The third time, she waved a hand limply. "The cabinet."

"Here?"

"Yes."

"You stole from the Martellis' liquor cabinet?"

"Julie said . . ." Her head bobbed, and intense rushes of pain surged in and out of my empathetic body, weakening in the ways she was weakened. "Julie didn't say," she backtracked. "Don't tell her. She didn't say I could. But I filled them with water. Shhhh." Usually, she'd have laughed, but she didn't even try. "Advil?"

"No." I was afraid of how many Advil she'd take if she got her hands on them.

"But Pete said."

"Pete lied."

"Oh," she murmured, deciding to sit up. Her body slumped against the cold, white bathtub, Gramp's old T-shirt gathered around her waist. When she got this way, she liked to be petted, but just softly enough that she could hardly sense it. I dragged the tips of my fingers along her thigh. "We'll sit here until you feel better."

Baby A and I sat on the bathroom floor until I convinced her she'd be okay to sleep. The next day, she scarcely made the swim between the Martellis' dock and ours, then she slugged around the course like a corpse. It made me sick to think of just how much she'd had to drink, picturing her crouched by the cabinet, chugging vodka and then coaxing tap water into the long-necked bottle. Baby A just couldn't stay away from danger. She would ruin all of our bodies for it.

Only later would Baby A tell us what happened that night: that Julie was flopping her limbs around, hands near Baby A's thigh, twitching up toward her crotch. When Baby A edged away, Julie would press up against her, cupping the backs of Baby A's legs with her own. Baby A had startled awake to check Julie's sleep-guise, eyelids not fluttering, chest rhythmic—she veiled herself well. In the morning, Baby A was bunched like a peach pit, hard and round, in the upper corner of the bed. Even I had noticed. Julie woke with a stretch of her arms, like a cartoon, twisting at the hips, pretending not to care that Baby A had moved as far away from her as she could.

The benefit tournament left the grounds torn up. Gram let us have a day off, then set us to filling in divots Tuesday evening. Halfway through the task, Baby A disappeared. Baby C and I decided to go hole-by-hole on our own. A small plastic baggie of sunflower seeds in the breast pocket of my overalls rumpled audibly as I moved. As Baby C rose from slumping over the sand trap, I offered her a fistful of seeds, which she declined. Instead, she poked my puffed cheeks, so I opened my mouth. She recoiled with a slight burp, and I backed away, too. "You gonna be sick?"

She shook her head with a laugh, then laid her palm out in front of me. "Spit," she said. I spit the hulls in her hand.

She stayed very still so as not to move the spit seeds. "You're a sweet and understanding lover. Partners will appreciate your empathy and loyalty. As for money"—she paused, looking up at me, both of us focused on my spit in her hand—"you're healthy at least, and look at you, just grinning like a possum. But drink some water, goddammit. It's ninety-eight degrees."

She shook the seeds off her hand onto the ground and folded her shoulders inward. We stood for a moment, staring at the holes scattering the grounds. I was hoping what she said was true. We began walking to the next hole, both dragging buckets of sand.

"Where do you think she's off to?" she asked.

"Rich."

"I don't feel good about him."

I smacked my lips together. "I don't feel good about any of them." I meant it, returning briefly in my mind to Pete in our kitchen, the glass in Gull's hand.

Baby C had strode in front of me, but at this she paused, looking back at me expectantly. "Well, except for Q Johnson," I added.

"You don't have to just say that."

"No, I mean it. He's the best one."

Baby C smiled as she bent with her bucket to pack a clump of sand into another hole. In a low, reassuring voice, she repeated to herself: "The very best one."

IT WAS DARK AT THE BOAT DOCK

Pete had begun appearing everywhere the girls and I seemed to be. He joined Jason's pickup basketball group, showed up at the driving range most mornings with a rusty seven iron he swung back and forth for a hapless hour, and one sweltering evening when we'd made plans with our friends, Pete managed to wedge his way into Wendell's good graces. We found him waiting that night with the rest of the boys at the boat dock.

"Heard you patched up our little brother," Baby A said to Pete as her legs dangled off Rich's tailgate, Rich's empty beer can in her hand, holding it like something she'd manifested.

Pete stood near the canoe rack. He gave Baby A a brief nod, then turned to me, standing alone, and asked, "Do you want a beer?"

I looked around, confused that he seemed to be speaking only, and confidently, to me. Then I shrugged and let him hand me a bottle. He slipped the sharp cap into his shirt pocket as he watched me hold the beer I had no intention of drinking. Baby C and I hadn't had a drink in months—not so much in solidarity with Baby A as in fear that by some twisted miracle, the twinge would find its way beyond us to our sister's envious stomach, her lustful mouth. The bottle perspired against my skin. I felt Baby A's eyes bob around the rim as if they were her tongue, her hands gradually crushing Rich's can. Rich nudged at her legs and reached past her for one of the soup cans filled with shrimp tails he'd brought in a plastic bag. On his shifts at the Shrimp Shack, Rich had begun to collect the tails for a foolish game the boys had invented years before, when Cart worked there, too. He grabbed the can of shrimp tails and a homemade slingshot, while Pete and Wendell sifted through the boat dock gravel for sizable rocks to use when the tails ran out. Q hovered as if he was looking, too, but he never bent down.

Q and Baby C were trying very hard to look uninterested in each other. If Baby A found out about them before Baby C told her, all hell would break loose. She'd torment Baby C, embarrass her, probe her for information. I could imagine the envy in Baby A's eyes as we held beers, steady on our feet. And more than that, there was a churning around the boat dock, maybe fish in the water or a storm in the clouds. As I looked around at all these boys, I felt cornered. Pete—why was he there? Peering over at me, offering me things. It didn't feel delicious, like the girls made it seem; it made me squirm. I asked myself: Was it enough, because I wanted so badly to *be* wanted, that Pete wanted me? Did I even understand what it meant to be had?

I walked my beer over to Baby C. "You have to tell her."

Her face was warped with anxiety, arms across her stomach as if it ached. Q was waiting for her to make the initial move, to break the news to the group. "It doesn't have to be *a thing*," I said.

"She'll make it one."

"She won't. Look at her."

"Yes. *Look* at her."

Baby A was still gripping Rich's empty can, wanting what she couldn't have, trying to be good but needing any excuse, like a secret from a sister might provide, to go off the rails. It was almost embarrassing to watch Baby A attempt to be so composed. It went against the very grain of her chaotic being.

Rich presented the group with an egg carton of perfectly halved, empty shells. He flipped open the Styrofoam lid, and the boys applauded, then balanced the fragile cups in a perfect line on the picnic table. Baby C winced away from me toward our sister, laid a soft hand on her own thigh and walked silently past the boys' parked trucks. Baby A followed with a look of worry. It was too dark to truly see them once they'd walked beyond the row of cars. The boys orbited me; Pete with his arm drawn back against the makeshift bow, distended veins the color of ripe berries. Wendell sidled next to me, squawking in my ear. "Blah blah blah your fucking sister, man," he seemed to say. Rich was fidgeting with the egg carton, his eyes flitting, panicked, around the dock as if he'd had a premonition that someone was about to burst out of the bushes, hack us to pieces. His behavior compounded my already unsteady feeling.

I envisioned the girls' shadows beyond us, layered in fog, Baby C's arms still folded in on herself, Baby A jumping up and down, hurtling her imaginary silhouette onto our sister's. I heard the point of a shrimp tail strike an eggshell precisely. I heard the thing bust to smithereens. Wendell still in my ear, "Blah blah blah blah. I get it, dude. Blah blah I totally get y'all girls, man." Then the sound of more broken and breaking eggshells.

I whispered to Wendell, "What do you think of Pete Martelli? Why is he here?"

"Said something 'bout—" Wendell paused, looking into the distance. "I don't remember, man. He's a cool guy, I guess. Runs a hell of a football. Damn smart. Smarter than any of us."

"That's not true. Not smarter than me. Or Baby C."

Wendell scoffed. "Come on, babe."

"Don't call me that."

Baby A swayed back into the light. She pushed Baby C violently into Q, who was standing beside Pete, listening to him explain the inner workings of the slingshot. The boys, still orbiting, hollered and raised their beer bottles, even Pete, who I could tell, despite all the anarchy, had been watching me talk with Wendell. Rich pulled Baby A into his chest, pressing her hard against him.

Wendell walked away to hang all over Q in congratulations. Pete swooped in, handed me the slingshot. I felt anxious as he put his hand over mine where I was supposed to clasp the bow; I couldn't stand to be touched, all those boys touching all of us at the same time, hands on hands on bodies on hands. It wasn't even that Pete was the one touching me, it was all of them, their inability to leave us be. Pete's hand was cold and dry. He stood behind me, and I thought back, oddly, to the *Cosmopolitan* quiz I'd taken on Julie's bedroom floor years before as Pete hovered over us, knowing I was pitiful in this realm of sexual wanting, confused as to why Pete was doing the work for both of us, coming back even as I engaged minimally, felt only a small warmth, a small possibility, when I looked into his angular face. Q and my sister orbited each other with such unpolluted desire between them; it was painful to watch, even more painful to feel the surges of him against her skin, the rush of fervor in her chest as he looked into her eyes. I yanked my fingers from beneath Pete's without a word and stumbled toward the tailgate of Rich's truck, where I pulled myself up like I'd just emerged from the bayou after swimming without enough air, and squared my breathing the way Gram had taught me.

I expected to see Pete looking punctured, but he didn't seem concerned that I'd abruptly walked away and hadn't let him touch me longer. Instead he glanced over at my sisters with the same flat look.

The bow got passed to Q, who'd done what Pete had wanted to and brought Baby C's arms up, her hands around the device, his palms over hers, their arms drawn back together, such sharpness propelled through the thick air.

My voice echoed in triplicate. Pete faded into the light, outside it. There was no telling where anyone was. Rich would call out for Baby A, "Babe, watch this one," as he groped in the dark for her face. I couldn't imagine how she stood his slimy touch on her polished skin. I hated that the ripples he created in her chest pulsed through mine. I wanted to take it all back; the shrimp tails, the broken shells, our bodies. I wanted to take our bodies back. I wanted to break my sisters and myself free. I wanted to take Gram with us, and Gull. For us to decide, the way we only mused about, that these boys weren't worth us, and I wanted us to stick to it. It was dark at the boat dock; I couldn't see my hand in front of my face.

"How's your orange tree?" Pete asked, leaning against Rich's wheel well.

"Sour."

"Well, how's your brother's hand?"

I let myself look into his eyes before deciding what to say. He had barn-owl eyes, hazel as mud clumps. He was really wanting to know. He was leaned in. "Healing," I said.

Pete moved to sit next to me on the tailgate. The energy between us was potent, almost awkward.

"Why did you come tonight?"

This made him smile. "Why did you?"

"Well, I live here."

"I live here, too."

"No. You come home on breaks."

"What's the difference?"

"Tearing up the floorboards when it floods, coating yourself in bug spray to do the yard work, only getting three restaurants to choose from when you can't stand to cook."

He laughed, looking at the ground. "I still need bug spray in College Station."

"Are you going to go back and tell them about how you flung shrimp shells around with your hick friends from home?"

"Is that what you think of yourself?"

He'd been looking into the side of my face as we talked. I'd been looking ahead, but at this, I reared my head back to stare at him. "What?"

"Do you think you're a stupid hick?"

"Of course I don't."

"Then why do you think I would say that?"

This stumped me. For the quiet, odd boy, he was speaking sharply to me in a way I hadn't been prepared for. "Because I don't know you," I said. "And you don't know me."

"I'd like to. I'm trying to."

"Why?"

"Jesus, why does anyone want to know anybody else? Because why not? I'm sure you're interesting and funny sometimes. Tell me if you're not, so I don't waste my time."

He was smiling, so I let myself grin slightly, and then we laughed. I don't know if I trusted the laugh or meant it. Either way, we laughed. "Friends?" I reiterated, and he nodded. A moment later, Pete took a deep breath, as if he were about to say something, then let it go.

The town was peeking into the rooms of their children, making sure their chests rose and fell with breath. The town was unloading the dishwasher while watching TV. Long-haul trucks crossed the bridge. Warblers, late for migration, pushed their wings through the dense air.

The boat dock was littered with sharpness. "We better pick these tails up," Baby C said, lingering beneath the arc of Q's arm. "Someone will cut their foot." She was glowing with a new joy, but hesitant, her face still blinking at mine and Baby A's as if to ask: *Is this okay?* I understood. We'd made such summer banter about Baby A's stuckness on Rich that I knew Baby C was afraid we'd turn on her, the sweet sister, the one who tried to tell our futures so we wouldn't be wounded by what was to come.

Wendell, drunk, slurred, "You girls the only ones walking 'round barefoot." He looked down as he wobbled. Ours were the only bare feet, pink nail polish shining in unison. Q knelt and began to gather sharp bits in his hand. Wendell tried, setting his beer down against the picnic table, but couldn't find his balance. Soon enough we were all hunched over, sifting through gravel with our beer-buzzed hands. Baby A sidled up to me, leaning over to feign picking up tails. "So what's up with Pete? He's hot in like a distant, cool way, right? What do you think?" We must've looked like kids scavenging through the innards of a busted piñata. Or buzzards picking at thick bits of bone. Iridescent snatches of shell and tail and gravel shone against me like treasure. It was dark at the boat dock. We'd worn similarly cut T-shirts.

"I think I'm going to start the swim back home," I said as I touched Baby A's shoulder.

"No." She held my hand against her where it'd landed. "We'll go together, soon."

The warmth my sisters' bodies had created, being nuzzled and kissed, dampened my insides in the warm-wet way a faint does, just before spotty vision takes you fully into emptiness. Gull needed us, I thought. Or Gram. There was an emergency. There was some reason we needed to leave. Suddenly my body was panicking. "Really," I announced, "we've gotta get home."

I peeled myself away from the fold their drunk, foggy bodies made. There was something foggy about Pete. The feeling reminded me of old men kissing us square on the cheeks, far too close to our mouths, before scurrying out of the clubhouse. Sure, it was a kiss, and they were old, it was meant to feel sweet or harmless, but it never quite did. Always like they'd timed it for when Gram was in the kitchen and one of us was alone.

A sweaty hand nestled along the small of my back. I turned toward it as the hand pulled me, forcibly, lips smothering mine suddenly before I could think to inhale. The hand held me still, even as I squirmed to pull away. I pushed my palms against the chest in front of me, twisting my bare feet on the gravel. I heard Baby C gasp. "Stop," she yelled. "Stop it, you prick."

Someone shoved the lips away from me, and when I opened my eyes, I could hardly strain to see. In the same divided second I'd opened my eyes, the truck headlights had been flipped on. Rich Goodson was standing in front of me, being struck repeatedly by Baby A. The beatings of her palms against his chest snapped like flip-flops on concrete. "You son of a bitch," she wailed. Baby C pulled me toward her by the arm, both of us watching in horror, utterly perplexed. She stroked my hair with her hand as I shook against her. Wendell pried Baby A off Rich after she'd begun scratching his face with her chipped black nails. I began to tremble, staring at the moment as if it couldn't have really occurred, left to stand alone in the middle of it like a pariah. I knew then that I would never be more than one of three to them. A dupe to exploit when they got bored. And though Baby A was raging against Rich, clawing at him midair, my instinct was to blame her. That stupid game they played. How she put on our faces and names like it was something she could take off and pretend had no consequences. I was crying, reflexively, and though everyone was consumed by Baby A's show of fury, it felt like they were staring at me.

Pete was transfixed, the way I imagined I looked when a patron hit off the tee with a crazy but effective swing. He looked like he'd seen someone perform a trick and was trying to recall how it had moved so he could teach it to himself later. I ruminated over the look on his face for a long time—for years it was all I could wonder about, if there had been a clue in that moment. But as I lived inside it, stood barefoot against it, the moment didn't last but a blink, and then my attention was drawn to the mechanical hiss of Q's truck, Baby C calling for me to get in.

Wendell said in an instantly sobered tone, "One more hit, okay? One more." Baby A slammed her knee up and between Rich's legs. Then she stood over him as he crumpled.

Wendell tried to calm her by rattling off at the mouth. Out of the headlight glare, Pete stepped toward me with surety, keeping his hands well away. "He thought—" Pete began.

"No!" Baby C snapped. "He just wanted to see."

All this we exchanged as Baby A screamed into the gloaming, "You sick bastard. I hate you. I fucking hate you," clawing the air as Wendell held her like the defensive tackle he'd been bred to be. She said she'd kill him, over and over, she said it. This nightmare had been—according to the tauntings of our deepest fears—inevitable. Rich stayed on the ground as Wendell pushed us toward Q, reappeared behind the wheel of his truck. Baby A turned her fury on the rest of the boys. "Cowards. You sick damned cowards."

Rich wiped his mouth and looked up at us, satisfaction across his bleeding face. He would go on to say to anyone who'd listen that he'd hooked up with two out of three of the Manatee's girls.

In the swirl of it all, I'd kissed him back.

Wendell bouldered past Pete to load me into the front seat of Q's truck. The permanence of how used I'd been had begun to calcify inside me, weighty in my chest. I felt dispensed. But in an almost-sick way, relieved, too; the worst thing I could imagine had happened, and I'd survived it, would continue on through it, even if numbly.

Baby A sobbed in the back seat under Baby C's wing. Before the truck began to move, Baby C pushed the door open violently and leaned out to throw up across the gravel. There was so much noise, so much frustrating fog, nobody seemed to notice as our sister did what she needed, wiped her mouth, then resumed the comforting of Baby A. Q asked softly if we'd like the radio on as he handed Baby C a crumpled fast-food napkin from the glove box.

What else could we be? If being what they wanted got us kicked around like this—

Baby A's sobs became louder, flared. I felt, for the first time, a twinge of real and true hate for my sister. This was her fault. She'd taunted Rich with this very thing; what had she expected? We rattled across the train tracks and through town with the white noise of the engine. Q's truck smelled like Whataburger and sweat. A pine-scented air freshener long used up clattered against the rearview mirror. Baby A was hunched over, grasping her ankles, swearing into the soda stains. As I stared out the window, I realized what the heat was doing to us; the palm leaves wilted, the grass crisped to a barley pale, it was trying to sweat us out. We were stuck in its pores. It was hard not to think that all roads led back to Gram. Or Murphy. Her lips were my lips were Baby C's lips were the Manatee's girls' mouths. Look what the hell she went and left us to.

Q parked in the middle of the clubhouse driveway beside the golf cart shed and got out. He moved to collect Baby A from the back seat to find she was already standing on the gravel, Baby C holding her upright. He stepped back to open the car door for me as if one act of bare-minimum courtesy could be a balm. Even though there was nothing on them, I wiped my lips with the back of my hand. The automatic light flicked on as Baby C shepherded our sister through the clubhouse door. Then it was me and Q, standing in the wasted night as if we were naked, humiliated to be witnessing each other this way.

"You've talked about it," I said.

I expected this to shock Q, but it didn't. His face was gentle and controlled; he pitied me.

"Well, haven't you? Like locker-room talk." A bit of fear, like reflux, gathered in my chest. I hunched over for a moment, afraid I'd be sick. The thick night air pressed into my side.

"I've heard it before . . ." He hesitated. "But I never said nothing. And I never heard plans. I didn't know this was going to happen, I swear to God. I wouldn't let them do that to you. Or to your sister."

I knew he wasn't talking about Baby A.

The creak of the clubhouse door sounded like a page being torn from a book. Baby C melted onto the yard and toward us like a liquid sunset. The whole night leaked. I turned to Q quickly. "You ever done anything out of anger? Like, pure rage?" Baby C neared, too close for him to answer audibly without her asking us to repeat ourselves, so he shook his head no. Then Baby C took my place in front of Q, and I moved up the yard toward the clubhouse.

In our room, Baby A was curled on top of her sheets, our cell phone nestled next to her cheek as she stared at the wall beyond the phone screen glare. It blinked rhythmically without sound. Rich was surely blowing up our phone with apologies exclusively hers. She mumbled when I sat near her, pushed the phone toward me. "I haven't even read it. Only tell me what he says if it will make me furious or make me forgive him."

Another surge of anger charged through me. "I'm not going to read text messages to you like an infant."

She lifted her slanted head from the pillow, eyes swollen and red. "You're mad at me now?"

"Yes, I'm mad at you now."

At this she sat up and scrunched her face dramatically, strong-arming my forgiveness. "What about this is my fault?"

I threw my head back in frustration. "Don't play stupid. This is the fruit of your gross game. Your little mockery of us. Rich Goodson isn't smart enough to think of a thing like that. This was your sick idea."

"You don't have to be smart to be a conniving bastard."

"No, but you do have to be a conniving bastard to enjoy a thing like that."

She flickered as if I'd struck her. In the moment, I was afraid she might strike me. Our voices were raised. Our eyes bulged with resentment. Baby C had managed to slip in the room.

"You don't get to be the only victim in this! He did that to both of us, B."

"Yes!" I slammed my hands down on the comforter between us. "But he used *my* body. For your sick game. *My* body."

"Why are you angrier at me than you are him?"

"I'm angry at both of you."

She gritted her teeth. "But equally."

"Is that what you care about right now?"

"Why didn't you rip his head off? How dare you come for mine."

"How dare——"

We were sweating, chests shaking. The rage, when angled outward toward the town or even those boys, felt as if I were boiling over just to burn myself. When angled at my sister, though, it was satisfying, as if I were being vindicated. I wanted Baby C to jump between us and break up the dogfight, or at least talk us out of it with soft, steady logic, but instead she lingered beside our dresser, fingers fidgeting with a knob. "What is it I don't know?"

Baby A glared at me. Silence settled. Baby C kept turning the dresser knob, and I fixed my gaze on a pulled stitch in the comforter, trying to unravel it with my eyes. Baby A began to sob again. "Rich made this game—"

"No." The thud of my voice sent an ache to my brain. Baby A's shoulders folded inward. She sobbed harder.

"Don't break our hearts with lies. A thing like this happens, and you want to lie? Try to think of us, please." Baby C sounded soft, maternal, still keeping away from us. It amazed me that Baby A and I were close enough that our knees almost touched. If one of us moved an inch, our entire existence risked imploding. Baby A explained, through stubborn tears, the game she'd created for Rich, the whole time fiddling with her pinkie toe, tearing the nail down to the quick. Baby C listened, her face neutral, almost contented, and when Baby A was done talking, she sat between us and forced us into a huddle where we cried into each other's hair. We shared a truck, a phone, chores, a face, a body, a life, a body, a face. That was how it reeled in my head when I thought of us. I prided myself on the idea that it bothered me the most out of us girls, the sharing, though I knew it destroyed us all, just differently.

[ENTER] FRONT PORCH CHORUS

When Murphy was in middle school, Isadora and Harriet Shrub often shopped the Seeglow's aisles to stock the church fridge, where we once overheard Isadora have an outright fit: "I can't handle this child, Harriet. She's plumb nuts." Harriet, in her nasally way, replied, "Let her run wild, honey. She'll get it out." But Isadora refused. "Her running wild is the problem. She's steeped in trouble. Stealing from the offertory. Shaving her legs with her daddy's face razor—all that precious peach fuzz, gone! She threw a golf ball at JoeBeth Hallowill's head. Gave her a goose egg for the ages." Then the two laughed, stalled in front of potato sacks, Harriet clutching her gut. "There's nothing like the fluff of little kid leg hair."

Isadora, still laughing, shook her head. "I kept telling her it'd never be that soft again. That it'll come back darker and thicker than ever. She said, 'Good.' Can you believe it? I'll never understand why they want to grow up by force."

Harriet grabbed a sack of Yukon Gold to inspect, tilting her head as she let the bag spin. "They wanna be like us. 'Cause they love us so." As we eavesdropped from aisles away, we heard Isadora suck at the inside of her cheek with a squeak, voice absent of the laughter that'd just doubled her over. "I know, Harriet. That's the part I can't understand."

JUST BABIES

Long before the alarm clock was to wake us the next morning, I rolled out of bed and crawled across the floor on my palms to our swimsuit drawer. For the next hour, in the barest sliver of morning cast, I laid out each bikini top and each bottom, ranking them from loveliest to least, switching them around to see which combinations worked. There were heart prints, zigzags, solids, and neons, but I was too numb to appreciate even the floral prints. The suits wouldn't make me feel lovely or whole. They wouldn't cover me in the way I newly needed. I wasn't sure how to wear clothes anymore, or that face, or those legs—I wasn't sure what it looked like to be Baby B.

At the back of the drawer, rolled like towels, were a pair of one-piece suits in muted green and blue, backless: our mother's. The lining was detaching from the fabric, fuzzed up in pills. I'd seen pictures of Murphy and Gram in these and had never once wondered where the suits were. Quietly, I put the blue one on. It fit like dipping comfortably into a secret memory. I didn't want to share my body in this suit with anyone, even Gram, so I decided to swim alone.

As I lowered myself into the water, I listened. The fish were docile. No wind to move the trees. None of the animals howled in their pasture luxury. My body merging with the water made the first real sound of the morning. I hated to do that to a new day— break it in.

The water separated for me as I swam, pulling myself through with cupped hands. For a moment I considered stopping at Aunt Rachel's and trying to talk this through with her, but then I'd have to betray my sister, which, even as angry as I felt, would only worsen the muddle of my feelings. So I swam past the house and farther, farther, until I was clutching the side of the midway buoy and the sun was rising to pierce my eyes. I'd been there countless times before, but never alone. I was disconnected from my body completely and felt hung out to dry in the ether. The previous night, after Baby C forced the three of us into a reconciliation huddle, she'd crept into the clubhouse when she thought we'd fallen asleep. There she sat on the stained carpet in the farthest corner, clubs hung above her like a child's mobile, and dialed from memory the number of a telepsychic, who she talked to for over an hour. I sat on the middle landing of our winding stairs with a slight view of her, listening hard as I could. She began their conversation in a whisper: "Can a soul be split in three? I feel everything they're feeling." After minutes of listening intently, she replied, "Will it always be that way, or can I cut them off somehow?" My chest panged with a deep sense of loss when she said this. I imagined the psychic giving specific, betraying advice. I wanted to yell down from the stairs, *What you're wishing away is love*, but she could never know I was listening. The wooden banister cooled my cheekbone as Baby C and the psychic talked. She mostly listened, nodding her head against the textured wall.

I knew the catalyst for this was Q Johnson—she didn't want us to feel what she felt with him, the way we felt those boys palm and suck at Baby A. The pang of loss curved into a warmth of disappointment, that desire for others was creating a rift in the bond between us. It wasn't like I didn't want the separation, too; it just hurt to hear her say it, and to a stranger, no less. If she had asked me, I'd have said, *We can. If we each end up on opposite ends of the county, the state, the country, it certainly couldn't reach us there*. I'd say it because I wanted it to be true. I knew the only way to stop it was to die, which was a thing that could never happen to my sisters. They would be—had to be—eternal. Unnatural girls. Baby A was breathing in steady sleep upstairs, and my chest hummed with her peace. What we were grappling with, Baby C on the phone and me hunkered by the stairs, was the conflation of sharing and sameness. How to feel what they felt without ownership. How to let it pass through without stowing it away, to fester beside our own festerings. There is a special kind of grief in this—wishing a good thing away simply because you don't know what to do with it.

As I bobbed with the buoy, alone, I thought about the boys and the boat dock. I wondered if Baby C was asking the psychic those questions for my sake, after seeing what the mirror of our bodies had brought. Thoughts of the gossip that was surely already making its rounds tugged me down like an anchor in my suit bottoms. At some point, from a patron or Harriet, Gram would hear. Then Aunt Rachel and Jason and Julie, if Pete hadn't already told her. My thoughts stalled around Jason. God, he was going to be mad. Maybe I should swing by their house on the swim back, tell them the whole story. But I didn't. I ended up in front of the Ace Hardware store, having dripped down three blocks of sidewalk from the boat launch beside the church where I'd pulled myself out of the water. Q was working the early shift at the fix-it counter toward the back of the store. Through the window of the door in the outdoor plant section, I saw him hunched over a bent piece of metal, trying to flatten it with the round end of a wrench. I cracked the door open a hair and whispered his name until he looked up, startled, and walked over.

"It's just me—uh, B."

His eyes stirred with embarrassment, which I assumed was for me. "Here to talk, I suppose."

I nodded. "I guess, I just don't know what to make of it, Q."

He tied and untied a knot in the lace of his waist apron. "I haven't been here long, you know, but all I can think is Rich is angry. At himself. Angry he can't tell, and that he wants her—or y'all—real bad. It's all self-hate, really. With Rich." His eyes circled his hands, working the knot.

"And Pete?"

Q breathed out heavily, craning his neck up to crack it sideways with a reverberating pop. "All I heard was Wendell ask him about college slu—um, girls—and Pete said he hadn't been dating much. Said he was happy to be back here for a while and that he wanted to get to know you."

"The girls and me."

"No," Q said swiftly. "You."

I was stunned by the specificity of both Pete's wants and Q's words. Silently, I considered that maybe Pete had thought of us while he was away, my sisters and me, our differences instead of our insurmountable similarities. I thought of how often Julie was around and wondered if he ever asked her about us, what she said. Surely Julie said backhanded or outright hateful things brimming with jealousy, though I was never sure what of ours she was jealous of, having demeaned most things we stood for or upon. But it was jealousy and meanness in Julie. I wondered then, as Q reached out to a nearby plant and let his hand slide down the leaf like it was the long, soft ear of a hound dog, why Pete was intrigued by me, having witnessed us slink from their house so many times to swim home with our toothbrushes in plastic sandwich bags. What of mine did Pete think he wanted?

"If it makes you feel any better," Q said, "Wendell gave Rich a busted lip and ribs after we cleared out."

"Broken?"

"Cracked."

Q's nervous fidgeting had ceased as he intuited that the conversation was ending, and it began to make sense to me why I'd longed for him; he was always petting the world around him. "Do you need me to buy a cactus or something?" My eyes roamed the pitiful garden section, sparse but green, spared by the rainless summer. I asked this, knowing he'd wave me off, no money stuffed in my soaked swimsuit. There just hadn't been anything else for me to say. Q shook his head. I watched as he retreated into the hardware store, back to his fix-it counter. I turned to walk to the boat launch, but just as soon as Q walked inside, he walked back out, holding a towel that he handed over and car keys that he used to drive me, wordlessly, home. I could see the shine of Baby C on his face. Though I was happy that she'd found what we were all searching for in Q, I was still jealous, not only that she'd gotten Q in the way I'd wanted him, but that now there was someone else that I had to compete with for Baby C's affection.

Q dropped me at the mouth of the driveway because he couldn't be gone from work long. I snuck into the side door of the clubhouse. The whole place was quiet save for early-bird patrons sitting politely in their cars, engines shaking the gravel. After wandering around, changing into my polo shirt, I noticed a formation near the fifth hole. As it neared, it became a clearer portrait of my family. Amazingly, they'd all gone on the morning swim, Baby A and Gull included. As they walked, towels draped across them like silks, Gram and Baby C swung Gull between them. They were singing "London Bridge," signing choppily with their free hands: circulating an L by their ears, pronging two fingers in an upside-down V at the base of their elbows, then bringing it to their wrists. It was sweet to watch. I looked between my sisters' faces and began to feel, concretely, that after the previous night, we'd never be the same sisters again. Even before the worst of what that summer would bring was upon us, I began to mourn the girls we had been.

Gull laughed as he swung on their arms, taking pelican-mouthed breaths between chortles. Watching him swing with such intentional fury made me desperate to know what it was like, for him, to be the youngest.

Gull did not look like any of us, even in half-light. He had rich tones, sharp and enlarged features edging him further toward the unique. We knew Gull was the Rodanthes' child, that Mrs. Rodanthe had an affair with the artist in residence at the Bryan Museum whose exhibition she had curated. She'd gone on an acquisitions retreat shortly after, returned a year later with extra skin folds and thinned hair, resolvedly quieter. She'd had the baby—Gull—at home and paid the midwife to stay quiet, but of course the neighbors saw her come and go with a birthing ball. News of a baby made its way to Gram via the nun who sometimes showed up to watch the altar guild play bridge. "He's an unresponsive one, Isadora," she'd said. Gram said she'd covered her mouth with a splay of extra cards because it was so hot, they needed fans, and said, "Let me give him a sweet look."

Gram won that round, and the round after, poured the women some wine and won a little more. The next day she showed up at the orphanage with heavily beaded bracelets, donning a pair of low kitten heels she only wore on Easter. The three of us were allowed to come along but were left to play with the older kids in the cemetery, running around the headstones, standing blasphemously atop, shouting, "Ready or not, here I come."

The nun set baby Gull on the play mat as Gram stomped around, jingled her glass beads, and clapped loudly behind her back. When the sound was concentrated to his right side, he turned toward it as if to catch a bug that'd zipped by. When the noise was on his left side, he didn't stir. Gram went back and forth, clapping and talking real low. She inched close to his clear, burnished eyes and told us he grinned so wide, so accepting, that she couldn't hardly stand to look away. "Oh my." Gram gathered him up and let him pull at her earlobes as she mumbled into his left ear, then his right, stopping to admire his face in between as he kept on tugging at her skin.

"I guess that's it," the nun said. Gram started to laugh so loudly we heard her in the cemetery. Our ears perked up, sensitive to her smokers' hack even then. Baby A climbed on the radiator beside the nursery room to peek through the window. "Look," she said to Baby C and me on the ground. "They're laughing." And they were, both Gram and Gull, his chortles foggy and off-pitch. It wasn't a week before she brought him officially home.

"I love this baby, and he is your brother," she'd said to us in the clubhouse den, the baby Gull on her knee. Baby A tilted her head, snapping her fingers, then squinting at his unturned face. "How we gonna love him if he can't hear it?"

Gram sharpened her gaze and for a second, I thought she'd poke Baby A's sternum with her hard, callused finger. "Don't you start that with me, girl." That was about the only time I could recall that Baby A stopped along the controversial trail of something she wanted to argue about.

Later we snuck into the spare room, now functioning as a makeshift nursery, to look at Gull on our own. We'd poke at his chubby skin, bubble our mouths to make him giggle, say his name over and over. I was not convinced, even after the spare room was painted Baby Boy Blue, that he was a permanent addition. As we dangled over him, distraught with fascination and confusion,

Baby A remarked, "How come Gram wants him, when most days she doesn't even want us?" Which we thought about real hard, though I can't remember any of us answering, nor can I recall it coming up again. The trio of us girls and the shiny new addition that was Gull orbited skeptically around each other a few years, until Gramp passed, really, and it became clear we didn't have a thing in the world but this family.

"Look who's back," Gram said, heaping her towel atop my arms as I stood in the clubhouse doorway. "Happy to skirt morning chores, I bet."

"Gram—" Baby C had protested impulsively, letting it go when Gram shot her a look. Baby A hurtled past us all down the hall to change.

I volunteered for the weed trimming before Gram could assign chores; it was more work but could be finished quickest if I hopped to it. Baby C had stepped instantly into airing up cart tires, monitoring the holes, gathering trash—the mosey-paced but daylong jobs. Baby A stood at the clubhouse counter as Gram flitted about, already coated in dirt at the fingers. "Gull, you come back around one for lunch," Gram called as he stepped into his Velcro shoes, poised for the clatter of neighbor kids scuffing their in-line skates against cul-de-sac curbs. He'd grab the pair of in-lines the girls and I had shared when we were younger, given them by Harriet Shrub, her son's old set.

I trimmed the weeds and myself into oblivion, patrons with their club bags jostling like windchimes. I didn't bother with earplugs; my mind was too gone to feign focusing. I started on the fairway, blade swinging so sharp and fast it could lop my leg off in a blink. The destruction it could do to my body, I considered too intently. If I had a big scar, I thought, they'd definitely know which girl I was. Horrifyingly, I knew my sisters had both entertained the idea, too.

I trimmed outward toward the brush and forestry, toward the neighbors' yards. I'd trim the earth until it was bare as I was. I'd trim my mind until what was bare was the truth, as I entertained all of the outcomes I could create for the night before: if Jason had been there; if it had been Pete who'd kissed me—maybe I could have wanted him; if Baby A had stopped Rich before he reached my mouth. The greenery swirled like a dirt devil. I waited for it to levitate me aboveground. As I hacked into the buttonbush, I heard a commotion from the clubhouse just a few yards behind me. I'd long finished the chore, so I began my way back, Jason's energized silhouette coming soon enough into view. He was spouting off at the mouth, he and Baby A furiously in each other's faces. I couldn't discern if they were angry at each other or just angry, together. Jason charged toward me. "Why didn't you tell me? I had to find out from Pete at the pickup game this morning. I'm going to beat the piss out of Rich, that stupid prick."

Baby A leaned into him, riled. "You should."

"Jason, it's no use. It's done." I surprised myself with this, but I'd meant it.

"It's not done!" Baby A's face was red. "Goddamn it, why is Jason the one saying he's going to kill him? Why not *you*?"

She squeezed her hips, arms akimbo, and sharpened her eyes at me. "You have my permission, Jason, to hurl him into oblivion." She picked up the weed eater and chucked it a few feet away, then stormed off toward the truck. The sound of keys in an ignition lit the tepid air after the sound of the weed eater crashing against the ground had settled. Jason and I stood a moment, staring in her direction.

He gathered me into a hug where I couldn't make myself cry

for his sake, knowing that was what he wanted from me, a display of all I was feeling in the visceral way Baby A could. I set my head against his shoulder, smelling the ripeness of the morning pickup game in his armpits. Gram waltzed up with a few discarded beer cans in hand to tell me I'd better get back to it, and since Jason was there, that he could help, so we scattered fresh mulch across the flower beds and fixed a glitch inside the ball-dispensing machine. Jason had himself wedged laterally behind the machine with a smattering of tools at his feet as I thought of Q, flattening metal with a wrench in the hardware store, saying Pete had asked about me and only me. I'd known the simple fix for the ball machine, but I let Jason immerse himself in the problem to prolong our time away from other tasks. I sat on the concrete, wanting to ask all the questions that choked me, but I held them in my throat. It'd have been selfish to spoil such good quiet.

After too long, I tapped Jason's shin and took his place, forcing my arm down the pipe the balls traveled to pop a stuck one out. It clicked against the ground as it bounded off the concrete and rolled into nearby grass. Jason sat against the wall, dripping, lightly dazed from having lain sideways for so long, blood rerouting through his face and body. He found a deserted bottle of water and drank from it. "You girls going to do the Bluegrass Festival this year?"

I shrugged. "Not if she stays this mad."

"Well, she's not mad at you."

"She's mad at everyone, which includes me and C and Gram."

Jason finished off the water bottle, twisting the plastic loudly into a compressed disk. "Do you think it'd really help if I did something? Went and talked to Rich?"

"Wendell already beat the daylights out of him. Now I think all we can do is avoid him."

"In this place? Good luck."

We sat across from each other, both exhausted. I lined up the soles of my sandals with the soles of his Nikes and we stayed that way, legs outstretched, making a small and silent joke of our monstrous confusion of duty and pain. "Are you embarrassed of us, Jason?"

He lifted his head from leaning back. "No way in hell am I embarrassed of you. I'm embarrassed for *them*. Not knowing one from two from three."

"But even you get confused."

"Well, sure I get confused, but I don't stay confused. That's the difference." Jason leaned his head back again, and I pulled my feet away. "Rich isn't stupid, though, B. He did this on purpose. That's why she's so mad. I mean, how would you feel?"

I tried to imagine giving myself to somebody the way my sisters both had. Then I pictured Pete, mind lingering on his difficult face. "How did Pete describe it?"

"Just said Rich grabbed you and kissed you, then grinned like a loser while Baby A tried to hit him. Said Wendell held her back and Q drove y'all home."

"What did he say that *he* did?"

Jason paused a moment, looking stumped. "He didn't."

Good, I thought. At least he wasn't lying to save face. "I talked to Q this morning at the hardware store. He said Pete wanted to get to know me. Me specifically."

"Why?"

"Gee, Jason. Thanks."

"Sorry. You know what I mean."

I exhaled, wrung out by it all. "I'm not sure what to think."

Jason scratched his kneecap. "He's a stand-up guy, I've heard. Do you think he likes you? Or—I mean, what kind of sense do you get?"

The air between us lightened, and we smiled, having never spoken this candidly. "The sense is . . . he's hard to read, and I'm afraid of anyone related to Julie, but I'm not sure what there is to lose. Especially now."

The ring of Gram's cast-iron dinner bell shattered the stillness of the trees. I hopped to my feet and pulled Jason up, dropping an armful of tools in the shed before slogging into the clubhouse. Baby C was at the stove, heating leftover taco soup in a pot. Gull rushed Jason's legs and tugged him over to the carpet to show him the roller skates he'd mastered that afternoon. I leaned behind Baby C in the kitchen, resting my chin on her shoulder, both of us gazing into the oracle warmth of corn kernels floating in peppered tomatoes, pounds of ground beef. "Where is she?" she whispered into the side of my face, swirling a wooden spoon through the soup.

"Still gone." I recalled our sister throwing the weed eater against the ground, the sound of the impatient car engine clamoring to leave as both my guts and Baby C's sank with a feeling that wherever Baby A had gone to that afternoon, she would surely never completely return.

Baby C pulled a corn bread from the oven, in a cast iron pan that molded the bread into the shape of corn husks. We picked apart a bushel of cilantro together, breaking open the stench of earth in our hands with a flat clap. Then, in a passing way, my sister looked at me with my very own eyes. It was almost a hateful thing, and a beautiful wonder, how this way of being a woman, ashamed of ourselves though we'd done nothing wrong, had been passed down to us as if an heirloom dress. And we passed it between us, this uncertain shame that, even though we'd scratched our name into its tag, didn't belong exclusively to us.

Gram ate with her elbows on the glossy wooden tabletop. Jason had more corn bread than soup, relishing the corn-husk shape of it. Baby C picked at her plate, not much making it to her mouth, and we listened as Gram and Gull recounted chasing the neighbor's chickens down the road through the back gate the other day. Gull chuckled so wholly, I reached over to pull the fork away from his face, afraid he might laugh his way into it. Jason cackled so hard at Gull's contagious laughter that tears streaked his flushed cheeks. "The neighbors were in the window just watching us run around with bells, arms flailing," Gram said, bouncing her shoulders with a chuckle. "If this place ain't the living end."

[ENTER] FRONT PORCH CHORUS

Once, we looked at them. *Really* looked. Isadora had the girls, babies then, in a stacked stroller in the church lot after Sunday service, three pairs of the same eyes glowing up at us like fish nudging the water's surface. There was a nearby mother—Wilma Earle—with her little girl against her hip, pointing up at the morning. "The moon is out! Look, it's the moon!" the baby said, which was all-in-all very cute. We looked back to Isadora's girls, still staring, still glowing, no charming baby babble, just gazing clear as cloudless sky. They were seeing us. *Really* seeing. We pitied our Manatee. Saddled with strange, motherless babies. Even worse, Isadora knew we shunned her a bit for their sake, because they made us so uncomfortable. Because when we saw her with them, we didn't quite know what to do. Couldn't recall the girls' names. Couldn't conjure up a single polite thing to say. Isadora forgave us our shunning eventually, and we warmed back up over the years, to Isadora anyway. We try not to shiver when the girls look at us now. We try to understand why they don't out us for shaving points from our scorecards or nudging the ball from the bunker before swinging. It's a shame Isadora's girls have to be so disconcerting, because we could have loved them. There is another world, in which we do. We really do.

FISHTAIL

Baby A washed up from her disappearance about midmorning, slept in her bed facing us instead of the wall. Her tenor had shifted. She had stowed her intense fury somewhere out of view, wanting us to buy into the act that she was miraculously resolved of all distress and was to be regarded as perfectly content, no longer angry at us or them. I asked if she'd heard anything from or about Rich, and she said flatly, "What's to hear? He's dead to me."

Our cell phone had begun to ring for Baby C. She'd started to carry the flip phone at her hip in Gram's old belt clip. It was Q who told Baby C about Bailee's party, coaxing her to come. "I'll pick you up," he'd said on the phone. "Or y'all."

She broached it with me first, hesitantly, as we washed up the kitchen. "Just for an hour or two. It'll be fun. Q swears that Rich won't be there. Says he's been banned from the Shuggarts' house anyway."

Baby A had snuck behind, edging her ear to hear. "Well, we can't just leave her behind," I said, to which Baby A pushed physically between us. "I'll come wherever. Where to?"

Baby C and I looked swiftly at one another, then to our clamoring sister. We could both recognize that the eager shift in her was artificial and would likely only last until the hourglass ran out. There was an unease in Baby A that moved just as fluidly through Baby C and me; she was teetering on the edge of rage, and we knew the smallest disappointment could encourage her over. We were afraid of some asshole boy saying the wrong thing, or some girl bringing the gossip up out of nosiness or spite. We were afraid that we couldn't control what entered Baby A's sphere. Her fragility shone like fish scales under a flashlight; it would draw so many in. We needed to be there, to yank the fishing rod away from the fishing people and say forcefully, *Put that one back. She is ours.*

And our girl stood there, manically smiling as Baby C told her Bailee was having a party, that Rich was banned from the premises, and that Q had offered to pick us up. Baby A squealed, took the phone from Baby C's belt clip, and texted Q: Be here @ 9;). Then she toppled the day's chores over with her exuberance, rushing about with such distracted speed that I was afraid to slow her down, to ask how she was doing—really, tell me—and to have to dissect, or simply stomach, the lie she'd give in response. We let her flutter about. Even Gull, who'd spent the afternoon trimming hedges with clippers he could barely lift, would pause as she whisked by, staring into the wake of her motion, trying to riddle what exactly was going on. "She's moving like a witch," he said to me when I bent to help him balance a big cut.

"What do you mean?"

"It's like—" he began, hands moving as timidly as his mind until he dropped them away, deflated that he couldn't find the words, and pulled the clippers out of my hand.

As we got ready for the party in our room that night, Baby A drank two bottles of water and ate croutons by the fistful from a plastic bag with the same frenzied energy. All that was on country radio that year was Tim McGraw, old Garth Brooks, and sometimes Carrie Underwood. We turned the volume up and down, oscillating like ocean sounds. Baby C wore our heart-print bikini top beneath a woven see-through tank and linen shorts. I, wanting to stay behind but having agreed to go, planned to arrive translucent in a mid-length halter dress our mother had worn as a cover-up to

Galveston Beach in her teens. I'd styled myself as closely to her as I could, referencing one of the photos on the clubhouse mantel, masked by stacks of *Golf Digest*. In the photo, Murphy's hair was unspooled almost completely from a braid. Baby A calmed herself enough to make an intricate fishtail of my hair. After she tied off my hair, Baby A forced herself into a denim miniskirt we'd received from a classmate that didn't fit any of us quite right. We tried to show her that the button was too strained against her hips, but she wasn't bothered. She said, looking at herself in the mirror, "I like it this way. This tight." When we coaxed her out of the skirt later, after Gram carried her up a flight of stairs, there was a blistered red circle above her navel where the copper fastener had pressed against her abdomen. I pointed it out to her the next morning, and she said, "God, of course I wasn't feeling a thing."

Q parked his truck at such an angle in the Shuggarts' ditch that Baby A and I slid into each other along the back bench seat. The charged warmth of her leg against mine was a comfort; she'd been stingy with her affections lately. The Shuggart house thumped with music and laughter and movement so audaciously that I could feel the bayou water rippling in response. Baby A seemed to have a vision for herself, wobbling through the mess of people toward something specific. Q and Baby C sat very sweetly in a corner by a bookshelf, discussing the ones they'd read and the ones they hadn't. Q's palms were turned upright in my sister's grip as she rubbed the lines etching out his life with her thumbs. They seemed to understand each other in their silence, and they seemed to find silence in even the loudest of places. I stood by the wayside with a clump of dress in my hand, considering the out-of-town boy who sat on the couch, all the coy touches and small flirts I could try out on him, because he wouldn't know that there were two more of me moving about the room. I could tell him my name was Anne or Teresa, and we'd talk without investment, because he wouldn't be staying and I wouldn't be real. I'd say ridiculous things: *Don't you know they faked the moon landing? Really. They really did.* And with a finger to my glossy mouth, *Does David Allan Coe only have the one good song?* It was satisfying to look at him and imagine, but soon enough I became disappointed in myself—in this goddamned place—that the only way I could imagine being wanted or feeling free was to play another game of lies with a plain-faced, dull boy who wasn't even from here. Shame and frustration blurred into a formless melancholy that blanketed my bare shoulders. Then Julie walked through the front door, gripping a bottle of bourbon by the neck, hoisted it in the air, and screamed with glee as the party received her with the same holler. I expected Pete to be not far behind, but there was nobody else, just the door left open for a fleet of daddy longlegs to waft in.

"Your skirt is really short. Cute," I said to Julie, hovering behind her.

She looked at me with a curled lip. "What is *that?* Did I give you that dress?"

"Oh, no. It was our mother's."

"Ah. Sentimental. Makes sense, because it's like a total faded rag."

I smiled weakly and took the shallowly filled cup she handed me. I just held it. "Your brother didn't drive you?"

"Uh, I can drive."

"Well, I mean, he's not here?"

"Honey, no. He's hunting ducks with my dad. Probably killed like seventeen already or something. But no, he won't be back until Monday. Why?"

"I was just going to ask him about—"

"Oh God!" She planted a hand over her heart and slumped toward my face, keeping her voice low, a sympathy in her eyes I'd scarcely seen. "I heard. I mean, what the fuck, right? I could kick the shit out of him myself. From what Pete said, Rich's lucky your sister didn't club him to death with a tire iron. At least no girl will touch him now. He couldn't get a date with a cow in this town." Julie was looking away from me as she spoke, into the sea of people. "And Pete said Rich is lucky, too, that he and Wendell didn't break his fucking arm or jaw or something. He got away too easy with a couple of broken ribs."

"Cracked."

She looked over as if she hadn't even been speaking to me. "What?"

"Nothing. Your brother said he was with Wendell when they roughed him up?"

"Yeah. Said it was his idea. Apparently they threw him in the back of the pickup and took him home after. Better people than me."

I couldn't argue and say that Pete hadn't partaken in the beating, that it was only Wendell. Even though I trusted Q's retelling, I hadn't been there, nor had Q. If I pushed any further, Julie would tire of me or call me a liar, so I imagined it in my mind—Pete whaling on Rich Goodson and then driving him home—unsure if this made me feel any different or better.

For the next forty-five minutes, I played Ping-Pong with the JV baseball team, whipping our arms out and across with ferocity. "You should go out for the team," they said. "Come on, come on. We could use you."

I wondered if the boys remembered I had graduated. Then I wondered if the sound of my laughter would draw my sisters' attentions at all. "Get your sisters," one of them said. "Don't you want them to see?"

It was amazing to me how hugely they all seemed to misunderstand what we wanted from each other, us sisters. It seemed everyone believed that the three of us should be tethered at all times, like a paper cutout of perfect girls with hands connected to create some decorative swoop across this place's face. It seemed that for them, if we were going to be spectacular, it would have to be together. But we were more interested in the ways we could alter our courses, the ways we could help them understand that we were not of the same cloth, our hands weren't permanently connected, that any one of us could just saunter off, even though of course those things weren't as true as we wanted them to be.

The praise of the baseball boys did help me ease. One boy, some little brother, stood behind me to angle my arm just right, pushing my shoulder toward following through.

Beautifully, this was not because he wanted me. It was because he wanted to win, and we were paired up. The little brother said, "You can do it. We can do this," and I believed him. I imagined Gull growing up to be like him.

Then Wendell stumbled down the curved staircase and weaved through a careful arrangement of swaying bodies until he spotted me in the sunroom. I saw him see me, and it was obvious that it rattled him. He flicked his head around until he spotted Baby C still in the corner with Q, then looked between us until I got up and came closer. "Your sister," Wendell said, beer bottle in his hand, jaundiced glaze in his eyes sinking below the thick slowness to his voice, "is passed out in the bathroom. Can't get her up. To wake. I——" He rubbed hard at his forehead as if coaxing the slurred kinks from his thoughts. "I can't get her to wake up."

As he massaged his brain loose, I'd already leaned far enough into the room Baby C was in to motion her toward us more urgently. The beautifully polished wooden staircase banisters shook like trick branches as we wound around three platforms before we were let off. A stale cast of light poured out from the hall bathroom. As we creaked the door further open, Wendell loomed over us from behind, muttering nonsense. We saw that Baby A was sprawled across the bathroom mat, arms above her head, hair covering her face. Instantly I knelt to check her breath, putting an ear to her chest and two fingers to her neck. She was breathing steadily enough, but her eyes didn't stir open as we shook her, poked her sides, tickled the bottoms of her feet.

"Did she hit her head?" Baby C asked.

"What?" Wendell staggered. "No, she just passed out."

"And didn't hit her head?"

"No, Jesus, no. She didn't hit her head."

"Because if she has a concussion and falls asleep—" Baby C began, until Q stopped her with a hand on her shoulder, a quick squeeze, and said in an even tone, "She didn't hit her head. She's just drunk."

"Really drunk. Like, so damn drunk." Wendell lowered into a crouch as if he were evaluating a short putt. I surged with anger.

"Well, what in the hell did you give her?"

"Just beers. She had a few plastic cupfuls of some red thing." He pointed up at the sink counter where a plastic cup was, hollow. "I thought she could take it. She was bragging about her tolerance and laughing. She said she was lying down because she was tired. I thought"—he paused carefully as he looked into my dangerous face—"it was kinda cute."

I pointed to the door. "Get out, Wendell."

"No," Baby C said, lowering my arm with hers. "Get that rag wet with cold water and wring it out."

Wendell did as Baby C asked, handing the wet rag over and lowering back into that watchful umpire crouch as Baby C draped the rag across our sister's forehead. Baby A twitched like dogs do in their sleep, like small electric volts were surging through her. I surveyed the bathroom and grabbed a glass jar of decorative potpourri, holding it beneath her perfectly round nose. In a forceful jolt, she twitched herself awake and blinked at the cold towel. We pulled her into a slump, situating her back against the tub. Wendell got in the tub to deal with her hair, tying it up with an elastic I'd pulled off my wrist.

Then Baby A forced her stomach against the rim of the toilet bowl, heaving dryly. "You've gotta throw up, honey," Baby C said, adding the *honey* in hopes it'd remind her of Gram and increase the urgency.

"I know," Baby A whined. "I can't."

"Stick your fingers—" Baby C slowed her hand toward our sister's mouth and didn't cower when she swatted and pulled away. "You have to. Or they're gonna pump your stomach again. You want them to pump your stomach?" Baby A started bawling, shaking her head. I reached to hold her bobbing head still as Baby C forced her own fingers past our sister's teeth, not retracting them fast enough to miss the rush. I wasn't surprised Baby C was familiar with this.

Baby C washed her hands off in the tub with a bar of soap as I fixed the limp bun Wendell had mangled Baby A's brown-blond waves into. Her body shivered with cold sweats as she vomited repeatedly into the toilet. I gently situated her hair into a braid and then spooled it in the center of her head so the tail wouldn't swing to catch any of the mess. "Goddamn you, Wendell!" she started to scream. "Please, God. Wendell! Why won't you do it? You fucking—you coward. You—"

Wendell's face had gone white. "What is she talking about?" we said. "What did you do?" Wendell shook his head, trying to comprehend what our sister was saying, his face as perplexed as ours. All of us began to cry, even Wendell, whose confusion seemed to devastate him. Q, standing outside the door, moved farther into the bathroom to get a handle on the commotion.

"Can you get another boy?" I said to Q through tears, rubbing circles on Baby A's shaking spine. "We'll have trouble carrying her down ourselves."

He returned a moment later with the Ping-Pong little brother, who looked at us in a messy pile on the floor with piercing pity. He carried our sister in his arms, as if she were a child who'd fallen asleep in the car, while Q walked alongside in case she shifted her bodyweight and threw the little brother off balance. Wendell stood at the top of the stairs, watching us descend, paralyzed by something Baby A and he must have exchanged, something she couldn't get him to do. We weaved through the party with our limp girl as everybody stared and gurgled with inebriation, which made everything they said sound like a joke.

"Who the fu—"

"Look at—it's the three."

"God I feel so bad for her—them."

"Yeah but like, that's kinda trashy."

"Bailee!"

"She'll throw it all up, dude."

"That one is fucked."

"Hey, what'd I say! She'll throw it up."

I heard Julie's voice crow "Par for the fucking course" as she cackled at her own joke.

The boys laid Baby A across my lap in the car as Baby C tried to turn the keys in the ignition with shaking hands, recalling suddenly that this wasn't our truck. Q peeled the keys from her grip as if she were holding a knife. Frustratedly, she began to cry again, which made Baby A sob into my side with empathetic wails. Baby C climbed over the front seat to be in the back with us as Q drove the group of us, once more, home.

"How are we going to tell Gram?" I asked.

Q leaned into the wheel with his chest. If he had been mine, if I'd been Baby C, I'd have reached for him. But her heart and eyes were stuck to our sister, who was folded over, her head between her knees. "I can't think of any lie," Baby C said. "It'll be worse if we lie."

"There's no way she won't be hungover within an inch of her life tomorrow."

"And she'll probably throw up again," I agreed.

"I should've known," Baby C said, deflated. Before I could look at her quizzically, she added, "Horoscope said: 'Invest in others but guard yourself. Be understanding. Be skeptical.' But I couldn't tell her. Oh, I wish I had told her."

My brain wouldn't wrap around what she'd said. "What were you supposed to know?"

Baby C quieted, and our sister stirred in my lap. I'd wanted Q to turn the radio on or roll down a window, get something moving in that crowded space. Baby C exhaled. "Gram is gonna be beyond angry."

I nodded, not touching Baby A, curled in my lap. She'd said my skin nauseated her, slapped me away. It occurred to me to look at the clock. Our curfew was set generously at midnight, since Gram stayed up that late to watch talk shows with the tee-time book in her hand and a map of the course, penciling across both as she laughed intermittently. It was thirty minutes past when Q pulled into the drive, soon enough that Gram wouldn't have started calling us but late enough that we were in trouble. Baby A moaned as I unbuckled the seat belt I'd stretched to cover us both. Baby C went around the side to open the door to see if she could carry her. We could, but we'd have to cradle her between us. Q swooped in like a bird, stretching his arms out wider than I'd ever considered they could go, and moved to lift our sister up. Baby C stopped him with a hand on his shoulder. "You probably better go. Gram's gonna be real mad. I don't want you to see."

Beautifully, in a fashion I hadn't expected, Q helped drape Baby A's arms over our shoulders and instructed us to hold her at the waist like a limp marionette before getting back in his truck and pulling, albeit slowly, away.

"Can you walk?" we asked our sister. "We need you to walk." We made it a few joint, heavy steps before Gram emerged from the clubhouse, having heard Q's truck rumble away. She flicked on the porch lights and pushed her reading glasses up on her head in disbelief. "What in the world?"

She neared us quickly, careful not to say anything until she'd decided what was really going on. Baby C's and my eyes were bloodshot, begging her to go easy on us. Baby A's head was slung so far down that Gram had to lift her by the chin to get a full look. "Oh, Baby." Gram reached between us and swooped Baby A up, lugged her up the stairs toward our bedroom. She'd made it seem simple, like if there was enough conviction and care, you could just lift any old body up to carry them home.

Baby C and I didn't bother looking at each other. We half

expected Gull to languorously happen into the clubhouse to distract us—what a gift he'd have been in that moment. But of course he was fast asleep, and all we could do was gentle our tired bodies into the room, watch as Gram got Baby A into a nightshirt and wiped the frosty makeup off her face with an oiled cotton pad. That was when we saw how deeply the skirt fastener had pressed into our sister's stomach, nearly cutting the skin. I hoped it wouldn't scar. Pink welts were already rising around the rim, in a shape I could only compare to a shotgun shell.

Gram pulled a trashcan to the bedside. "She got most of it out, yeah?"

We nodded.

"Shouldn't have trouble after she falls asleep, but in the morning she might. Careful if she upchucks again."

"Yes, ma'am."

Baby A's head rolled heavily like a marble to one side of her pillow. Gram stroked her damp forehead and left most of the comforter pulled back. I expected her to say, *We'll talk about this in the morning.* Or to look at Baby C and me and say, *You better count your lucky stars blah blah blah.* Instead she pattered down the stairs into the clubhouse, where she flicked the television back on and settled into the couch. In the moment, it felt like mercy. When I think back on it, it makes me wonder whether, if Gram had taken more of a stand that night, leaned into Baby A about what exactly had happened, what exactly was wrong, things wouldn't have ended up the way they did.

I'd thought, when Baby A was stilled and asleep on her bed, I'd heard her mutter: *I wanna die.*

I woke up the next morning convinced I'd figured it all out: Baby A, for some reason, thought being the miserable one would make her unique. It was my fault and Baby C's fault for not being different enough. She'd be the one who got shit-faced at the party, but at least she'd be the one. I found myself contemplating her esophagus and mouth, wondering if they were bruised or rotten smelling, trying to sense the state of my own.

Had she torn up all our bodies the night before? My throat was scratchy and dry. I was sure none of us girls, the next day, would utter a word. What destroyed them destroyed me.

LIGHTNING SNAKES CRASHES

Baby A kept to herself the days after Bailee's party. Her punishment from Gram was to mow the entire course alone. Usually we set off on two separate riding mowers, with the leftover sister running about to pick up sticks or obstructions. Alone, it took Baby A two days. Then Gram began to send her on weekly errands about town to pick up dry cleaning, haggle down prices with the fertilizer supplier in Texas City, and a host of other tedious things. We knew Gram sent her to these places to mask Baby A's newly mandated appointments at the church to have "talks" with Reverend Olivia. This was the method Gram had used on our mother. Throughout Murphy's whole pregnancy, she'd had a standing weekly meeting with the reverend, who during Murphy's time had been an older man named Reverend Alson. According to Aunt Rachel, the two had gotten close and the reverend had celebrated Murphy's babies, which Gram hadn't joined in. The current reverend, Olivia Josephine, was young, eager, and not entirely trustworthy. Mostly, I didn't want her to have the parts of my sister that she wouldn't share with us. I imagined Baby A and the reverend separated by a large table, Baby A's arms crossing her chest, the reverend peppering her with questions that went unanswered.

When Baby A came back from her daily errands, she had grocery bags, mail for Gram, and a to-go cup of sweet peach tea. She went, most times, to the Sonic drive-through to chat with Julie, who worked there that summer before she left for college, scuffing her skates against yellow curbs. The rumor was that her dad was being made to retire early because of the many safety infractions that'd occurred at the plant on his watch, even after the big explosion. In July alone there'd been two men that'd lost fingers, a woman who was severely burned, a team of men whose hearing had been shattered. Mr. Martelli walked around town with no shame at all.

The retirement package they offered him was more than any of us would see in a lifetime. Julie was serving cheese sticks and diet cherry limeades to fund the spray tans she drove thirty minutes to get in Webster and the lace-trimmed tank tops she never seemed to wear twice. Baby A would return with a single drink for herself, walking past us, bent over by the toolshed, or wrangling up a string of carts, sweating. She'd talk at us about the gossip she got from Julie: whose parents had sent their kids to Ohio to stay with relatives after busting their weed stash, which girls had an STD and which boys had given it to them. Julie claimed that Jason and Bailee Shuggart hooked up in his truck, and Baby A assured us she'd told Julie to go to hell with her bullshit lies, but we were never sure. One afternoon Baby A came back with old clothes stacked up to her forehead, rushing them down the hallway to our room. I assumed it was a pity-haul from Julie, who often gave us trash bags full of clothes she'd grown out of, but Baby A never mentioned them, and I didn't find the clothes anywhere in our room.

"It's the weather, I bet," Baby C said.

The two of us sat on the dock with a bucket of golf balls beside us. We were supposed to be diving for strays, but we didn't have the heart.

"What about the weather?" I looked up and around at our same slack, hot sky. "It's the same all year except three weeks in January, if we're lucky."

"I don't know." Baby C kicked at the brown water. "Maybe she's taking the boat dock personally."

Maybe she was. I didn't have anything to say or argue, so we sat, watching the opaque surface. "That's a big fish," I said as a fish jumped high in the air and then another, and another.

"Hey, how is *Big Fish*?"

"Oh. It's good. I finished it. It's about fathers."

"Oh," Baby C said.

We didn't know anything about fathers.

"Do you think by default we have daddy issues?" Her face was clouded with true worry, eyebrows pinched together so tenderly that I replied with a laugh, "We have issues, but they're not just about having no daddy."

"True."

I could tell she was rearing up to actually tackle our task, placing her palms on the edge of the dock with her knees bent. She was the better diver of us girls. I sat back on my heels to watch her launch diligently into the water, but she lost the nerve, turned her head toward me. "Why do you think she screamed that stuff at Wendell?"

I was surprised to hear her ask this, thinking we'd decided to attribute it to drunkenness. I began to shrug my shoulders but stopped, looked deeper into the umber water, algae clumps skirting the top; the most fibrous thing I'd ever seen. "She wanted him to do something, she said. But what the hell is there for Wendell to do? He already did what he could to Rich."

Baby C wobbled slightly on her ankles, poised to dive. "Do you think—well, I think she might be wanting him to kill him."

"Who to kill who? Wendell to kill Rich?"

She nodded.

I tried to push the squabble with Jason away as it pressed

against my forehead like an ache. "She did say something to Jason kind of similar. But I think she's just angry. She doesn't have that in her, C. You know that."

"We all have everything in us." My sister moved her focus to her feet, picking dead skin from her nails. Our pink pedicures had each chipped into unique oblivions, as they usually did between constant swimming and walking about barefoot.

A gull swooped down from a perch and skidded against the surface with its opened mouth, scooping up water like a bucket. We let it comfort us. We let it, just briefly, be taking in its mouth and away from us the worry for our sister. As the bird turned with the bend in the bayou, disappearing into the trees, what we'd wished he'd taken with him was suddenly back in our laps. Baby C regripped the dock to steady her form, grasped the wire bucket of balls, and broke her body gracefully through the film of dark summer muck. I was thinking I should've emptied the bucket in the grass before she dove. All that extra weight she'd have to lug around.

The first time it dawned on us that we could lose a sibling was with Gull. He was four and fell in the bayou while taunting some crabs caught in a net. A decomposed wooden board gave way beneath his feet as he teetered on it, leaning over the water's edge. He fell in quickly and quietly, none of us watching him. Gull had known how to swim since he was two years old. We'd all helped teach him, bobbing around him in the water like a wreath as Gram held him, kicking. But Gull wasn't taught how to unhook water-logged jeans from a nail attached to a board, dragging him farther into the murk. Coach Lyell Keith had seen big splashes as he tried to chip out of a sand trap and strode over calmly until he saw it was little hands making the splashes. He dove in with everything on, cell phone clipped to his waistband, wallet in his pocket, and never said a word about it. Coach Keith yanked Gull out of the water so hard his little jeans ripped off.

By then, the commotion had gathered us. Gram sprinted from the clubhouse and hijacked a cart halfway. My sisters and I arrived at the dock in time to see Gull spout water as Coach whacked him on the back. Gull coughed wetly, then spewed all over the dock as Coach kept on patting.

It'd been silent. We'd let Coach do it all, not one of us or Gram trying to take over or intervene. We were stilled.

Eventually Gull took a few clear, confident breaths, enough for Coach to scoop him up and sit him beside Gram in the golf cart. We ran behind the cart as Gram drove, then sat on the couch and listened to Gull tell Gram and Coach Keith what had happened. He swore something jumped up and grabbed him, that one of those crabs must have been holding him down. Gram ushered Gull toward us to rest on the couch, watch some TV, while Coach recounted what had actually occurred. He spoke low, in a generationally southern voice, as Gram nodded.

Coach didn't leave that night until it was well dark out, waiting around to make sure Gull was truly okay and that we'd all calmed. We wished he would stay. We wished he would take over for Gramp, who had passed just a year earlier.

Before leaving, Coach Keith and Gram hugged in a way that reminded me they'd known each other their whole lives. Gone to school together, been at each other's weddings, a trust between them that came from deciding to be good to each other for that many years in a row. I knew Coach was nothing special, and neither was Gram, in the grand scheme of things, but in our small town, they felt like the world. When they were young, Coach was *the guy* and Gram had been *the girl*, and they'd hugged knowing what it felt like to carry that into every mistake they made. Now Coach Keith had gone and saved her baby's life. Gram hugged him with all she could give. It made me wonder if he'd been there after our mother died, though of course he had. Gull hugged Coach before he left, too, and Coach ruffled a tuft of his hair.

"You'll be alright," Coach said to Gull. But really, Coach was saying that to all of us.

Gull became fully our own that day, no more adopted brother about him. As the girls and I fidgeted, wired with nerves, Gram rocked Gull to sleep in the recliner.

Baby A waved us girls to the back door and onto the first hole. "We've gotta go get that net." So we walked all the way to the water's edge and tugged the crab net up, which took all the strength in each of our grips to do. We hoisted the net, and Baby A tumped the crabs out harshly, slamming them into the water. "You get out of here," she'd said over and over, low-toned. "You go on."

As we walked wearily back, Baby A dragged the dripping net against the grass, sounding as if she were rubbing a balloon against an oven door, that rubbery crackle of wet grass. We hung our heads for what we'd nearly gone through. Baby A passed the net off to Baby C, who held it above the ground to her chest, soaking her sternum cold.

"I miss Ansley Deer," Baby A offered like abstract bait.

"Isn't it crazy that the water took her so fast?" I marveled, ashamed.

Baby A pointed for a furious small moment at the sky, yelling, "Look what it almost did today!"

We shushed her, and she let her arm fall dramatically beside her. I remember the air smelling thin and crisp that day, the way it usually did before hurricanes. When we happened into the clubhouse, Baby A clutching the net, Gram shook her head and looked at Baby A in a way she didn't often turn on Baby C and me. She looked like she wanted to say, *Girl, you're just mad about being born.*

We lived on from there, afraid, diligent with Gull's floaties and earplugs. As for myself, I expected to be dead any second for any reason when we were little. Until I was about nine, I was just sure I'd be kidnapped. "Don't let them get you in the car," Gram had told us sternly. "Once they've got you in the car, you're dead." So we practiced dropping to the ground and becoming dead weight. We did it in the bayou, sinking to the bottom as long as we could, not to play underwater tea party but to outweigh the bad people. I was best at it. Immovable. Not a thing could get me out of the water or off the ground, not tickles or threats. Even with this skill, I had more fear than faith.

Gram had the dock reboarded, even though we couldn't afford it.

When I talked with Baby C on the very same dock about our other sister's secrecy, I'd wanted to bring up that day with Gull, but something kept me from it. Gull had only given us a scare that big the one time, but Baby A was always playing chicken and lying. I was afraid to create an anxiety between Baby C and me that I couldn't take back. And anyway, Baby C was saddled with her own load.

She had slowed down in every way, Baby C. Walked slow, talked slow, her thoughts slowed, but nobody was worried. Her vomit was everywhere in little splashes. She'd started to only eat one very specific meal that didn't upset her stomach: broiled unseasoned chicken, a side of lettuce with carrot slices, and water with a hunk of lemon. For breakfast she had nothing unless Gram bugged her, then she'd concede to a banana. She was afraid of food hurting her, but more afraid of us noticing she was behaving this way. Gram had pulled her aside a few times for a talk, even had Harriet lug over a pot of Baby C's favorite spaghetti sauce, which she ate only to be nice. Later that evening, I felt the onions burn their way up her esophagus.

Gram said there wasn't anything really wrong with Baby C, that she was just self-conscious like all young girls, but I could tell that my sister hated herself for this sickness she couldn't control. I could tell she was trying to get better. It seemed as if Baby A got all the destructive attention, and there wasn't any left in the well for Baby C. Gram had passed on comprehensive allergy tests for the eat-and-find-out method because our insurance had lapsed. As a safeguard, Gram stocked up on the Gatorade and saltines, and I watched as every week and a half, something mysterious made Baby C sick.

Of course, Gram had always known there was something wrong with all of us. She didn't talk much about losing our mother, or Gramp, or how we were conflated, but years later, when all was confirmed and what was left of us had grown up, when it had become less painful to talk about the ways we'd hurt ourselves and each other with our neglect, Gram would ask abruptly, "And you?" She would be cross-legged with a mug of cold coffee, the two of us in lawn chairs on the back nine, taking a break from tidying up sand traps. "What were you struggling with back then?"

"Everything we did," I said, "was together."

"Until it wasn't," she replied.

It would hurt me to acknowledge that yes, until it wasn't, everything my sisters and I did was entirely together, even when that was unfair. Gram couldn't have known the way we felt each other's pain, the deep pulsing unity that kept us up at night. And if she had, she could never have let us know, because we'd have resented her for not being able to fix it.

Later that day, Aunt Rachel called to say a rogue spray of dry lightning struck the tree in their front yard and near massacred the house. It fell to the wayside "at the last minute, Isadora," Aunt Rachel said with shock. Firehouse volunteers came by to clean it up because we'd donated our old woodchipper to the department, which was originally why she'd been calling.

Gram got off the phone and turned to all of us gathered on the clubhouse couch, except for Baby A, who'd stowed away in our room. "That stuff is scarier than anything."

"Lightning?" Baby C asked. "Than anything?"

"Than anything," Gram confirmed.

"Not scarier than snakes," I said.

"Lightning and snakes, then."

Gull piped up, colliding his hands in the air as he said, "Crashes."

"Lightning, snakes, and crashes."

We could agree on that much because we didn't know about other things, awful things. Things already waiting for us.

That night, I woke for water and found Gram at the kitchen island, hovering over a map of bills. Water bills, soil and fertilizer bills, tree cutting bills, energy bills, golf cart part bills. Gram tried to keep them from us, but we fetched the mail. We noticed the pile of letters that remained unopened, as if they would go away if she didn't let their reality enter our world. The course saved on labor fees because the girls and I did most of the big stuff, but during the previous school year Gram had to outsource. There wasn't a big membership fee, and we didn't charge much for the driving range. Gram refused to raise the prices, even though the nation was in the middle of a recession. "People come here for the bargain," she'd say.

As she hovered over the papers in her *Who Shot JR?* T-shirt, I got to watch her for a few unfiltered moments before she felt my presence and looked up. "What are you doing awake?"

"Water," I said as I moved to get a glass from the cupboard. "What's all this?"

"Don't be coy." Just as quickly as she'd said it, Gram exhaled and clutched her eyes shut. "I'm sorry. It's just business as usual, I'm afraid."

"Gram," I began hesitantly as I held my glass under the faucet. "We don't have to keep doing this. Someone would buy it."

She flattened her hands on the island surface and bit her lip. "I am sick of you girls saying that. You don't wanna work? Is that it?"

"No, Gram—"

"Where would we live? We sell the course, and we'd be selling our home. I don't have retirement or stocks. We ain't rich. We get by, and that's fine."

"But Gram, you're tired. And that's okay. Let us take care of you. We could buy a small house in town, or a double-wide, a real nice one, and you could rest."

She swallowed hard. I couldn't recall a moment she'd been closer to tears than then, standing over the overdue bills, knowing. "I don't need to rest."

"Oh Gram," I said as I set my water glass down, moving to touch her shoulder. "Of course you do."

She said nothing back. We stood for a few beats with my hands on her and her neck hanging over the stacks, both of us unsure if there was any digging the golf course out of the hole it was in. I said with such confidence that *someone* would buy it, but I didn't know if that was true. The world had changed. Homes were in foreclosure; everyone seemed to be in debt, losing jobs. It wasn't a luxury to have time anymore; it meant you were lazy, or at least Gram held steadfast to that idea. I saw suddenly that worry had chipped away her last few healthy years. It was as if, in May, we'd had a spry, swimming Gram who was optimistic and rough, then we looked away just a minute to turn back and find it was August, and Gram was covered in cancerous sunspots, pale, slow to the step, and trying for all our sakes to hide it. We'd looked away, those few moments, to get better understandings of ourselves and to study each other. There couldn't be guilt in that. But it was sobering to stand in the kitchen with a woman I'd clung to, even if out of sheer necessity, and realize she was no longer the gathered, shining person she'd been. The one the town loved and the men chased. Would they notice? Well, of course, no. She would be eternal and ethereal to them, in the way that my sisters and I were fused; the town could not be bothered to see any of us for what we were.

Quietly I walked my water glass back to bed and fell asleep, exhausted by what I couldn't control and knowing the only thing that could fix it was money. Where was I going to get any of that?

The next morning, as I reordered tee times for canceled groups, Pete walked into the clubhouse with a handful of tinfoil packages and his driver, which he leaned against the wall in the corner like a wet umbrella. He wore boat shoes without socks, a bright-orange collared shirt tucked loosely into his shorts. As he neared me, leaning against the counter, he slid one of the tinfoil packages over.

"I thought hunting was about blending in," I said before I

could think the remark through. Pete tilted his head in confusion. The hazel of his eyes swelled the room.

Waving my hand sillily through the air, I stammered, "Julie mentioned the other day. Ducks."

"Ah, yeah. I almost forgot about that. Yeah." He eyed the tinfoil squares. "Don't worry," he said, "these aren't them. Pulled pork from the meat market."

"Oh, thank you." I placed my hands on the warmed foil as my stomach roiled with hunger and confusion. "We could eat in the kitchen. Or outside on the bench."

Familiar as he'd been when Gull cut his hand, Pete walked both sandwiches into the kitchen and found us plates. "Paper, please," I cautioned. "Gram doesn't like to clean more than we need." We sat at barstools across the kitchen island from each other, eating our barbecue sandwiches, the mood a bit stilted. "So, the ducks. Did you get any?"

Pete laughed, reaching behind him to grab a paper towel to cover his mouth with as he kept laughing. He tore an extra for me and handed it over. "I guess you could call it 'getting,' but mostly, we, well, uh, we kill them. With guns. From far away."

"That makes sense." My face pinked. "How many?"

"Combined, my father, cousin, and my father's friend made out with about thirteen when the weekend was over."

"And you?"

"Well, I like to limit myself to just one. For the day, at least."

"But isn't it a sport? Aren't you supposed to get as many as you can?"

"To some, yes. There are laws, too, about how many you can kill in a day, but to me, focusing on the one lets me appreciate it more."

"Hm, I don't know if that makes you humane or strange."

"Maybe we can settle somewhere in the middle?"

We. I shuddered. My *we* was on the driving range, scooping up golf balls in a shuttered cart. My other *we* was across town talking to the reverend. There had never been a *we* that wasn't my sisters and me. I bristled visibly enough; Pete's eyes searched the room for what he'd said incorrectly, settling his wrist against the table's edge. I took a swig of iced tea like medicine.

"I came by to see how you were. Julie told me what happened to your sister at Bailee's party, and there's the Rich thing, of course. It's been a rough go for you, hasn't it?" His tone was like a doctor's, condescending and edged toward the diagnostic. I nodded hesitantly.

"What did Julie say happened?"

"Well, other people told me, too. Just that your sister got cratered and had to be carried out. I can only imagine. People were saying shitty things. I wanted to see for myself that you were alright."

I thought back to that slumber party years before: Baby A leaned over the toilet, Pete staring into the back of her head, then just as quickly walking away. "We're fine. *I'm* fine. But yeah, rough night."

"You deserve better friends than my sister and Bailee Shuggart."

I scoffed and took a bite of the barbecue sandwich. "Where do you suggest I get some?"

He nodded consciously. "Fair enough." This made me feel I had a bit of a leg up, almost like I wasn't being ambushed at work with a random sandwich. "You could join a Facebook group or the YMCA. Send letters to soldiers at war."

"Facebook?"

"Funny." He smirked. "I thought it'd be the soldiers that'd stump you."

The door creaked as a group of men walked in loudly, sweating all over the carpet. I excused myself to give them receipts and book their next tee time. We made small talk about the oppressive heat, and one of the men handed me a five-dollar bill that I stuffed in our shared tip jar. Baby A would've taken it for her own, but I wasn't her. When I returned to the kitchen island, Pete had made a fortune teller out of the paper ring binding our napkin and plastic cutlery, no bigger than a quarter. Somehow, he was able to put his football fingers into the pockets and open it, close it, open it, though nothing was written in the mite-tiny flaps.

"How'd you do that?"

"When I was little," he said, "I'd get nervous when we'd go out to restaurants and I'd refuse to talk, so my uncle taught me how to make these out of paper napkin rings to take the place of conversation."

He unwrapped another set of utensils and showed me, step by step, how he made the miniature fortune teller. There was no way I'd be able to re-create it, but it was fascinating to watch as he made creases in the paper with one precise pass because "more than one fold will rip it." I wondered what he would write in the flaps if he could, and how he was ever satisfied, even as a child, with a fortune teller empty of words. I had over- or under- or misestimated him, I realized. There was something shockingly tender in the way he manipulated the paper.

Pete finished the object and slid it over. "Baby C is going to love this," I said.

His face faltered. "Don't you girls get tired of each other?"

"Uh . . . yeah."

There was quiet because I knew what he wanted to know, and I couldn't bring myself to say, *I'm a lonesome loser, just like you suspect.* Instead, I said, "It's hard to make friends. It's like, in nineteen years, nobody has bothered to learn our names or how to treat us like separate human beings. Feels like crap, frankly. So yeah, we get tired of each other, but it's not like there's anyone other than Jason or our aunt to go to."

"I don't think you give people enough credit."

I laughed. "Sure you don't, because you're one of them, and you want credit." At this, he laughed, too.

We'd finished our sandwiches and I'd begun to fidget with guilt that I should get back to work. Fidgeting, also, with anxiety that Baby A would wander in and have something to say to Pete about his behavior at the boat dock, realizing then that I hadn't told either of my sisters that Julie had said Pete tussled with Rich that night. Though it wouldn't have made a difference.

"Listen—" He patted his hands against the countertop. "I'll get out of your hair, but I want to know two things."

I tried to arrange my face to reflect indifference.

"First, what would you like me to call you?"

"When?"

"No, *what*?"

"Oh." My cheeks warmed. "My name, Baby B. Or B."

"Okay, B. Second. Want to go fishing with me on Friday?"

"Well . . ." I imagined this in snapshot; he and I floating aimlessly in a canoe with hooks and flopping fish, stinky raw hot dogs as bait, the must of the water murk. If it got awkward or I got a surge of anxiety like I had on the boat dock, how would I leave? All I pictured was my squirming in a life jacket and his looking into the water, ignoring me. He laughed again before I could answer. "How about a walk, or I can join you on a swim? Heck, what if I just show up around this time? I'll bring another sandwich."

"I'll be here."

"Good. I'll text you if something changes."

"Oh . . ." I reached my hand across the table, and he put his hand atop it for a few seconds before pulling away. "I don't really text. Only Baby A does. And now Baby C for Q, I guess. It's best to call. Our cell or the clubhouse is fine."

"Then I'll call." He gave a cursory grin, exhausted by the back and forth, I assumed, and balled up the tinfoil remnants of our lunch to stuff them in the trash.

After Pete left, I checked out the clubhouse window to ensure neither of my sisters had seen him. I wasn't ready to explain why he was there because I was certain it wasn't to be just friends. He had plenty of those in College Station, where he was headed back to in a few weeks anyway. I also wasn't ready to explain how I felt about his being there. His hand on my hand. The questions and the fishing.

It had been almost a week since Pete stopped by and left me with the idea that he would call. Radio silence. I'd insisted on the shifts at the desk by the phone, and watched our cell clipped to Baby C's waist like it was going to transform into Pete himself, to no avail.

One morning we returned to the clubhouse after our swim to a message on the answering machine, blinking like a beacon. Gram beat me to the machine, shooing me into the mudroom to step out of my suit before she pressed play: *Isadora. It's Curtis Mitchum. I just wanted y'all to know the Coast Guard has said the bayou's pH is too high, and well, I know this is 'bout the time y'all get back from swimming, so it's probably best y'all take showers and steer clear. Anyhow, I'll be by for my tee time, so I can bring y'all some of that scrub Jana swears by. Alright now.*

"Girls," Gram called. "Go take showers. We're not swimming for some days. Throw those suits in the wash."

Baby C rushed out of the mudroom to get Gull to the downstairs tub, herding him with a towel like a matador. Baby A had been midstrip in the laundry, tilting her head to listen in on the muffled machine message. I snatched the suit from her hand. "Go."

With a smile, which I hadn't expected, she kissed my cheek and ran naked toward the stairs for our bathroom. I filled the washing detergent cap with soap, glancing my arms and legs over for rashes, hoping the others were checking themselves, too. In a flash, I pictured Pete eating jam on toast with a heap of scrambled eggs at his Casa Grande marble countertop, preparing to bring me a sandwich, or preparing to never speak to me again. I'd been thinking of him in spurts since he'd stopped by; Pete on the putting green in shorts, Pete in his truck driving to me. The more I thought of him, the nicer the idea of him became, even if there were considerable gaps in my imaginings, even if he hadn't actually called.

As I rinsed the detergent cap out in the water stream, I realized there were no clean towels in our bathroom, and Baby A had just sprinted there bare as a buck. I grasped two rolled rag towels from the shelf beside the washer, closed the lid, and pressed the "delicate" button.

Our bathroom mirror was fogged with steam when I poked my head in. "I got you a towel, wild woman."

She laughed. "You gotta shower, too."

"I got two towels."

"Or we could share?"

It was my turn to laugh. "Or—we could not."

Baby A pulled back the curtain, just her head exposed, and smirked. "Come in, jeez. I'm almost done anyway."

"I'll wait."

"Why? A waste of water if you ask me. Prude."

"You're almost done anyway, right?"

"What if I was Pete?"

The water steamed from behind her head like volcanic fog as my back stiffened. I had been careful not to mention him to either of my sisters, or to look at him too long when he hit balls on the driving range. Baby A looked back at me with a meddlesome expression; she was proud of herself for figuring it out.

"What, have you been spying on me or something?"

"B, your stomach is doing flips all day. It's like a permanent knot in my gut."

"A taste of your own medicine, then."

"Anyway. I don't care. I want to know. Like, what's going on? You like him, right?"

"Yeah, I think so. But he hasn't called. And he hasn't stopped by."

Her face scrunched with dismay. "Did he say he was going to call?"

I nodded.

"What a fucker." She reached her hand out of the curtain, and I put a towel into it. Then she stepped wetly onto the bath mat, wrapped up and dripping, still angry. Angrier than I was expecting her to be over a boy not calling me. It was like we were standing at the boat dock again, Baby A raging and me standing by the wayside, hurt and confused.

She sighed. "Why are men so disgustingly awful?"

"I don't think he's awful. I think he's ... actually—" I dropped my towel to the floor before stepping carefully over the puddles she'd made into the tub basin, the water far too hot for me to handle. As I bent to adjust the temperature, Baby A walked out of the bathroom, saying, "I'll make him call. Don't you worry, B. That boy is going to call you." And I believed her.

"The Bluegrass Festival is coming up, girls." Gram pushed a big bowl of yeast rolls toward the center of the kitchen island. "End of August. Starts the twenty-eighth."

Gull perked up and moved to Baby A, whose legs dangled from the counter. He tugged on her arms until she laughed, twirling him in a dance hall circle. "The prize this year is a million dollars," Gull shouted as he stamped zeros in the air with a cupped hand. Baby C reached to ruffle his hair. "Just a thousand, silly." He was still twirling in Baby A's grip, grinning into the motion. Then they began, in a collective brainstorm, to list songs our mother had sung when she'd competed as a teenager. My mind was too fogged to help. The pollution of Gull and Baby A's spinning laughter plugged my ears.

The thing about my sisters and me singing at the festival was that we sang together—no solos—cattled around a microphone while the band sawed on fiddles. For me, if I sang in a group, I couldn't be heard as much, which felt safer, even if I still death-gripped my dress hem and swayed side to side with nerves. Baby C closed her eyes when she sang, drifting far and away in a manner I envied. Baby A loved the attention, unsurprisingly. She especially valued the charade of getting ready, hovering backstage and being clapped for. My sisters were magnetic and gorgeous and would lilt onstage while I stood rigid, leaning as far as I could into their shoulders. In past years we'd worn matching dresses and pulled our hair back the same way, but that year felt as if it was destined to be different, if only because we'd grown away from giving in to the idea of us as three carbon copies put on

God's earth to tootle around a golf course and sing old songs. There was prize money to be had, which caused, for the first time, the possibility of winning to permeate our motivations. It was the year we seemed to really understand what a thousand dollars could do for us. And—I figured, though never confirmed—each one of us girls thought we'd get the thousand all to ourselves to spend however we pleased. It's amazing that we thought this, because we knew in our bones that it'd be split like everything had been our whole lives. Then Baby A would blow it and ask us to lend her funds in twenty-dollar increments until she'd blown our portions, too. Odd, what you can imagine when you really let yourself.

"I think . . ." Baby A trailed off, standing in front of our bedroom vanity mirror a few nights later. "I think we should wear minidresses, or even miniskirts, or"—she whipped around to face Baby C and me, lying across the beds—"we could wear our course uniforms. Hot, right?"

Baby C was instantly torn. "Isn't that kind of strange, though? Like making it sexy."

"Golf *is* sexy," I said with a snort.

"Be serious." Baby A was trying to pull her long hair into a perfectly messy bun atop her head, wobbling on her knees like a buoy in rough water. Julie had been smuggling spiked teas to her and replenishing Baby A's flask with whatever hard stuff was in her parents' wet bar; we could smell the odd mixtures on both of their breaths. Gram had told Baby A, after Bailee's party, that if she were to sniff even a whiff of alcohol in the house that wasn't residual beer drippings from the patrons, she'd send our sister to the Spring Center in the city. When Gram threatened rehab, even-toned, Baby A had nodded respectfully to Gram's face, hanging her head as she should've, just to walk away unbothered, knowing we didn't have health insurance and couldn't otherwise afford it. In the mirror, Baby A kept clawing at her scalp with a taut hair tie. I scoffed out loud. She turned to me with a vengeful look in her eye and taunted, "C'mon, do it for Pete."

Baby C looked sideways at me, surprised.

I wanted to take the shoe off my foot and throw it at Baby A's head. I wanted to tell her to go to hell. But a lump welled in my throat, and I felt more embarrassment than anger. I wondered for a moment if she might turn the same question onto Baby C, grill her about Q. But no. Baby C and Q were real. Even Baby A couldn't pick that apart. And anyhow, Baby A was dumb. Didn't she know, even if it felt like we sang for the men who watched us, it was always for and had always been about our dead mother?

Baby A kept clawing at her scalp, tugging her hair upward. "We need to look like women," she said. "We're not girls anymore. And that doesn't sell."

"Are we selling something?" Baby C asked, pressing against her right hipbone. She did this, pressing it so often and so hard that she had a persistent bruise as she tried to feel for how thin the skin had gotten during particularly rough spells of her sickness.

"Don't be an idiot. We're trying to win money, and it's even better if it gets people to come to the course. We've always sold something. And I'll make the outfits, anyway. You won't even have to worry about it."

"You're going to *make* them?" I said, still wilted by her meanness, the way such conviction overtook her face and was a second later washed away. I'd thought we'd had a real sisterly moment earlier, outside the shower. That I could trust her with this. I could never parse when Baby A was my ally or my enemy.

She rolled her eyes and kicked her foot back like an irritated horse.

Baby C pulled her T-shirt up higher, kneading a fold in her lower belly. "Why can't we just win because we're good singers?"

"That's not enough for this town. For anyone." Baby A fastened the hair tie finally, angrily. She'd meant, *For me. It's not enough for me.* She moved away from the mirror to sit beside Baby C, stacking her hand atop Baby C's. Her eyes were weighty with the whiskey we smelled, but when my two sisters locked eyes, Baby A's sobered. "We are beautiful and talented, and that's a good thing." Her voice was soft. "Why are you afraid to be beautiful?"

At this, as I knew she would, Baby C went stiff and rolled off the bed, hurrying out of the room and down the stairs to the bathroom in the clubhouse to avoid the one we shared.

"Goddammit," I said as I slammed my hand against the comforter.

"I thought we weren't supposed to say *goddamn*," Baby A said with a curl.

"Why'd you have to do that?"

"How was I supposed to know she'd get upset?"

"Don't be a bitch. You know! You know how she is." I shoved her shoulder and got up.

"You don't have to go and save her, you know." This rang in my ears and spun around my head and has ever since. I hated that this was who my sister was becoming; bitter and resentful and angry, even at us. Hiding things.

It took a few minutes for Baby C to let me in the clubhouse bathroom, and when she did, it was already done. I could tell by the smell; she always flushed toilet bowl cleaner down after to negate the stench. We stared at each other. There was no use talking about it, then. I let her push past me in silence and walk back up the stairs.

The golfers screamed for their balls to "Sit! Sit!" and "Get in the hole!" They called the trajectories of their putts, "Right, right, right," while they begged the balls to curve up an impossible slope. They cursed themselves. They threw their hats on the ground in defeat. It dawned on me that golf was an angry game, all of us shouting at ourselves to do the near-impossible.

That night Baby C sat on the driving range in Gramp's oversize T-shirt and called her psychic. I watched her from the bathroom window, standing on top of the closed toilet lid as she stretched her long legs out, let sweat drip down her neck, and asked the psychic if we'd win the festival, if Baby A would stop her indulgences, if she would stop getting sick, if Gull would—please—stop getting teased by neighbor kids; all of these words I shoved into her mouth as I watched her, hoping this was what she wanted to ask for, too.

Then I lay on top of my comforter and dreamed vividly. I was walking from Seeglow's grocery to the church while balancing a perfectly stacked pyramid of empty, green-shining tawny port communion bottles down the middle of the street. Police cars blocked off the intersections while children, teachers, and elderly folk lined the sidewalks, wrapped in blankets, watching expectantly. I could see the church a few blocks ahead, but it was as if the road was a treadmill beneath my feet, and going forward got me nowhere. They were rattling bells and cheering, tracking me with their eyes. I couldn't think above the noise enough to discern if they were cheering for me to reach the end or cheering for me to lose my balance so they could watch the glass shatter. A voice said, *You'll get to her. She's just over there. You'll make it. Right there. Come on, right there.* To which another voice hollered, *She's been waiting. We've kept her, all this time.* But I could not see over or beyond the tower of sea-glass green I was balancing, and out of my periphery I realized that I hadn't moved but a few feet beyond the grocery store. They kept screaming, *We've kept her. We got her. Come on, girl. She's all yours.* And when I finally woke out of brief paralysis to tears streaming down my cheeks, chest shaking with sobs, my instinct was to think they were talking about our mother. The longer I sat upright in the bed, letting my chest settle and trying my hardest to quiet down, the more I began to think that the person they were pointing me toward was myself, until I was thinking this with such assurance, as if it had been obvious, that I forgot I'd entertained the idea that it could be anyone else.

By morning, it was settled. We were going to sing our mother's songs at the Bluegrass Festival, and it was going to destroy us.

[ENTER] FRONT PORCH CHORUS

We didn't tell Isadora when we found Murphy behind the laundromat with a starter pack of cigarettes. Didn't tell her Murphy was walking the park bridge most midnights the summer of '88, humming along to her Walkman, alone. Never mentioned a thing about her and Rachel Ronsino—now Upchurch—stealing from the drugstore shelves: magazines, polishes, balms. That once Mr. Petro saw her scoop from the tip jar and slip coins into her coverall pockets. Said she jingled the whole way out. The teachers among us knew Murphy had a mouth, wrote as much on the reports home. And when we'd go by the golf course after work to drive a bucket of balls, we'd spot Murphy dutifully at the register or stringing up a bunch of carts. It was that image of her, doing exactly as she was told, that kept us from telling Isadora who had fathered those girls, 'cause we knew. Kept us from telling her, even still, after Murphy passed, because what in the hell would she do with information like that. We see her now, our Manatee, clawing herself through grief from one day to the next, right on past those little girls, right on past that boy, and we wish we had a way to tell her, in words that wouldn't sound like *I told you so*, that the girl was always trouble.

BUG-DAZE

Eventually, Pete called. We talked routinely with the home phone cord stretched around the kitchen corner as I ducked under the stairs, mumbling, but mostly listening. He talked about the hunts he went on and summer studying. Then he started to wash up at the course, and we'd kiss behind the golf cart shed. They were plain but sparked-enough kisses. So plain that I can't recall the first one. The kisses felt akin to our talking; mostly an indulgence of him. Odd pits of regret panged my gut when he strode away, back to the driving range, his clubs leaned against the bench. Of course, I assumed this was because I had no spark, or that I didn't know what I was doing, figuring we'd progress toward romance as things went on, or we wouldn't, and I'd learn to be fine with that, too. Pete had a school to return to, a life out there that most likely reminded him nothing of Longshadow or me. I wondered often if I was the kind of girl who couldn't feel kisses the way other girls seemed to. I wondered, less often, if it was Pete with something missing. Pete without the flicker in him.

Baby A was sneaking out at night when she thought we were asleep. She'd check, hovering her hand over our chests and watching to make sure our eyes were staying closed, then she'd shimmy out the window with loads of lip gloss on, wearing one of our cotton nightgowns like a slip dress. At first, I hadn't thought much of her leaving. I figured it was to see Rich, and that she was too embarrassed to confess; they tended to make up, even when he did horrible things and wasn't sorry. Then I'd taken to thinking she was sneaking around with Julie, vandalizing things or sitting on the greens to talk. Looking back, it seems obvious where she was going. I'd live on to hate myself for feigning sleep, stilling my chest as her hand floated above, clutching my eyes shut so she'd be convinced enough to leave, then watching her trot across the yard without stopping her, letting her sink further and further into the dusk that would eventually steal her completely away.

On a morning within it all, Baby A jostled me awake. The bedside table clock blinked 6:07 a.m. "Let's swim," she whispered.

"It's too early. And the pH," I said as she began to tug the sheets away.

"I want to go without the others. Just you and me."

The warmth of my bed was promising, but the idea of getting my sister in the water, just us, won out. She offered me a combination of swimsuit pieces, and I dressed in the hall bathroom. Then we stepped into flip-flops by the back door and began to trudge across the holes, sloping with their slopes, ebbing and flowing as if already in the water. Baby A didn't walk ahead as she seemed to have done most of our lives. She stayed in step with me, shoulders back, eyes ahead. It was her gaze that threw me the most. She had always looked where she was headed and only there, but that morning, her eyes wandered. She moved fluidly, naturally, as if nothing were off kilter. Unnerving, the way she slipped into this method act convincingly. I wondered who she was trying to imitate, or what, with her actions, she was trying to make me believe. At the edge of the dock, she stacked two towels side by side near the metal ladder, waiting for me to plunge first.

"To the buoy and back?" I asked, dunking quickly underwater to soak my hair flat.

"Whatever. I'll follow you." She was already a bit breathless.

We swam toward the midway buoy, pulling ourselves forward

with the length of our arms, kicking and breathing measuredly. Gram had taught us all the perfection of stretching our bodies, pacing our limbs, how to be with the water, not in it. Though our walk to the water had unsettled me, it felt like Baby A and I were aligned when we swam. There was nothing to hear except our own breathing and the sounds of our feet against the surface. Between strokes I could see that we'd kept even pace with one another from no effort of my own. Baby A was about a yard away from me, our faces occasionally meeting when we turned in the same direction for a breath.

When I looked at my sister moving through the water, it felt like she was wearing my face. Almost as if she were chasing me, gasping for air. The feeling passed quickly from my mind but stayed as a small burst of panic in my chest until we reached the buoy and grabbed the side of it to rest. "You're not so fast today, huh?" I said, watching the way wet hair stuck to her neck like the tentacles of a sea creature. The disheveled parts of her shone in the rising sun.

Baby A leveled her breathing and smiled as she panted. "I didn't want to make it a rush. Nicer this way, staying with you."

I smiled back, and we waited at the buoy longer than usual; she should've raced off a few beats in, already yards ahead, sprint-swimming for the clubhouse, but we bobbed there, both of us wanting to say something about the morning or our feelings and neither quite sure how to phrase it.

"Do you think," I began cautiously, "you're feeling better?"

She nodded slowly as she focused on the water's moving, a chaos we'd created with our bodies. "I think so. I don't think about it much at all now."

"That's good." I didn't know if she meant her habits or the boat dock, but I couldn't bring myself to ask.

"I guess," she said, still focused. "I still feel . . . not myself."

"Is the reverend helping?"

Baby A scoffed. "No. If Gram had ever talked to her the way she makes me, she'd come home fuming and say, *What a foolish woman.* All the reverend wants to do is get to the bottom of things."

"Well, what's the bottom of things?"

Baby A had expected that, I think. She scanned the exposed half of my body. "You."

I was suddenly aware of the wet of my grip against the buoy, the possibility of my slipping or my sister deciding to race ahead of me as she was used to. Then she took a deep breath in: "And Baby C, and Gram, and Gull, and Ansley Deer, and the reverend herself. And all these damn, dumb boys. Everything. This place is the bottom of it."

I let myself chuckle, trying to keep in step with what she expected of me, or was comfortable with me doing. As if a bird I'd been admiring from afar finally landed on my windowsill, I was afraid to scare her away. "This place is the bottom," I agreed.

Later that afternoon, I was helping Gull soak dirty flagsticks in the kitchen when Pete Martelli walked into the clubhouse with his dad and uncle. He was wearing a wool driving cap that looked ridiculous on him; I wanted to rip it off. The caricature of it. "Petey," his dad said. "Get the keys for the golf cart. Meet you on the first hole." Patrons by the driving range glared at Mr. Martelli; the exact figure of his early retirement package had finally gotten around. He smiled flatly back, kicked at the grass in his saddle shoes, smug.

Pete walked up to the counter and rang the handbell. I shook both flat palms to the side at Gull to sign *finish* and walked behind the counter, grabbing a set of cart keys out of the drawer to hand over. "The tires are a bit low," I said, "but you can still make it over the humps." There was no giddiness or deep understanding between us, like Baby C and Q exchanged. No secret smile.

He looked at me keenly and scooped up the keys. I'd noticed that Pete never seemed to stall at the sight of my face in the way even Gram and Jason did; Pete recognized me. Or was darn good at convincing me he did. "How about lunch after?"

I blinked a few confused times as I closed the drawer. We'd never gone *out*. "Oh, okay."

"What?"

"It's just, we've never gone anywhere before."

I wobbled against the moment. Pete laid his hand on the counter as a bridge between us. "If you can get away from this place, let's go to the Shrimp Shack like you mentioned."

Like I mentioned? Baby A's silhouette out of the corner of my eye caught me. She was teaching a helpless young boy how to grip a putter. I blinked her away. "If you come find me after your round, we can see how much I've gotten done."

He spread his arms like wings and motioned around. "What's there to do to this beautiful place?"

I smiled and chose to believe him. How earnestly he seemed to love our run-down place, how clearly he seemed to be seeing, or looking at, me. I stepped back and tried to soften my flustered voice. "More than you can imagine. That's what keeps it looking so good."

He knocked a knuckle on the counter and walked onto the course, smiling. For the remainder of the afternoon, I tried not to wonder what hole his group was on, or what Pete was shooting. His short game wasn't great, but he sure could drive the ball.

Baby A sidled up to me and squealed in my ear as she walked

a bucket of mulch to the shed, having seen Pete whiz by in a cart. I tried not to react, to keep my hopes dampened as they'd been. Instead, I listened for the cart engines, the thwacks of golf balls smacking into trees. I listened for the woosh of irons through static Gulf Coast air. They sounded like birds do when they scoop into the bayou face, just as quickly as they lift away from it, with fish or nothing in their mouths.

Pete and I ended up at the Shrimp Shack that afternoon. We had just stepped inside when a torrential downpour unleashed holy hell for about fifteen minutes. Then we sat in a booth by the windows, watching the lot swell with water. I ordered a bowl of fish gumbo, and Pete said "Same."

"When do you head back?"

"Few weeks."

The waitress set down glasses of water and two bowls of soup.

"Excited to get back to your charts and dissections?"

"Definitely. I feel like I've lost my edge over the summer. Out of practice, you know?"

"Doesn't the hunting help?"

He shook his head as he lifted a brimming spoon to his mouth. "Meat market takes care of that. Sometimes I do what I can in the field. If there's something lodged or stuff to be cleaned up. But mostly we just wrap 'em up and drop 'em off."

As I pictured this, my gumbo had suddenly become unappetizing. "And you'll be there till Thanksgiving? School."

He nodded, already fiddling the paper napkin ring into tiny, fortune-holding squares. "It's a nice drive up there. Not long. You could always come visit."

"For what?"

The sound of rain against the window and wind lifting the

cheap shack shingles said what he couldn't. I gazed at the bends
in the napkin ring paper, wanting to cast words of tomorrow onto
them with the confidence that Baby C would if she were me. Were
we just each other in different shades? Well, no, we weren't. But
I wished I had her wisdom in me. I longed to see what was ahead
for Pete, so I could decide if he was worth it. Then, shamefully,
I realized he'd probably considered the same of me. Wondering
what I was worth.

"Your sister hates me," I said, unsure why.

"She doesn't hate you."

"Well, she thinks we're trash."

Pete's eyebrows ruffled as he brought another spoonful of
gumbo to his mouth. "What are you talking about? You hang out
all the time. She goes to the course every evening after she gets
off at Sonic." So that's where Baby A was going at night, I con-
cluded. Onto the green with Julie.

Pete paid at the counter while I peered outside to see sunlight
drying out the fifteen-minute storm. He held the door open for
me and, after letting it slam behind us, took my hand and guided
me not toward the truck but behind the drive-through, where he
put his hands on my waist and kissed my forehead. We stayed
like that for a minute, his chin against my head and my hands
then on his sides. We kissed, and he held me in the exact way he
was supposed to, signaling like he didn't want anything more, so
maybe he didn't, but my body didn't believe him. Then his hand
fluttered up my shorts, clawing at the waistband. He tugged and
kissed at my neck. Pete held our bodies together as our fabrics
rubbed, he panted into my jawbone in a way he hadn't done before. It had changed—the way we had been together was never
like this, wasn't insistent. There was supposed to be ease, or if

anything, indifference. It was supposed to get more romantic as we went on. Against the side of the Shrimp Shack, I felt like a stand-in for someone else.

I pulled back for a moment to get a read. The face was Pete's, and the voice was Pete's. The hands were what seemed foreign. The way he was being with me was all wrong. It was like we'd had an entire togetherness that only he recalled. He was trying to convince me of the way it was, things I'd done and said that I could only take his word for. *You like it this way. Don't you remember, Baby? Remember that time on the ninth hole?* Only I didn't remember.

Still—it was Pete's face and Pete's kiss, so I let him paw at me and I kissed him back, wondering when it would feel the way I imagined.

We were together behind the Shrimp Shack quickly, all at once. Then we kissed and kissed, and Pete drove me home with his hand on my thigh. I let him drive all the way up to the clubhouse because I didn't have the energy to hide. It was dark by then, nobody on the course. The sprinklers crowed.

Pete laughed at something I'd said and forgotten as we stood in front of the door. He gazed into my forehead instead of my face. "Can I see you tomorrow?"

My throat was thick with confusion. I could feel my face had paled. "You can see me at the Bluegrass Festival."

He pulled back, expression contorted. "But that's next week?"

"There's a lot going on around here." I grasped the humid-wet door handle. "I'll see you then."

"Then you can expect to find me in the front row." He grinned.

I watched Pete carefully as he drove away, hoping he wouldn't feel my eyes. I hated the way his smile made me feel, hated that it made me hate myself. He—this endeavor toward romance—was supposed to make me feel beautiful, more my own. This self-loathing I'd become all too familiar with blanketed me, dragged me toward the bottom. Instantly, my hair became intolerable. I wanted to rip it out, throw my large and small intestines up. I wanted to never receive a birthday or Christmas gift again. I wanted no one to ever look at me, or take my picture, or say my name. I was not good enough. I was just fodder, just fish food, just a body pinned against the Shrimp Shack wall.

When I creaked the door to our bedroom open, Baby C saw me in the hall light. She waved me over to her bed, and I stepped lightly past Baby A, whose head was folded entirely into sheets, only tufts of hair and tender snores escaping. Gram had always maintained that it was most difficult to tell us apart when we slept.

Baby C had a small keychain flashlight shining onto three circular, color-coded charts spread across her comforter.

"Look," she said, pointing at the highest point on one of the charts, *Baby A* written across the top. "Our midheavens. You and me—we're the same, but Baby A's is different." She ruffled through papers and pulled out a Seeglow's receipt with scribbles across the back. "I called Aunt Rachel today. She told me our time of birth. Said legally we had to be a minute apart, even though it was all at once, really. Baby A's midheaven is in Sagittarius, and ours is Capricorn. Do you know what that means?"

I blinked at the colored circles and all of the intersections she'd traced across them, symbols and numbers dotted around. "C," I said with a daze, "I don't know what midheaven is."

"Oh, well, I just learned it today. Bought this kit through the Scholastic catalog that lets me make birth charts. The midheaven is the southernmost point, see—here, at the top. It determines how people see us. It says, 'Midheaven is you, under spotlight. How you're seen, not only because of what you wear or how you talk; it is the concept that society has attached to your name. MC'—that's midheaven—'might manifest in career ambition, fiscal attitudes, or the people you attract in close relationships.' " She lifted her head to make sure I was still listening. "So, you see? Baby A's is all wild and lusty and hellish. Yours and mine—we want loyalty, security. We want peace. It makes sense now. Yeah?"

My head was spinning. All I could think, and say, was, "If it's the southernmost point, how is it at the top?"

She paused, searching the chart. "You know what"—she laughed—"I don't know."

"Hmm."

We gazed into the charts.

"You know what I've been thinking?" She was careful to keep her voice low. "Since the midheaven is supposed to tell us which parent we take after most, maybe Baby A sucked up all there was of our mother. Maybe you and me are like this because we got the scraps of our dad."

I soured. This was something I knew for certain was impossible. "Baby C—"

"I know, I know," she chided herself before I could. "I just want a reason, that's all."

"Does this"—I skirted my fingers just barely across the chart she'd drawn for me, *Baby B* written across it in pink marker— "mean anything? Really?"

Baby C deflated at the shoulders. "I sure hope so. I mean—it must. It has to."

"It doesn't *have to*."

"Yes." She flattened her hand across the comforter in a silent slam. "Yes, it does." Her face glowed in the flashlight battery wink. God, she was beautiful. Not her face, but *her*. "Baby A's just been so angry. The boat dock really messed her up, and I don't know how to help."

I nodded. "A different kind of angry, though."

"Yeah," she agreed. "Like she wants to ignite things with her eyes." We were quiet. I fiddled with the paper as she stared at it earnestly, in search of an answer. She'd used string and tape as a protractor, had color-coded the chart elements with an array of pens and markers. I'd thought for a moment, with a sting, that she'd made these charts because she saw us as a pet project, but that was just the eager meanness of my judgment. We—Baby A and me—were her whole world.

After a while, she said, "You were with Pete today."

"You felt it?" I was still squeezing my own tense gut.

"Saw his car in the drive."

For the first time in those few minutes, we looked each other in the eyes. I loved her so much, it was indistinguishable from that human instinct to survive; if she lived, I lived, and the same with Baby A. We were a web of dependent heartbeats. I touched the back of my sister's veiny hand, and she sandwiched her other palm atop it.

"Do you think he's a good person?" I asked, hoping there was honesty in her to give.

She grinned flatly. "Is Q?"

"You're the one who said he was the best of us."

She looked up and past the bug-screened bedroom window. "No. That was you. Anyway, I do agree that he is. Better than us all."

"Why do you think so?"

Her eyes went glossy with Q, a gloss I'd never known. She was thinking of his face. She was thinking of his spirit. She was longing for him to materialize, to join our conversation and blanket us in his organic humility. "He doesn't want a lot from people, or life, it seems. Not even me. He just lets me be. It's amazing. Odd, but amazing. Maybe we could all be better if we didn't want so much."

I sighed, my hand finding hers again in the dark. "All I do is want."

"Yeah." She squeezed my pinkie finger, rolling the skin around. "Are we good? People, I mean."

I said "Of course," but neither of us were entirely convinced. We would move unholy mountains for each other, and that wasn't a pure feeling. For me, it felt tenebrous and vast. Baby C and I stared together at the whirring, perforated night until she rolled off the bed to brush her teeth and I followed to change into my sleep shirt. The bug trill was constant and ambient as we settled into bed, and even louder as I tried to block it out, praying myself to sleep. I prayed for Pete and me, for clarity. I prayed for Baby A. I prayed for Gull and Gram and for the weather to give us a semblance of reprieve. I thought about midheaven. Being exactly between here and there—stuck at the lip of an astrological chart. I considered myself, my truest self, under spotlight, but couldn't stand the thought for more than a moment. My mind drifted back to the golf course. A flash flood that afternoon had pushed everything to the surface. The next morning, we'd have to remove the sediment and reapply the herbicides with masks across our mouths. For weeks after a flood, we had to be prepared to tackle massive infestations of weeds.

In the morning I found Gram lingering in her robe by the kitchen coffeepot. She was murmuring in a melodic hum. I stood in the hall's archway watching her, hesitant. Rarely did Gram seem so still. She didn't often get the chance to just be, and I felt bad aiming to pull her out of it. I sniffled a bit and moseyed up behind her, softly touching the tattered collar of her robe. She turned a bit, still murmuring, and set down the piping cup of coffee she'd poured. Then she reached into the cupboard and pulled out a mug for me, filling it up just the same.

"You're up early, little critter," she said. The affectionate tag *critter* had been passed to Gull when he became the baby of the family, so when she said it to me, I felt little again in a tender way, like I could hug her leg with my whole body, like she might swoop me up in her arms with ease. I looked at the backs of her hands then, tensed to hold her mug. They were wrought with frighteningly bright blues and purples, tiny bruises.

"Couldn't sleep," I said.

She rubbed my back with her free hand. "Then coffee is just what you need."

I took the cup she'd made me, poured in milk and cane sugar as she watched, shaking her head. She drank her coffee black. Gramp said it was because she was a young girl during the Great Depression when sugar was scarce, and all the sophisticated women Gram knew drank their coffee black anyway. It was funny to think of Gram wanting to be sophisticated.

"River Joanie was asking after you at bridge the other day. Couldn't believe you girls are nineteen."

"Welp," I punctuated. "How's she look?" River Joanie had been our mother's nanny during the first five years which is how Murphy and Aunt Rachel met. The town tended to pass River Joanie around from family to family as babies were born and their mothers went back to work or elsewhere. Gram and Aunt Rachel's mom agreed to let the girls be nannied together in the clubhouse, so long as Gram never had to take Aunt Rachel home.

Pictures of River Joanie holding babies in a big squirm litter the few baby albums we have of our mother. River Joanie had seemed ancient even then, with tightly curled white hair and broad shoulders, a feeble but lullabyish voice. A voice that was nearly gone by the time we'd grown. When we saw her at church, she strained to say our names.

"Just the same. Old, you know? You three will always be babies in her mind, I think. Was devastated we couldn't pay for three. Part of me thought she'd show up one day and offer to watch y'all for free."

"Why didn't she?"

"Well the woman has gotta eat," Gram scoffed. "And anyway, she had Jason your early years, so she saw you enough to soothe the sting."

"What sting?"

"Oh honey," Gram said, a plain but frank look on her face, "she loved your mother as much as me, some days."

"You really think?"

"Yes." Gram nodded, then paused. "I was such an angry mother. So angry, in fact, she ran away once, your mama. Over to River Joanie's, in fact. Kept herself there for four days before she would come home." Gram was speaking into the countertop. She lifted her head slightly to look anywhere but my eyes. "She was fifteen, and I'd told her she couldn't go to the Houston Rodeo with your aunt Rachel after they'd won tickets calling into the radio to see the Judds. There wasn't any reason, really, other than I plain didn't want her going. Your aunt Rachel showed up in her turquoise cowboy boots with a damn bolo tie around her neck the night of, idling in my driveway, trying to start trouble. I stood by that door in front of your mama as she screamed herself red.

"Told your aunt, 'Go on,' but she wouldn't leave. She sat on the gravel until dusk, hoping I'd give in or your mother'd sneak out. Sat waiting even after the Astrodome was long filled and the concert was over. I fell asleep on the clubhouse couch with the long-handled broom in my hand, waiting to catch your mother, almost hoping to. And the next morning, I sent her to the auto parts store, and instead she camped out at River Joanie's until that Thursday, crying herself to sleep, River Joanie said."

A scurry of bugs interluded.

I didn't know what to ask except, "What happened when she came home?"

Gram smiled a little, mostly in pain. "She didn't want to talk to me for a few days, and I wasn't real keen to speak to her either, but she ate at the dinner table and started to say 'I love you' before bed. And we just went on that way until one or both of us forgot to stay mad."

Rarely had Gram presented herself to us with bare honesty, and there she and I were, exchanging deep shames simply by standing in front of each other. I could feel this was a purge for her, that she'd needed at least one of us to know that she hadn't done it right the first time, and that she knew she wasn't doing it right this go-round, either. It only lasted a flicker, like watching a candle flame dance, but as I looked at Gram, I saw how youthful she'd been, how beautiful and shapely and how much there had been for her to live up to. I saw her in school dance clothes, with a wide skirt and curled hair and gloves on her hands, and I saw the ways she'd given her best self to my mother, who was sharper, funnier, and altogether more. With a shatter in my chest, I saw that Gram wasn't sure which one of her granddaughters she was holding on to. It was in her eyes, a quick searching of my face, a panic. Gram saw me seeing her. She dropped our arms to hang low in a cradle.

"I'm doing the best I can," she said.

I knew she meant *I'm not her, can't that just be okay?* And I wanted to say *Gram, it's not even her that I want*, but that wouldn't have been true. If my mother had lived just nineteen years longer, us girls would have been better. We'd have names and understanding and a source text to pull from instead of an idea to guess toward, a woman who was just a girl that we couldn't help but feel left by.

Gram rounded the kitchen island and hugged me tightly. We stayed wrapped up for a few good moments until something outside barked or sang or turned on loudly, and she let me go.

We rehearsed like wild for the festival. Sang as we filled the ball buckets, as we tidied the kitchen and clubhouse, as we dried off at the boat dock when we swam our way to visit Aunt Rachel. There was a parity to our chorus, something we'd navigated as little girls cooing in the bathtub, fighting for the radio dial when Gram drove us to school. Sorted by instinct into song. It was nice to have a goal again after being out of school, knowing I could probably never go back.

Baby A was keeping the alterations she insisted on making to our festival outfits a secret. She wasn't much of a seamstress, not precise by nature, but this seemed to mean something to her. She'd steal herself away after dinner to our room to lock herself in and us out. I imagined she was just crudely stitching something frilly to the hems of our skirts and tops, and I'd allowed myself to know that this was an opportunity for Baby A to be alone with her habits, flasks, and small jars under the bed. Our mouthwash bottles had suddenly emptied. The Advil in the cabinets was disappearing in fistfuls, the Midol, the Motrin, Gram's diazepam and Flexeril. I pictured our sister sitting on the floor above us, loose-limbed, with a threaded needle in her hand. And I did nothing. I told no one. As we sat on the couch those nights, eating saltines with slices of cold ham and watching *Jeopardy!*, Baby A and Gram and I, having each discovered an empty bottle of our own—and each having kept it to ourselves, as we later discovered—never moved to check on her. Instead, during commercial breaks, I daydreamed about us months ahead, Bluegrass Festival winners like our mother and a thousand dollars richer. Everything solved and fixed and elevated. I couldn't push away how smug Pete had seemed behind the Shrimp Shack. How sure he'd been while I was in his grip. I'd begun to check the mailbox each night, even though I'd told Pete to stay away, because I had wishfully convinced myself he was the kind of guy that might deliver me a coded love note, and in that love note would be everything I wanted to hear, though I wasn't even sure what that was. Of course, each night I walked back to the clubhouse with nothing in my hands and pattered down the hallway, hating myself for being at his beck and call when all that I was doing was an attempt to reinforce that I was, in fact, not.

On one of those nights inside the swell of it all, I had a nightmare. Pete and I were behind the Shrimp Shack, as we'd been, but in this dreamtime, Pete had me pinned. His knees were wedging my legs apart and his lips were at my neck, but he was biting me, hurting me. I felt it, in my sleep, the deep pain he was causing, and all I could think in my dream was *I thought he liked me I thought he liked me*. It was all wrong.

His face was Pete's face, but it was corrupted, distorted. In the dream, I screamed and cried and clawed at him, but the blows didn't seem to land and my voice didn't carry. I felt like a shell, in my dream, like the sand dollars Gull lifted to his ears to hear the ocean, screeching for whoever would lift me up to listen. My voice was washed out by waves. Then I awoke in a rush. Sweat matted my hair in clumps, and I was already crying into the world. I looked to the beds on either side of me to find my sisters sleeping, noiseless. How had the panic that shook my body not stirred in theirs? I wanted to rattle them awake. To scream at them: *Can't you feel this mayhem inside me?*

Instead I walked down to the clubhouse and slept on the couch.

I didn't know what to do with the dream, so I rebuked it. Anytime my mind tried to pull it into focus, I shook my head and banished it further into the recesses of memory. If I did this enough, I figured the dream might undo itself. How could your own mind pit the very worst thing against you and make it happen, even if not really, but feeling altogether real?

I traded worry for Pete for worry over my sisters. Why hadn't they stirred at my nightmare? And why hadn't I been able to sense what Baby A was doing upstairs as she made our costumes? And when Baby C returned home from a date with Q, why was I surprised to realize she'd even gone out? There was a rupturing. Something in our guts and bones and veins had muted. My sisters and I were wading in the water of a disconnect. Everyone in town was dangling their wires in my face, trying to get me to plug back in. The racoons screamed and the peacocks screamed and the bugs bit the shit out of my legs. All of it was an anvil. Something ambient and poisonous was floating above our heads.

STUPEFIED

The Bluegrass Festival flyer was tacked to the fridge, low enough for Gull to circle the part that emphasized the thousand-dollar performance prize in purple marker. He and I felt the same about the money—it would save us.

Baby A and I had slipped into a habit of getting ready for the day side by side in the bathroom mirror. She'd sidle up to me in the mornings as I clutched a scrunchie between my teeth and brushed my hair into a manic ponytail. She would watch diligently and wait for her turn with the brush. Just as diligently, I'd watch for unsteadiness in her limbs, a slur in her voice, a detached droop to her eyes. She'd sift through our drawers for another scrunchie or fix her fingers lightly on the strands of hair that'd fallen from my grip. Most mornings, she seemed fine. It was later in the day that she went rummaging through the cabinets or summoning Julie over.

As we stood together before the mirror, I'd shimmy into my clothes or blot my oily face with toilet paper. If I tried to leave before Baby A had finished, she'd say "Wait!" in an incredibly wounded way. I'd stand in the corner of the bathroom where the door met its hinges to watch her pull her hair into a ponytail as messy as mine, dabbing the same oil pools from her pores. We were very much like the deer that stashed themselves in the woods beside the highway. All just trying to find the right way to reveal ourselves.

The humidity flattened us near completely most days. Wednesday night, three days before the festival, when Gram was at bridge and Gull was at the neighbor's, Baby A charged into the clubhouse and gathered Baby C and me in a huddle. "I need to get high," she said. So, even knowing that Gram had threatened rehab, that our medications were vanishing in fistfuls, that the twinge of liquor already coated Baby A's breath, we got high.

"Why did you do that to your hair?" Baby A's voice was slowed as she lay sprawled across my lap, looking up at me. We'd opened the window for the pot stink to dissipate.

I was boggled. "It looks exactly like yours."

Baby A laughed hysterically for at least two minutes. She was pulling at individual pieces of hair to stretch them across her face. "It isn't exactly, though," she said, still tugging the strands in a coded arrangement. "I have to get it—" She paused as if she'd been stonewalled, blinking at nothing, then let giggles overtake her. "It needs to be just right."

"Why?" I brushed the hair away from her eyes as she laughed so hard the air escaped her, wondering if it was the high or if she really was behaving as strangely as it seemed.

"I need to sell it." She brought her elbows to the sides of her breasts, pushing them together and shaking like a can-can girl.

Baby C sat toward the corner of the room, picking at her feet. She tended to get sad or paranoid when we smoked. "Do you think we'll win?" she asked quite seriously.

Baby A popped up. "Of course we will, dah-ling." She moved to Baby C and started to tug her hair up and around her face as she'd done to herself.

Baby C swatted her away. "I'm serious."

Baby A plummeted to the floor as if a heavy rock had just been tied about her waist. "So am I." She wiped the back of her hand across Baby C's face in a brief caress.

"How can you be so sure?"

"Sometimes you just know. Even if we don't win the festival, we're going to win."

Baby C pulled away at this, waving her hand around as if she'd just walked into a spiderweb. "What does that even mean? What—what, um, is that even?"

Then Baby A began to sing "The Winner Takes It All" as loudly as she could. We tried to shush her, not wanting Gram or Gull to find us blazed, but Baby A moved to the bedroom window and opened it, singing to the golf course, the whole of Longshadow, when really I think she was just singing to herself. In that moment, I think we faded from Baby A's worldview and she was just a girl, in her bedroom, singing out the window of her house.

It felt like we were high for the next two days. Baby A was in a stupor, unable to overcome it with excitement or preparations for the festival. She was dizzy, like someone who'd spun around a lot and tried to walk straight; smiling and convinced that what she was moving toward was in fact in front of her, that it was not her falling over but the world, the ground, and she was straight up, standing still.

A few nights later, Baby A and C washed up the dishes after dinner as Gram plucked unused silverware from the table. Gull was chasing frogs beneath the elevated ramp of the golf cart shed because some boys had told him he had frog eyes, and he wanted to check for himself. I feigned helpfulness, gathering used paper napkins in my fist, floating around the perimeter of the table. I lingered by Gram's side and leaned, distracted, against her shoulder. Silverware clattered in her fist. She patted the side of my head once and said softly, as she looked toward the kitchen where my sisters stood over the sudsy sink, "I'm worried about her."

"Me too."

"She's been too quiet."

I lifted my head to look at Gram with confusion. "What are you talking about?"

"Your sister—she hasn't said anything to anyone these last few days. Nothing of purpose, really."

I looked through the cutout into the kitchen and saw that Baby A had walked away discreetly, leaving Baby C to scrub burned pork bits from plates.

Gram sighed. "You two never did understand her."

"We understand her completely."

Gram shook her head. "Not ever. She was such a quiet baby, so sad. Practically had me carry her everywhere. Hid behind my legs. She's just the same now. I thought the festival, or Q Johnson, would excite her, but . . ."

And you think you understand her? I wanted to say. *You don't know what it's like to be us.* But we stood in silence, staring at Baby C, until Gull came barreling into the clubhouse, squealing, a toad slipping out of his fingers. The mayhem overtook the moment then, but some days it feels like I'm still standing there, watching my sister do the dishes alone, convincing myself that I knew her. Something in me shattered irreparably. I'm still not sure what to call it, that realization, but it comes close to desperation; desperate to rattle away my selfish daze, the pot stink and daydreams, to bring my sisters in at the hips and huddle like cold animals in a forest, waiting for their mother, who's gone to gather food, to come back—but the moon has announced itself and the dark has darkened, and those huddled animals realize they're all they've got, that no food is coming, that every creature comfort has evaporated with their mother. Maybe it is always about mothers.

Baby C was a riddle folded inward, even when she wanted others to think she wasn't, smiling and swearing in jest. I wondered if Q's company was a balm we could never create for her, then I scolded myself for being so self-absorbed. Of course it was. After all, that was what we wanted from those boys, what only lovers had. The tension, the buildup, the adoration that was every day a choice and never obligatory, like family. Someone to look at us and see just the one, not as a sister or multiplied face but as a young woman with her own brain and heart and slew of things to say.

I waited for Baby C to finish the dishes, and when she walked toward the hallway and our room, I draped my arm around her shoulder, nuzzling into her cheek with a laugh. She smiled. When we walked into our room, Baby A was flopped on the bed with our cell phone, furiously texting someone, a smug grin across her face. I tried to be exuberant for Baby C's sake, yelling "Who's that?" as I tackled Baby A, and we tumbled over.

She said, "Nobody, nobody—well, okay, it's Julie."

My mouth dried with my disdain for Julie, which had grown considerably that summer.

"Yeah, I'm texting her pretending to be you. She thinks you stole her striped top."

I snatched the phone from her and scrolled through the messages.

I know you took it, B.

Of course I didn't, J.

IDC give it back.

I don't have it. Honest! You're just jealous.

Jealous? In the mailbox by tomorrow! Serious!

Back and forth, uselessly.

"It kinda does sound like me," I admitted. "What's the fun in this?"

"To see if she'll buy it," Baby A said with a wry smirk, typing away.

Julie was hard to fool and always in a fit, thinking Baby C and I had taken things from her, never accusing Baby A, who was the only one who had actually stolen from her, swiping countless knickknacks for the sheer thrill of confounding Julie, who had many times shown up at the clubhouse, demanding that Gram allow her to search our bedroom. When Gram refused, she would have her mother call: "Isadora, we need to talk." After hanging up, Gram would mock Mrs. Martelli: " 'We need to talk,' " she'd mimic, then throw her hands up and say some variation of "Such an ugly woman." We'd laugh with her, drooping our faces and fiddling with our make-believe necklaces the way church women did when they wanted you to know they might be flustered, but more importantly, they had pearls.

Baby A and I giggled at Julie's uproar. Baby C sat on the floor, picking at the carpet threads with a flat, unconvincing smile. I was filled from tip to tail with worry for both of them.

The night devolved as it usually did, until we were each asleep in our big T-shirts. I dreamed about nothing and hated myself for it, longing for clarity about my sisters, Pete, our collective fate.

Wasn't God supposed to speak to desperate people in dreams? Wasn't I desperate?

Julie had agreed to help Baby A with the sewing for our festival costumes. The only insight we got about the process was Julie's occasional "Your sister is shit with a needle" remark. Baby C and I agreed to let it be a surprise, not to snoop for clues. We'd sensed it was a heavy, important lift for our sister, who kept the outfits secret until the night before the performance, when she burst into the clubhouse after dinner to demand Baby C and I follow her.

Our sister was sparked as she led us down the hall, scissors in hand, face glowing with her experimental generosity. To make us outfits with her own hands was as much a surprise as it was a comfort—that maybe there was hope for her to outgrow her bad habits and rages, to stay with us in this town until we grew old at the very same speed, instead of stealing our truck and our cell phone minutes to run off with some boy to somewhere.

In our bedroom, Baby A had garments laid flat on each of our beds like the displays in Foley's. We'd expected her to transform our existing clothes into crude yet fashionable new onetime wears, but as Baby C and I neared, we saw our sister had used aged fabrics with grunge florals and faded dyes. I picked up the miniskirt beside my pillow, brushed my finger across the bows she'd pulled from our old teddy bears and hot-glued to the hip. Baby C loitered above her outfit just as hesitantly with an undecided smile, feeling the tactile differences between the joining of the fabrics, how haphazardly stitched together the pieces were, like debris. Baby A had made herself the most modest outfit of all: a dress with puffed sleeves and a sack shape, mossy green with patterned patches of other fabrics hot-glued across. It was like nothing she'd ever worn before. None of the garments were. They were loose in weird places. Baby C's with cutouts that'd surely expose the bruises on her hipbones, and mine a mid-thigh barely-there thing. Just to imagine it on me made me squirm. Each outfit was hemmed with a hot-glued strip of craft-store velvet ribbon. An eager silence cloaked the room.

"Do you love it?" Baby A asked excitedly after a few moments.

I nodded slowly, still touching. "They're cute, actually. Strange."

"Actually?"

"Well . . ." I hesitated. "You know. I was expecting less . . . vintage."

Baby C remained quiet, studying the one-shouldered top and

mid-length skirt she'd been made. Her hand floated along the velvet ribbon we shared, then moved to the patchwork borders between swatches as I'd done, picking at the frays. "What are these made from?" There was disbelief on her face, awe in her voice. "Where'd you get them?"

"That's the best part." Baby A moved to the closet and dragged out a heap of cloth. As we crowded around the pile, I realized what it was. I moved both hands to my neck in protective instinct, stepping slowly away. The back of Baby C's head bobbed slowly as she realized, too. I looked at our other sister in panic, trying to catch her eye.

Baby A just rolled her eyes. *She'll be fine.*

"But where did you get these?" Baby C asked again, stepping back as I had. She had recognized the dominant motif in each of our outfits: the fabric of our mother's homecoming dress, the one that Baby C had worn at Aunt Rachel's. Baby A had cut it into ribbons and cobbled it together with other items of Murphy's, clothes we'd seen only in photographs.

"Aunt Rachel gave them to me."

"But only to borrow." Baby C began to gather as many garments in her arms as she could, her face wrenched with fury as she pulled the clothes up from the pile, only to realize that each was reduced to scraps, defiled in a matchless way.

"No—no, she said I could keep them."

"But not cut them up!" Baby C screeched as she moved wildly, arms laden with the clothes of our mother's youth, all we had left that had touched her body, that had smelled of her skin, that she'd sweated in and lived in and worn when she faced the people in town. Not long after she passed, Gram had purged Murphy's belongings, stuffing them into trash bags to be donated. Aunt Rachel, luckily, had secreted away what she could, preserving it for us, at the time still feeble squirms in NICU pods. But now Baby A had reduced our mother's life to a pile of tatters stowed in the closet, expecting us to smile. Baby C began to cry hysterically, clutching a glorified pile of ribbons.

Baby A stood firmly beside the pile, looking at it and then us as if she'd labored to bake us a cake, and we were saying it tasted all wrong. "What the actual hell is your problem?" She moved toward Baby C and began to tug at the rags she was clutching, the girls ending up quickly in an awkward, tearful wrestle. I stood solidly in my shoes, which were all I felt sure of, watching, crying tears I wasn't sure were for them or me.

"You had no right!" Baby C screamed, pulling the clothes away from Baby A again, then dropping them and striking our sister, ramming her hands into Baby A's shoulders, pushing her away with both feet. Their bodies thumped against the hard-wood. Soon enough Gram's footsteps sounded on the stairs and she appeared in the room, face primed for an emergency until she saw the girls fighting on the ground, me frozen by the wayside, a color wheel of sadness strewn about. Gram reached for Baby C, who sat squarely on top of Baby A, slapping at her face. Wildly, Baby C reared her elbow into Gram's cheekbone and knocked her into the bedroom door. This snapped me out of my daze, and I rushed to help Gram pull Baby C away. She resisted but was eventually coaxed onto her bed, still moving her limbs hap-hazardly and swearing. Baby A stayed on the ground, slumped against the dresser with her knees pulled up, whimpering.

Through tears, Baby C explained to Gram what Baby A had done, pointing at her on the ground. Gram stared around the room in shock. "I—I don't know what to say."

Gram held Baby C's bowed head against her stomach, hands comforting her back. Baby A yelled from the floor, "You always take her side! Nobody in this family ever believes me. You hate me!"

"No," I felt myself say shakily. "No, you could have asked, or saved—something. Anything. You destroyed it all."

Tears began to streak Gram's cheeks, though she tried not to let on. It was a charged mess of disappointment and the fiercest anger I'd ever felt coming from all sides like a kiln.

"I can't wear this," Baby C sobbed. "I can't wear it."

"You can," Baby A pleaded, her hands stretched toward our sister as if she held a platter. She'd been looking at her hands while our sister was crying. "She'll be with us, don't you see? That's all I wanted. I was trying—"

"I can't. I just can't."

It took eight milligrams of melatonin and a bath to eventually calm Baby C down, which Gram took charge of, carting her out of the room to the clubhouse bathroom so they could have space. I was left with Baby A sprawled on the floor beside me, as devastated as I'd ever seen her. "I didn't mean to mess this up," she said, slumping into my lap. "This was the one thing I wanted to do *right*. God, I—"

I brushed against her greasy hair with my hand, trying to listen for Gram and Baby C downstairs. Were we still supposed to be angry, or were we allowed to move on toward trying to understand? Baby C's body sent me no signals. The sister in my lap began to spurt tears and snot across my ankle, warm with live-wire emotion. Gull, having watched the whole scene from the doorway, stepped gently toward us and curled into my lap beside Baby A, wrapping his small arms around her.

That night, Baby C slept downstairs on the couch. And Baby A, for the very last time, snuck out of our bedroom window.

[ENTER] FRONT PORCH CHORUS

From this far, it always seemed as if a many-faced person was jogging through town, sitting outside the Ace, scraping snail shells off the bulkhead with an oyster knife. They're a blur we never bothered to untangle. They nearly blend with the green of the bayou's algae, the electric pink of the evening's sunset. Those girls drag their long shadows behind them like prom dresses and don't see—can't, from their vantage—how they fuse together. Stranger than their ominous presence would be if the Binderup triplets *were* properly distinguished, if they weren't just a meandering three. What would we call them when we talked about them? By their names? Those temporary yet eternal names. We don't know how Isadora does it. And truly, there are some days we're convinced even she doesn't know how to tell those girls apart. Not the way a mother could.

SPECTACULAR GIRLS

I woke feeling no more resolved. And worse: it was performance day. The girls had reconciled in the night, Baby A having slept next to Baby C on the couch after she returned from wherever she'd snuck off to. I imagined they talked after waking, gummed each other's skin in their soft hands, wanting more than the satisfaction of being angry to forgive each other. Gram had posted special hours on the clubhouse door, noting we'd close early to attend the festival.

Downstairs, as we readied, Gram cooked anything she could pull out of the pantry: biscuits, sausage, eggs, grits, all the jams and syrups lined across the countertop. The house was still tense with the night before, Gram cooking like the blazes in silence. Gull layered three biscuits with butter and blackberry jam, balanced them against his chest up the stairs, where he distributed them between us. Baby C was sitting at the floor-length mirror in our bedroom corner, chanting under her breath as she flat ironed her wavy hair: *Manifest YOU. Fulfillment IS. All signs say success is here to stay.* Baby A and I were shoulder to shoulder in the cramped bathroom, Gull's biscuit delivery balanced on a soap dish that'd never ever held a bar of soap. I watched my sister closely, looking for signs. As I studied her, Baby A pulled out a stash of secret makeup and lined both sets of our eyelids, mine then hers, with steady hands and purple liquid glitter. Her face was flushed, but only artificially, and her breath was tinged, but only with sleep.

Soon enough I was standing outside the door as Baby C sat on the toilet lid, our sister lining her eyes the same way. Between them was a transformed understanding.

With a palpable resistance still between us, we pulled on the outfits Baby A had crafted from our mother's clothes. They fit beautifully, acutely tailored, but I'd begun to worry what Aunt Rachel would think when she saw us wearing them, recognizing the remnants of things she'd once saved. Baby C took one of Gramp's oversize flannels from the hall closet and let it hang like a robe over the outfit. Then we turned circles for Gram as she admired us. "You really do look pretty, girls."

Yes, I thought, *but do we look like her?*

Gram sent us off with a paper-towel parcel of biscuits, promising she and Gull would be there as soon as the morning groups finished their rounds. Here, if it were a pure kind of reminiscence, I'd say all that I could think about was Pete, but that could never be true. Even when I was living moments for the first time, my sisters were always weighty on my mind.

As she drove, Baby A sang along scratchily to a mix CD she'd burned while Baby C indulged us with soft smiling directed out the window. It was generous that Baby C thought so much of Q, but really, we knew she was the best one; even Q had to have known. I saw why others chose them—my sisters. I wondered what they saw in me, and I wished they'd tell me while we were together, unabridged, on our way. I needed to know what it was about me that did the world any good. Beside me Baby C was tying and retying one of the bows on her outfit, chewing a pit in her cheek lining. I could feel my own face cratering with the hole she chewed.

The festival was held in our church parking lot beside the boat dock, about two minutes down the road. I expected to see Harriet Shrub or one of her altar guild flock worrying about how these boozy, bluegrassy people might mangle their finely manicured lot. As Baby A swung confidently into a parking spot, I envisioned our mother on a green John Deere, swinging around with the same sharp confidence, cleaning up the lawn for us or for Jesus or just because she felt she had to. I blamed her for not staying. Which felt hateful, to blame our Murphy for being dead, but it blistered me—all of us—in moments like this, when we had to invent her body in our minds just to see her around town. Baby C lingered in the truck with me. I wondered if she was trying to see something that wasn't there, too.

Baby A banged on the side of the truck for us to get out, so we did, sliding our bare legs along the bench seat. We trailed each other in a line to the Sunday-school room where the performers were supposed to wait, then camped out in a corner at a rickety low table with short plastic chairs. Around the room were many of the toys we'd outgrown and donated: tricycles, a blow-up plastic Pooh Bear couch, the tiny cream-painted table with four wooden chairs trimmed in chipped gold paint that Gramp had made for us. We kept it in the clubhouse, though we often dragged it into the kitchen to be with Gram while she cooked, to help her with simple things like stirring. I remember when we outgrew it, the strange jealousy I felt seeing other little girls in their church bows and church velvet sitting ungratefully at our table as they slammed wads of Play-Doh into its face. I saw both of my sisters take a gentle swipe at the table set, running hands along it as they walked by, nudging it with their bare feet.

That morning we'd trimmed and painted each other's toe-nails Peachy Keen, the light-pink-orange polish Aunt Rachel had given us from our mother's stash in preparation for performing barefoot. Baby A had slathered a mixture of thick night cream and runny sunscreen on all our heels, saying we needed to look soft but stay protected. I'd thought that was true for us most days, in different ways.

Finally the coordinator came into the room and taped a list to the wall. We recognized most of the groups as locals who performed annually, as we did. There were the Bayou Banjo Boys, and a motorcycle group that yodeled while a burly man huffed rhythmically into a ceramic jug, many lone female singers, and lone men with Tobacco Burst–finished guitars. In total, there were nine acts vying for the thousand dollars. We figured it was between us and either the Banjo Boys or the blond woman who looked and sounded like Jewel—which was very much to her advantage, since everyone around there loved Jewel. We were eighth in the lineup, which gave us time to relax and eavesdrop.

I was feeling a bit icky in my sexy outfit, barefoot on the glue-stained church carpet. For the last few days I'd been thinking about what Baby A had said at the beginning of the summer: "You can be whoever they want." *They*. I wondered if that had been her grand plan, to turn us into sexy little whatever-they-wants. Whether we'd be up there signing songs our dead mother once had, wearing her clothes, and whether Baby A would be thinking about Rich, or some other small-town prick with a Skoal can ring rubbed into his back pocket. I looked at her as I wondered this. She was sitting on a turn-top stool with chalk in her hand, playing tic-tac-toe on a chalkboard with one of the lone boy crooners. Baby C sat nearby on the ground, braiding small sections of wispy hair to frame her face my face our face.

Did they know me at all? Did they know how much I knew they were capable of? What dark, evil, bottomless things they had the capacity for, just like I did. It felt like we were trying to whisper to each other through thick walls, like I couldn't tell them things I used to, and even if I did, they wouldn't be able to hear me. I'd never felt so distant from myself. Or my sisters. And I had no clue how to claw us back together, beyond following them onto the stage, the same way I would follow them into high water.

Q snuck into the Sunday-school room with a fistful of Ace Hardware daisies, wearing a button-up and church slacks. He kissed Baby C on the cheek as they stood with the flowers perfectly between them, nuzzling at each other, quiet. After they'd gotten over the first excitement of seeing each other, Q walked a cluster of daisies to me, then to Baby A, who said, "For me?" in a flirty way that wiped the glow from Q's face and sent him hustling out the door. Baby C had seen it, but she could only sigh in response. I settled next to her on the carpet as she twisted the daisies her boyfriend had brought her into a ropy crown.

Physically, we were sweating in the annex of our hometown church, but really we were crammed inside the uniquely selfish little worlds in our heads. Even then, I didn't see us ever getting out. Our stage name was the Manatee's Girls, because that's what they called us around town anyway. Isadora's girls. The Binderup triplets. Girls. Y'all. You three. After the twangy boy's voice stopped echoing from beyond us and the crowd finished clapping, we huddled. " 'Amarillo by Morning,' then 'Tennessee, 1949,' and we'll end with 'Cold Day in July,' the Joy Lynn White version," Baby A said.

"But we didn't practice that song," I said, stung.

My sister shook her head. "You know it by heart. I already told the band, anyway."

We took the stage in our foolish outfits, which elicited whoops and hollers. I despised all I'd allowed to happen, the prop of multiplied seduction I'd let my sister dress us into. I knew enough about my particular kind of stage fright to avoid looking for Gull and Gram or the Upchurches in the crowd, to trust that they were there and to realize that I'd be fine if they weren't, if they got caught up at the hot dog stand and missed our act entirely. It was like the town was watching us through one big eyeball. No matter whose face I tried to zero in on to ground me, it was like looking into the same face, with the same beady center and dream-blue iris. It was so disorienting and intoxicating, that one big eye, I was afraid I'd lose the grip I had on why exactly it was we were subjecting ourselves to their gaze, which was to better understand our mother by way of better understanding ourselves.

The sun was brighter than any stage light could have been. The velvet drapes seemed to push us forward. As we crowded the mic in birth order, Baby A and Baby C on the outskirts with myself in the middle, I fumbled to steady my feet. Yes. I was looking for Pete. The one big eye I was seeing was his. He was the only one I'd wanted to be there, and I couldn't find him so I turned the crowd into him just to have him see me even if not really. I'd said he could see me at the Bluegrass Festival, and he'd seemed too annoyed to wait. It should've been him bringing flowers like Q had done; Pete should have been in the front row, looking up at me. Yes, I was still confused by him. Shamed by him. But I knew we could get through it, beyond it, that he could go back to College Station, and yes, maybe I could visit.

In a blink, it seemed Baby A was giving the ah-one-two, ah-one-two-three cue and our voices were flowing from us, thrumming in song. The first two songs were seamless, unfolding melodically just as we'd rehearsed, the three of us harmonizing and keeping even. The floating heads of the crowd nodded, hoisted their bottles in the air. The instrumentals were steady, the saw of the fiddle gritted against me like scratch to an itch. I stopped seeing faces and started seeing a place, our place. The home we railed against and rattled within, the home that had held us all the while.

It was before "Cold Day in July" that my stomach began to churn. As the band tuned instruments and my sisters and I took deep breaths, I got a rush of heat around the navel. My side ached empathetically with a deep, rising warmth, as if I were about to buckle over or vomit. I looked to Baby C in fear that she was about to be sick, just to see she was equally confused, staring worriedly at me. We turned to Baby A to see her smile beyond our existence into the crowd at someone. Her profile was startlingly sharp, as if she'd put on more blush or eye shadow when we hadn't been looking. She leaned into the mic and said with caricatured flair, "This is for you, Longshadow."

I reached for Baby C's hand swinging beside me and looped a few of our fingers together, our skirts concealing them from the crowd. I felt, through her skin, that she was swelling with heat, too, and anxious expectation. We sang on. And in the middle of our song, as we swayed onstage like cattails, a voice began to rise above us and curl around us, sharpening and volleying to be heard. Baby C and I turned without hesitation to our sister, who had a hand dramatically clutching her abdomen as she belted, albeit beautifully, far and away from the two of us. My voice wrapped around the lyrics dutifully but I felt detached from my body, as if I was floating above, watching us, three strangers. *You always said the day that you would leave me would be a cold day in July. Here comes that cold day in July.* The fiddles grated their final shriek, and the crowd erupted. Baby A pressed us into a huddle. Just as immediately, she let go, nudging us to the side as she stood in the middle of the stage, saying "Thank you, thank you" into the microphone.

Baby C and I followed our sister back into the Sunday-school room, dazed with emotion, as if we'd been suddenly woken in the middle of the night to trek through the forest without a light.

Baby A paused near the back of the room; she was lit from within. "We did it," she shrieked. "Wow. We were incredible. There's no way we don't win. We're so going to win."

I wanted to rip the clothes from my body. I didn't care if nothing was beneath, if my body turned out to not be there, if my ribs were a trick and I was just a floating head and heart slipping down the side of this illusion. Baby C's crown of daisies had blown off her head as we hustled from the stage. Baby A's was tucked safely behind her ear. She implored us with her stares to feel as elated, as otherworldly, as she did.

"What was that?" I said, looking at my sister, one of the few people I thought I knew implicitly, someone who would light the world on fire for me, and pictured her again, stepping in front of us toward the microphone. "We never talked about that."

Baby C stood silent, watching, having already boxed her round of this fight.

"Well, I just felt it. In the moment, it felt right."

"No. I could feel you preparing to do it," I said. "You planned that, didn't you? How could you?"

The room seemed to bubble up like paint separating from a wooden plank; we were moving in the wave of heat, the flux of people in and out, voices howling throughout the church lot. "You're selfish," I said, blinking the movement around us away.

Baby A neared my face with hers, all of me twisted in her angry likeness. "What is your deal?"

"You made us look weak. Like background singers."

"So what if you're background singers?"

"This wasn't part of our plan," Baby C said flatly.

"What plan?"

Baby C stepped nearer. "Us! We weren't supposed to betray each other. Not us."

Baby A withdrew from my face to turn with a scowl. "Oh, please. Don't be so dramatic."

"You did betray us," I said. "I just don't understand why."

Baby A redistributed the weight between her feet and knees over and over, indecisive, avoiding our eyes. She tugged at her outfit, pulling the collar away from her reddened neck. Baby C and I stared at her, more confused and deflated than we'd considered possible, feeling things babies weren't supposed to be able to feel toward one another. We were nineteen. It was the summer after high school. It was dark on the boat dock. His hands were on me. We weren't really there. We'd dreamed the whole summer up. We'd wake up, and it'd be April, and we'd be grateful, our mother's clothes still intact in our aunt's drawer, no flood weeds to pull. Baby A didn't reach to touch us or move her face to meet ours as we stood, acres apart, in the Sunday-school room.

"The only people I never meant to hurt," she said carefully as she angled her body toward the door, "are you." Then Baby A walked out, toward the person in the crowd she'd been singing for. At the time, I couldn't have fathomed who.

Baby C pulled me in with her arm, as I had prepared to do to her. Tussling with Baby A seemed to have strengthened my sister in a new way that I became grateful for. Or maybe it was Q's flowers. Though probably it was just the goodness in her. We listened to the Skoal-can men yeehaw across the water. After a few beats between us, she said, "Let's go find Gram and Gull."

We found them standing with Aunt Rachel and Jason beside the water balloon and dart booth, eating corn dogs and holding three extra. Uncle Henry was just returning from a stall with cotton candy for Gull, which he happily traded the excess corn dogs for. Uncle Henry handed the corn dogs over to Baby C and me, and both of our stomachs turned upside down in a knot of hunger, nerves, and the weight of our sister's sudden pretense. We ate them mindlessly while our family cooed: *You did so good. And wow, that note. Just spectacular, girls. You ought to win. Just spectacular.* Mostly, this was Aunt Rachel's voice, her eyes fixed on our clothing. I knew she recognized the fragments of cloth. I knew she was seeing apparitions of our mother as I had that day. The flurry of talk whirled us around, and Aunt Rachel reached for my sleeve, trying very hard to appear haphazard. "It wasn't us," I said, trying to get ahead of the issue. "We can give them back?"

Uncomfortably, Aunt Rachel shook her head and forced a smile. "No, you girls look better than she ever did. She had a bit of a belly, you know." Often Aunt Rachel said the very right thing, and just as often the very wrong. Her eyes, narrowed with thought, revealed her disappointment in us, in her old friend Murph, for leaving her to tend to this mess. I wanted to have a peek at the memories of our mother swirling around Aunt Rachel's head as she looked at her best girl's old clothes. I wanted to dip into those moments and pull my mother out, ask her questions: *Are we always going to feel so low without you? Do you know our hearts from where you are? Can you protect us?*

Jason, wobbling with Gull on his shoulders, had begun telling us of all the drama we'd missed. A fight broke out between some vendors over an electrical outlet that caused a small grease fire at the funnel cake stand. A couple boys in a truck smoked out the parking lot and gave some poor child an asthma attack. And Julie came around wanting to see the outfits on us, but Jason didn't know where to say we went, other than backstage. At this, I swiveled my head around, remembering to be consumed by the very idea of Pete. I pawed the sides of my body, where there should've been a pocket with our phone in it to text Julie, but it was gone.

Baby C saw me, put her hand over mine. "She has it."

I'd expected our sister to gravitate back, shamefully, before the announcement, but as the drum rolled and the presenter began his spiel, Baby A had yet to materialize. The presenter accounted for the triumphs of each act. The Jewel impersonator. The twangy men. "And those Manatee's Girls," he rallied. "They're one of a kind!"

I scoffed, and Baby C knocked her shoulder into mine, both of us depleted by the irony.

Aunt Rachel had wrapped her arms around us from behind, a canopy over and uniting us. We hadn't won, or even placed at all. It was the Bayou Banjo Boys who took the thousand dollars. At the mic, one of them joked about how much they'd get to keep after taxes, and the crowd scattered toward booths and the beer cart. Jason smacked his lips loudly and protested a bit for our sake. Gull, from his perch on Jason's shoulders, began to pat the top of his head.

"Bullshit," Gram mumbled.

Instantly, I was embarrassed by how sure I'd been that we'd win, how clearly and desperately I'd felt the need to. I didn't want my family to think us so fragile, so small-minded that they had to fear a loss like this would break us. They put on a show of disappointment so we'd feel less alone. Baby C, too, beside me, withered in embarrassment at having been so naive.

Q had pushed through the crowd by then, having spotted Gull hoisted in the air, and placed his arm supportively against Baby C's back. Watching them settle so seamlessly together sent a jealous ache through my chest.

When our family left, we kissed their cheeks and thanked them for coming. They maintained that the results were horseshit, total crap. Aunt Rachel, until the moment she was forced to pull away, had kept her touch against the relic of our clothing.

"Should we look for Baby A?" I asked my sister after the rest of the family had gone.

Baby C picked at the flesh around her fingernails, sucking in her cheek. "No. Or, yes? She ran off with the keys, I think."

Q lingered comfortably in the outskirts of our conversation as we riddled through the last few things our sister said, where she was likely to have gone. "Well, maybe if the truck is still here, that'll mean she never left," he offered, fingers hooked through belt loops like all the South's other boys. I let him last a bit longer in the circle my sister and I had formed, moving toward the parking lot past piles of spilled soda cans, the fighting scents of candle vendors, but the truck remained where our sister had parked it, just hardly between the white lines. Q stopped in his tracks, preparing to search elsewhere, as Baby C and I neared. We craned to see if she was inside, and then realized that the keys, course keychain and all, were sitting on the front left tire, in the shadow of the wheel well. They clattered as I picked them up.

"What the hell is wrong with her?" I said.

The halogen of lights strung up inside craft tents and around the food stalls singled us out like bugs beneath a microscope: Q, Baby C, and me, wriggling against the heat. I stood, clutching the keys, pretending to glance politely at the mayhem of the bouncy houses, while Q and Baby C kissed goodbye. I would always be jealous that Q had chosen her, I thought, recalling the flowers he'd given us. That hers were lost somewhere in the abstract carnival of the night made the jealousy worse. I knew in my spirit that people didn't deserve or earn other people, certainly not their love, but as I watched the children float and land inside the blow-up house, I told myself that I would never have been deserving of Q Johnson anyhow.

As Q faded toward his truck a few spaces away, Jason bounded back from the boat launch, where he'd seen the rest of the family off. "Girls!" he shouted at our backs. "Come have a beer. We can be sad you didn't win together."

Baby C had wilted with Q's departure. I turned to face Jason. "You can bring a few to the course," I said, surprised at myself, "but we don't know where Baby A went."

He hiked up his shorts with a lazy jump. "Couldn't have gone far. She'll turn up."

"We ought to be home when she does."

He shrugged. "I'll go grab some drinks from Wendell's cooler and meet you on the driving range."

Jason hustled off toward the boat dock, where the other boys were straddling an opened cooler, already blasted. The evening sun was setting behind the boys; radiant orange and pink dripped into the water's face.

Baby C offered to take the keys, but I couldn't bring myself to hand them over. As we bumped down the road for the few minutes it took to reach our house, Baby C found our cell phone wedged in the console at our feet, between a stack of Bayou Bloom brochures and a wad of receipts. I put the truck into park as soon as I felt it touch the parking block. My feet landing against gravel reminded me that they were bare. The lights in the clubhouse and the television were off. I pictured Gull and Gram snug in their beds.

Baby C dipped into the golf cart shed to grab a towel that we laid across the driving range, stretching the fatigue from our muscles. I took our cell phone from her grasp and flipped it open;

the bluish light pierced my eye and sent an ache through my forehead. I called Pete once, and he didn't answer, so I texted: Hey. No show at the festival? Then I waited for what I assumed would be a quick answer. Fifteen minutes had already passed when Jason walked across the green with a handful of bottles. He popped the caps off with his car key before handing two to Baby C and me, then sat next to us on the towel, buzzed. Baby C tilted the opened beer toward me with a look that seemed to be asking permission. I tilted the beer in my hand right back to her before taking a swig. We drank one beer, another, and then half of one more before flopping against the ground, where I tried to stabilize my whirly vision. The world around us was baleful. The world around us baled its bales of ominous hay. The world around us was closing in. The world around us—all the round way—was only this town, only as far and wide as Longshadow reached. Jason opened and closed his fist around the sharp bottle caps.

My stomach cratered. It roiled. It revolted. I jostled Baby C's limp arm and for no discernible reason blurted out, "Something's really wrong. Can't you feel it?"

Jason, who'd begun swinging a club against tall blades of grass, knelt next to me, hand on my shoulder. "What?"

Baby C floated a hand above her stomach to feel around, like doctors do with stethoscopes, saying, "Breathe in breathe out breathe in."

My mouth had gone dry. I tumped out the contents of the beer I'd been nursing, then held the cold glass of the bottle to the back of my neck. Baby C emptied her beer and did the same. I turned to her to help articulate what I hoped she was feeling, too. She nodded.

"We should start looking, then," Jason said. I clutched our cell phone in my hand, hoping it'd buzz with a message from Pete, or a message from Baby A via Julie's cell, or even, God forbid, Rich Goodson's. The confused disappointment I felt at Pete's absence was dwarfed by how visceral my worry was for Baby A. On our way to Jason's truck, we ducked into the clubhouse to slip on our swimming flip-flops. Baby C scrawled on the grocery pad magnetized to the fridge: *Gone to find sister.*

We went back to the festival, just minutes down the road, figuring there'd still be people mooning about. Jason parked by the boat launch, and we walked down the incline, shining our keychain flashlights on a group of Carhartt-clothed men drinking Lone Stars. "Have you seen a girl who looks like us?" we asked. They said, "Hey, you're the Manatee's Girls." We nodded. They said they hadn't seen her, so we cut across the boat launch into the church cemetery, taking big steps around tree limbs and stones. We didn't call her name or say anything, just left the loud crunch of dried leaves to resonate. Jason walked ahead in valiant fashion, Baby C and I straggling behind, next to each other.

"She's been sneaking out," I offered.

"Yeah, I know."

"You pretended to be asleep?"

"Yeah. You?"

I nodded. "Yeah. Where's she been going?"

"No idea." Baby C pulled both hands to her hips as we realized that our small town was much bigger than it'd ever felt before. Jason stood at a headstone, reading its face. We listed aloud places she might go: the Shrimp Shack, the football stadium, behind the Seeglow's lot, Rich's house, Wendell's, every new suggestion feeling more and more wrong, nudging us farther away from the place we'd find her.

Jason stopped when he reached the wire fencing around the

church playground. He turned, defeated, toward us. "Think we should call my mom?"

"Why?"

"Well—" Jason scratched his side, clicking his small flashlight off. "A's been over a lot, talking to her. She stops by after she meets with the reverend."

"Every week?" I gawked, looking into my sister's face, which was stretched with the same disbelief. "What do they talk about?"

"I don't know. They flipped through photo albums in the sunroom and laughed. I think my mom was just telling her stories about your mom. Didn't seem weird or anything." Jason stood in the church light, digging his sneakered toe into the mulch as my sister and I began to crumble under a sense of bewilderment so vast, it felt for a moment as if we might never again speak a coherent word, or breathe a tranquil breath. We walked back to Jason's truck and rode to his house, our flashlights pointed toward the floor, still shining, as we rehearsed aloud what he would say when he woke up his mother. The wire arch that we passed under to enter Casa Grande had always seemed like a promise, but that night it felt like we were ducking beneath it in a game of London Bridge, trying not to get caught in its grasp.

The Upchurch home was at the mouth of the neighborhood. Their porch light was weak, no brighter than a lightning bug's bulb. It shook—or our eyes shook—as we watched Jason slip through his front door, emerging minutes later with his mother, who'd stepped quickly into a pair of canvas overalls, a 1980s band T-shirt wrinkled beneath. I could see us the way she did; her eyes bulged as she walked toward us, rolling down Jason's window with an electric click.

"Me and Henry are going to head north until we hit the refinery plant. You girls and Jason stop by your friends', then south toward the high school." Aunt Rachel reached into the truck to pat the backs of our hands, piled atop one another. "Just look"— her eyes wandered into the past, recalling a moment that'd held a fear like this, that instructed her still—"behind things."

While we were on Jason's street, we walked to Bailee Shuggart's house, where nobody, including Bailee, was home. The Martelli house was on the cusp of the cul-de-sac two down from the Shuggarts' and the only cars in the driveway were Julie's VW Beetle with gigantic fake lashes on the headlights and the family Yukon. I thought about how Mrs. Martelli had always looked at the girls and me with dismay. I hoped that Julie would answer as I knocked against their moss-green door, which she did, in a long silk nightgown with her hair falling out of a slept-in bun. She winced in the light, eyes narrowed. "What? Oh, well, don't you look cute in *my* handiwork. Baby A told me she was going to wear that one, and *you'd* be in the sack-dress thing. Well, it looks better on you, anyway."

"Oh, um, thanks. Has she been around here?" I wanted to touch the silk of Julie's dress, wanted to fix the mess of her hair. I could tell she wanted to do the same for me, eyeing the inconsistencies in her stitches.

Julie's brow furrowed. She folded both arms across her chest for Jason's sake, her breasts bare beneath the slip. "I haven't seen her. I tried to find her after the performance. Bit scattered, by the way, your voices. I thought you'd practiced." She stepped back to turn off their entryway light, then relaxed enough to look harder into my face, recognizing the shadow of fear. "What's going on?"

"We can't find her."

"Hm. Weird."

"Is your brother here?"

"What's he got to do with anything?"

"I'm not sure. I just thought—"

She scowled, rolling her head for effect. "Look, I know you two had a date and all, but he's going back to school. And, I hate to tell you this, Wendell is going to set him up with his cousin Sara. Remember? The drum major? They're probably gonna go out. It's just—"

Julie reached out to touch my face. It felt like she was reaching across eighty acres, her hand brushing my cheek with a chill, her fierce need to make me feel, physically, as inferior to her as she was sure I was.

Before she could finish her thought, I pulled away and spit a wad of phlegm onto their doormat, which claimed *All Welcome.* "You're an absolute bitch, Julie."

Jason pulled me quickly out of the porch light as he bunched his face up hatefully at her, then walked me under his arm toward his driveway, where Aunt Rachel and Uncle Henry were turning their car around in the street.

The town was the same, but now stilled, as we begged revelations of it, driving ten miles over the limit. The halfway house beside the realtor's office, the string of auto shops across from First Baptist Church next to the Upchurch funeral home, the post office, the trophy shop inside the tailor's; I wanted to claw back the glycerin that held the place frozen to reveal its oddities, to perceive this space as if I'd never seen it. Our sister had encountered each inch of this town, if not with her body, then with her myth. Aunt Rachel's eyes, their widened fury, told me we were right to be worried, that maybe Baby A had divulged something to her that had seemed harmless then but had lunged into urgency now.

We pulled into the Whataburger parking lot, cruised slowly

behind the dumpster, where a racoon sifted through orange-and-white striped wrappers. I called Pete. When he didn't answer, I called him again and again. After about six tries, I handed the phone to Baby C, who took over the task. We stopped by Wendell's house, Rich and Cart Goodson's trailer, even Q Johnson's. Q wanted more than anything to help us search. "No," Baby C said as they stood on his wraparound porch, holding each other's forearms very properly, as if they were at an altar. "She'll turn up tonight."

It was understandable that Baby A might be playing a trick on us, frustrated as she'd been lately that we weren't as angry at the town, particularly their boys, for the boat dock incident and everything else. The festival performance, the destruction of our mother's clothes, seemed like perverted, poorly delivered jokes. We'd have to tell her when we tracked her down that she wasn't funny, that she had never been the funny one. It was Gull who made us laugh. She didn't have to be the world.

Soon enough, all our plausible leads spent, we were rattling down Oleander Road toward the peacock farm, an expansive property with no fence. The birds often wandered out into the street to stand defiantly for upward of ten minutes, no matter how loud the car horns or hollers. Jason pulled over, the truck straddling the ditch, and Baby C walked emptily beside me as we moved like a single apparition along the roadside. I could see a group of peacocks under a tree, huddled. "Ahhhhh," I screamed at them, but they didn't react, which infuriated me. All the emotions I'd wanted to point toward Pete, my sister, this place that was concealing them both, rose up in me. "Where is she?" I screamed. "You!" I pointed as I stood under a streetlight that had been crashed into, a harsh bend in its middle. "Go find her! You—go. Why aren't you helping us find her?"

Baby C put her hand on my shoulder. "Shhhh, you might wake the farmers."

I turned in a frenzy. "These fucking birds scream at the top of their lungs all fucking night for months, and you think *I'm* going to wake the farmer?"

Jason had strayed away, studying the horizon, opaque with pine trees. "She's right," he said as he moved to my side, still gazing out, then whipped his head away from whatever had captured his attention and glared at the birds. "Ahhhhhh," he started screaming, his head tilted upward. "Help us find her, you fucking monsters." He picked up a handful of gravel and started chucking it at the birds. Finally, just as I'd wanted, the peacocks started to scream, too. Then all of us except Baby C, who kept her eyes on the gravel, were screaming.

"If more people are awake," I said in a low voice as Jason and the birds kept on, "then maybe more people will be able to tell if there's something weird going on, like a car on their street, a person on their porch. We'll have better luck finding her if they're awake."

This hadn't been why I started screaming, but I'd found the intuition somewhere in the middle. It didn't make Baby C join in, but it did make her back off. She let us yawp and yawp until we were satisfied. Then we drove down the rest of Oleander, which connected the bayou neighborhoods in a big loop, spitting us back out at the center of town. For good measure, we drove past the festival once more, to cruise slowly past vendors tearing down their booths just to set them up again in the morning, dumping grease and deep-fried scraps into trash bins. Only a few down-turned, focused heads remained, cleaning up the mess.

It was two o'clock in the morning when Jason called it. Baby C and I could've searched for hours longer, but by then Gram was involved, demanding over the phone that we return to Aunt Rachel's. Soon enough we were drinking hot lemon water at her kitchen counter as the adults talked in a cluster beside the fridge.

"Should we print pictures?" Aunt Rachel said. "Is there any use? All of 'em know her face."

Gram sighed. "The child will turn up tomorrow, I'm sure of it. And I'll paint her back porch red, but she'll be here. No use making a fuss now. She's been wanting trouble lately."

"Well, do you have a picture?" Uncle Henry asked. "Just in case." In unison, they craned their heads to look at my sister and me at the counter, watching and listening to them, Baby A's face on our faces. Walking talking hurting pictures.

Aunt Rachel couldn't help but keep going. "Should we call Mr. Miller? EquuSearch can find anyone."

Beneath the countertop, Baby C touched her clammy hand to my leg. We knew they called Mr. Miller to find girls—bodies—in fields and marsh. Gram's resistance to urgency was a superficial comfort, but my sister and I, trying to console each other in the small ways we could, knew that something in the infinity that anchored our sister was off.

"Rachel," Gram said forcefully, taking our aunt by the wrists like a child. "We don't need horses, and we don't need police. We need to wait. Now, why are you so wild?"

Aunt Rachel tugged her wrists from Gram's grip and began pulling at the straps of her overalls as if they were suddenly intolerable. "Well, she's been coming over a lot during her errands, and she mentioned a week or two ago that she was seeing a new boy. Said he was older, that we knew him but she wouldn't say his name. I didn't think much of it, but when she talked about him, she wasn't giddy. It was like she was angry with him. She wouldn't really answer my questions, but I'm afraid he's older, maybe married? Something about it felt wrong. And maybe that's where she is."

Gram began to rub her temples, staring at the ground. Baby C opened her mouth and moved her lips around a few seconds before she spoke. "She didn't say anything to me." Baby C looked over to me expectantly.

"Not to me either," I added.

"Rachel." Gram sighed, still rubbing her head. "We just have to wait, honey. She'll come 'round."

Aunt Rachel was not assuaged, fiddling with her overalls until she burst into heavy tears. Uncle Henry pressed her to his chest. Gram looked over our heads to Jason on the couch, holding Gull's sleeping figure in his lap, and motioned that he carry our brother to the guest room. Then Gram draped her arms around Aunt Rachel's back to create a pile of brilliant, devastated women we'd long adored for helping us feel more brilliant, less devastated. "This can't happen to us again," Aunt Rachel cried into Uncle Henry's chest. "Not again."

Baby C and I slept side by side on the couch that night with the blankets kicked sideways, ready to get on our feet for news. I'm not sure if it was the whir of the Upchurches' real-wood fan blades or the creak of a door from someone going into the kitchen to grab water, but I only had one dream that night, and it was a screaming dream. We were all at the peacock farm where we'd just been: me, Baby C, and Jason. We were wailing by the roadside like we had, but this time the covert huddle of birds we were howling at began to loosen their mysterious canopy, and in my dream, they were standing over Baby A. Of course dream-me ran with cement-laden feet to reach her, but it wasn't just my sister's body there, but Ansley Deer's, too, stacked atop each other crudely, waterlogged and green. I pushed Ansley's body off my sister's and shook Baby A, but she was dead-weighting her body better than I ever had. I jostled her, saying, "We just want to take you home. Not anywhere bad, just home."

Her body was a boulder. Next to her, Ansley's body was, too. I knew she wasn't playing deadweight because she was afraid she'd be kidnapped; my subconscious knew Ansley was gone. But my sister . . . In the dream, I crouched with her bundled in my noodle-arms, shaking her while the peacocks screamed to high heaven, until finally, I woke up. The Upchurch living room was silent, Baby C was asleep at my side, and the place my mind had just sent me was a side of town we'd already been. *We looked there*, I said to myself.

[ENTER] FRONT PORCH CHORUS

We saw her on the boat dock with Wendell. No, we saw her under the boat launch bridge by herself. We thought we saw her in the church parking lot, feet hanging off the tailgate of a dented truck. We'll say we saw her leaning over the bridge, cars whizzing by. In our shared gut, we felt her moving between Oleander and Main where the peacocks scream, where she lay across Mrs. Deer those dog years ago, shielding that woman from the horror, offering her precious little baby body instead. We wish we saw her, wherever it is you're looking, we wish we'd seen her there, but the town had in its rollers and the town had put the children to sleep. The town had long stopped paying attention to the cars in the boat dock cul-de-sac, parked outside homes they didn't belong to. The town had their own daughters and sons to fear weren't breathing. The town missed not a bit of sleep that night. None at all.

SCREAM

In the morning we stared at plates of cheesy scrambled eggs we couldn't fathom eating. Instead we drank expensive coffee Aunt Rachel ground down from beans. Gram had gone to search the water on the boat with Uncle Henry. By then, things were full-blown: cops and fishermen in their scuba gear, volunteer groups driving slowly around town with lowered windows. Many festival vendors who should've been setting up their tents for that day's crowd were combing the grounds again, leaning over the boat launch to search the water's face. Gull stayed at the house with Jason while Baby C and I went back to the golf course to survey the slopes and sand traps. Pete hadn't returned my calls or texts. I thought of what I'd said to Julie, how hotly the words had burned in my throat, how much I'd meant them. My mind raced around Pete; it wasn't that I missed him, it was that he was missing, and so was she.

The police came around to do interviews and search our house. Officer Fenoli, who'd done the fire safety and stranger-danger presentations throughout our schooling, took pictures of the fragmented clothes strewn across our carpet, the state of Baby C's sheets, ruffled just so in her bed, as a pair of deputies stood in the corner and watched him nudging things with the tip of a pen. He asked us questions about where she tended to leave things, what she was afraid of and anxious about, questions that shouldn't have been difficult but fogged our brains; the answers felt very far away. When we told him she'd been sneaking out, the deputies in the corner mumbled into their radios, and Officer Fenoli put a border of blue tape around the window, left ajar to beg a bit of breeze.

They confiscated our phone and swept their leather-gloved hands across the dashboard of our truck, across the seats, inside the cupholders, as if dusting. I wasn't entirely convinced this was going to work, and they didn't seem entirely convinced, either. Most times I looked over, the officers stood staring down the driveway, as if they expected Baby A to waltz right up. Seeing us as hysterical women, they humored us, walking slowly around the clubhouse, moving pictures and curtains like fathers called in to look for monsters under a bed. Mostly they just stood with hands at their waists, intermittently pawing at their mustaches or adjusting the tilt of their wide-brimmed hats.

Gram fixed the officers iced teas and roast beef sandwiches on fancy crusty bread warmed in the oven. Baby C had been tasked with making a dipping gravy. The packet contents had hardly begun dissolving in the pot of cold water before she leaned over the kitchen sink and vomited extensively, as if she couldn't hold it back any longer. I took her place at the stove while Aunt Rachel draped a wet rag along the back of her neck. Baby C pressed her stomach tensely against the sink, heaving, spitting, crying. Aunt Rachel had taken off the shirt she'd been wearing, stood in a sports bra in the kitchen, and pulled the sodden one from my sister to dress her like a stubborn child. The officers pretended not to notice the commotion. They dipped their sandwiches in the gravy as they sat on the benches of the driving range, talking and laughing. The nerve they had, to laugh. One of them pretended to swing an invisible club, shading his eyes to watch the phantom ball soar. The others asked Gram for seconds, then stacked their plates on the counter for us to wash.

Our phones hadn't been ringing like they should've been. People should've been calling constantly, begging us to give them places to search, as frantic and desperate as we were. The grass blades stayed perfectly erect in the breezeless afternoon. Gull's chickens in the neighbor's yard squawked and flocked without any eerie sense that the world was shifting. I watched them from the kitchen window as I scraped bits from the officers' plates into the trash.

Aunt Rachel coaxed Baby C to lie down on the couch as Jason trudged inside, he and his mother secreting themselves in a corner when Baby C finally shut her eyes.

"I'm so afraid, Jason, that it's some vagrant coming in and out of town."

"Mom, it's not 1988 anymore. She's not *her*."

"Still! These things happen. And she was telling me—oh, she was saying how this guy is built and rich and is going somewhere exciting, that he is near obsessed with her. And she liked that, Jason. Once she said it was like a *game*. Her mother played games, too, goddammit, and I just—I can't remember if she told me where he lived or worked or—"

With my back turned, straining to catch their whispers, I could make out the sound of Jason pressing his mother into a hug, her wincing muffled by his shirt. Only mothers could share secrets with their children that way, a way I could only envy. I wished our aunt would say more, as I scraped nothingness from the dirty plates

Officer Fenoli stepped across the threshold of the opened clubhouse door. I was exhausted by him, by his stupid questions. Jason had been tailing him that day like a dog, in hopes that he could urge the officers to up the ante.

He stood a silent moment, one foot inside and one foot on the straw doormat, his face flushed with sun. "We're going to need y'all to come down to the station. We found—well, we're just going to need y'all to come down."

My body stopped being my body; it became this trapping,

shaking, loud thing that I couldn't stand to be in. If I could just step out of my body, I thought. This skin that I couldn't feel through. Blood pounded in my ears. I couldn't hear what Officer Fenoli was saying. Aunt Rachel was fumbling for car keys and grabbing for her purse. Baby C and I turned to each other, bleary eyed, knowing.

We rode in the back of Aunt Rachel's car, Gull squished between, then floated into the police station like summer bugs. Gull reached to grip our shirts, our empty hands, until Jason swooped him up and walked toward the vending machines.

They told us she was dead.

And we said, "Are you sure?" And they said, "Yes, she's dead." And we said, "Which one? Which one? Do you even know which one of us?" And the officer said, "Baby A Binderup. Daughter to Isadora Binderup." To which Baby C screamed—screamed in the officer's stubbly face—"She is *not* her mother. She is not our *mother*. She is our grandmother. You don't even know!" Which the officer took so well, so calmly, saying, "I'm sorry ma'am, you are correct. My mistake. My mistake." To which I thought, *Yes! This can be a mistake. His mistake.*

Why hadn't I felt it? I thought. Then Baby C said, "Why didn't we feel it?"

"Where is she?" I felt myself shout. "Take us to her. I want to hold her. I want to see her."

"She's not the same," the officers said. "You don't want to see her. She's not like she was." *Like us*, I thought. She's not like us anymore. In this—in death—finally, she got to be different. All we could do was conjure our own horrific imaginings of what our sister's body had become, our sameness violated by dying. Our guts were empty. Our veins were still. "I just want to go to her," Baby C screamed in the police station. "Let me go to her."

Our hearts flooded with water from the bayou, all the way to the top. And in our hearts were our mouths, and our mouths gasped for air that day and every day after. We rolled in grief, aimless and surging.

Then an officer pulled up the blinds covering a glass-walled room, and I saw Pete. He sat there gripping a Styrofoam cup with both hands. His wrists shone with handcuffs. His shirt was crumpled and stained. Nothing was dawning on me like it should've. An officer tried to shepherd us into a separate room, but I rushed toward Pete, pounding my fists on the glass. His warmly hued hair fluttered as his head jerked toward me. I kept saying his name, but his face didn't change; a blank, impotent look. Officer Fenoli put his hand on my shoulder and steered me away as the flock of my family followed. I must've asked him what Pete was doing there, why I couldn't talk to him, because Officer Fenoli said, "He's the one that told us where she was."

PART II

BRUISEY FATIGUE

She never asked Baby C and me to kill her. Just everyone else in town. We found out that the day after the boat dock was the day Baby A started asking.

It began with Wendell. They were leaning against his truck, he said, filling it up with gas, after she'd spotted him when she was out running Gram's errands. Baby A offered him sunflower seeds from a bag, bumped into his shoulder, arms across her chest. "Wendell, would you kill me?" she asked with what he called "charm."

They laughed, he said, while he fastened the gas cap. She didn't say another word about it. She walked from the Shrimp Shack to Harriet Shrub's flower shop and grabbed one of the high school football calendar leaflets kept by the cash registers in town. We found it later in her pillowcase, lines crossed through names and jersey numbers with a fingernail. Wendell reminded us of Baby A's distraught, drunken state at Bailee's party. *Goddamn you, Wendell*, she'd said. *Why won't you do it?* And she'd called him a coward.

I wished we could go back to relive it all, to see her in those moments and stop her. When Wendell told us these things, delivering a lasagna from his mother, he cried quite hard. We knew he was one of those men who lived to feel like they were saving women. We didn't feel sorry for him. We didn't comfort him with our hands or voices. We let him cry at the kitchen island, cursing him for keeping the truth to himself, for not seeing that our sister was serious.

"Did you know Pete was helping her?" I asked him, cold. "Did he tell you?"

Wendell cried harder. "I wasn't even thinkin' she had asked anybody else. And he seemed just fine. Normal. Just fine."

Margaret Wheeler's little brother said Baby A had asked him. Two stocky recent grads working for the city said she brought them sodas as they poured tar to pave the course's backroad. Reportedly she traced and retraced pink-tinted Vaseline on her lips as she asked the boys if they were good with guns. Junior Cruz, the Kinner grandsons, Mike B., and even Q. All said she kept her tone mellow, asked with a smile if they'd consider, maybe, just once, killing her. When Q admitted to Baby C that our sister had asked him, over and over again, if he was willing to end her life, Baby C started to slap him in the chest, the way she'd done to Rich Goodson on the boat dock, using her body to dispel what tears and screaming had stopped being able to satisfy. "I don't ever want to see you again, Q Johnson. I don't ever want to see you."

It was summer's end, and Q was headed for college anyway. His parents came to the wake and funeral, brought their Gull-aged son, but Q disappeared from our landscape that day.

I watched him and my sister as they argued and pushed at each other. After Baby C stormed off, Q leaned against the passenger side of his truck, facing away from the clubhouse, crying into both palms, flat against his eyes, for at least fifteen minutes. I thought back to the Sunday-school room, the daisies and Baby A's flirting, how disturbed Q had been. I didn't pity him, either. They tried so hard to get us to pity them or forgive them, but we knew what they really wanted was permission to forgive themselves. We didn't have that to give.

Rich Goodson didn't show up at the wake, the funeral, didn't bring any food or send flowers. He wouldn't talk to any of the local boys about Baby A. We knew she hadn't asked him, wouldn't have given him the satisfaction. We'd have been able to believe the whole thing if it'd been Rich Goodson that she planned her death with for weeks, but it was Pete sitting in the county jail, her blood on the bottoms of his boots. I wanted to cut off every part of me that'd touched him. I wanted to be the one that'd died.

We went with Uncle Henry and Gram to see the body—her body—but Baby C and I couldn't convince ourselves to leave the car. Uncle Henry had already identified her for legal purposes, but Gram insisted on a last look. The county coroner had once worked at the Upchurch funeral parlor, and he allowed Uncle Henry to cover some of her bruises with makeup, to sew up the cuts they'd made, even if they were just going to hack back into her. Gram didn't mention the hole in Baby A's skull, didn't tell us what color she was, that her perfect hair had been rained on, or that her dead-mother shade of fingernail polish had chipped with the force of the shotgun blast. She didn't bring anything back in a plastic baggie, like we'd thought, not our sister's dress or her hairpins.

Gram drove us home and parked outside the clubhouse, where we sat, still buckled in, knowing there was something Gram needed to say and that if we left the car, she'd never say it. Finally, Gram exhaled, staring ahead into the sameness of the truck's age-fogged windshield. "She could've been any one of you." Her fingers were still wrapped around the steering wheel. "It's always hardest to tell you girls apart when you're asleep."

We began waking in the middle of the night with headfuls of grief congestion. Jason, at his own insistence, was camping out indefinitely on the clubhouse couch and would wake at our footsteps in the hallway. He would fetch us glasses of water, wet rags for our necks, like his mother had taught him, and recite folk lullabies he'd learned from River Joanie, talking instead of singing them until we relented to sleep in the recliner. Very often, Baby C would happen into the clubhouse to find me already there, listening to Jason's droning with a cold rag across my forehead, arched over the couch edge. He'd keep talking as he walked backward into the kitchen to get Baby C's glass, while she nestled ritualistically next to me. Whoever had gotten there first would unfold their rag and settle it so it'd cover both foreheads, ears near touching. Jason stayed with us through the trial, deferring his college acceptance. Aunt Rachel and Uncle Henry seemed almost glad for that.

Uncle Henry and his brother took care of the wake. I remember, amazingly, laughing, weakly, around a closed and empty casket in the Upchurch funeral parlor. The Hollings brought a bucket of fried chicken, which Gull immediately seized, gnawing at a wing with a clip-on tie slung over his shoulder like a grown man. Baby C let me dab concealer over the bruisey fatigue that swelled beneath her eyes, brightening her face in a way that said *My skin is banana-peel smooth*, not, *My triplet sister is dead and we share an underwear drawer so these hip-huggers probably hugged hers*. It was only then that a real body had been lent to death. Before, it had been the myth of our mother floating above and around. As we painted our nails with clear polish to give ourselves something to chip at, dying ceased to be an idea and became a full presence in the room, taking up the space she'd taken.

Townspeople trickled up and down the velvet-carpeted aisle, standing in the parlor pews or bobbing like gaseous molecules around our cusp. Even the parade of the bodies that only emerged from their houses for weddings and funerals did not convince us that any of it was really happening. I had to be reminded she was dead. Shadow of a casket. Stench of Harriet's generous floral arrangements. A blown-up picture of Baby A's face leaned against an oversize easel. Uncle Henry had cut Baby C and me out of the photo on the computer.

The course patrons attended in a swift mass, ball caps held at their sides, taking each of our hands in theirs and holding us gently there. They didn't utter a word, which was just as well.

Mrs. Deer entered the room with a bouquet of peacock feathers in her hands. She looked like a flower girl in a wedding as she walked down the velvet carpet. Mrs. Deer laid the bouquet across the casket and then put a hand on Baby C's and my shoulders, knowing from her own grief that we probably hadn't wanted to be touched but needing, for herself, to touch us. "I know that just like others, I have spoken to you girls, thinking that you were your sister." She paused, and when she did, I realized she was trembling. "But I thank you for indulging me in those moments, and I hope you know—" But before she could finish, Mrs. Deer began to cry and cry, and she cried so much that she had to leave the wake room. I don't recall her coming back in.

Baby A had to die for the town to call her by name. It was all I heard: "Baby A Baby A Baby Baby Baby A." Baby C and I flinched each time, its tether to us so strong, an incantation to our own. I wondered if they would turn this trick for Baby C and me, too. Had they known us all along and just couldn't be bothered, or was this truly the learning curve? What I did know was that we were no longer the Manatee's girls, but the dead lettered girl's abandoned twin sisters. Gram had lived here long enough to always be part Manatee. At least she cast a sliver of that net over us.

Eventually, Baby C and I slinked into the grieving room, where Uncle Henry's older brother was, having stepped up to the task of town undertaker when their father died. He soaked hand towels in cold water, wrung them out, and laid them on our necks as we bent over the sink and retched. It seemed about the only thing that people in that town could do: cover us in cold water.

Uncle Henry's brother went to fetch Gull from where he clung to Jason's khaki leg and carried him into the room. Baby C and I knelt in our skirts, holding the wet towels, wrapped them about Gull's neck, and watched his shoulders soften with the slight comfort. It was like watching a bird do something heartbreakingly natural: emerge from water with a fish, or shed a feather. He understood everything. His hands were dry and tired. Palms out and down, as if about to play phantom piano keys, only to flip them both like griddle cakes—the sign for *dead*. He had learned it casually, inapplicably, until Gram pulled him aside that day in the police station, eloquently turning Baby A's life over with a deft swoop. He'd grabbed Gram's hands in the air like he could stop things mid-movement, then wept so hard he threw up.

We reappeared in the wake room like two uninvited ghosts, Gull having run ahead. Harriet at some point walked directly up to Baby C and me, unafraid in the way of one that had known too much dying. She touched and tilted our faces at once like she used to, but it didn't feel like she was still looking for her son. I realized, after all that time, that she'd been looking for our mother in us, which made me, for the briefest flash, pity Harriet in the way I pitied myself; both of us unable to stop looking for something we couldn't even name.

People in their Sunday best with bourbon breath tried to offer us their favorite things about Baby A, which turned out to be entirely generic witnessings that could be of any one of us, recounted sketchily, without details we might recognize as having been ours. Classmates recounted ways she'd cheated off their exams, ever so coolly and unabashed, or how double-digit late she always seemed to be. They'd sheepishly clarify, "Wait, that wasn't you, right?" with out-of-place giggles. Girls said, "She really was beautiful. Like, the prettiest girl at school." The town's mothers tried to rationalize with us in unhelpful ways: "Just seemed like she'd live forever, didn't she?" But no, it never had seemed that way. We smiled at the mothers, almost grateful ours wasn't there to experience this. People kept saying, "She *was* funny, she *was* seriously smart. What a travesty this is. Don't make no sense, that much I know. Man oh man, she really *was* something."

Under breath, a person or Baby C or God said, "She *was* undeniable."

Baby C and I couldn't stomach the vacancy. We talked about destroying all our clothes at the next local burn, dyeing our hair, finally piercing ears, noses, lips. Baby C had ripped down all the newspaper clippings she'd taped to the textured wall above her headboard. I'd thrown away Baby A's various stashes: a few blunts in the dresser drawer, plastic baggies of random pills, cold medicine caps still sticky with syrup. We searched pant pockets, skirt waists, and shoes for coins, slivers of paper, receipts. There were no answers in her billfold or beneath the floorboards. Nothing hidden on the bookshelf or under the bed.

"Do you know what *to predict* means?" Baby C asked as we sat on the floor, piles of papers around us like force fields. The birth charts she had drawn for us and her horoscope clippings were scattered among stacks of school papers, old magazines, and notes we'd written to each other.

"No."

"It means: *To estimate the consequence of something*."

She stopped there. I blinked at my floral comforter, then blinked at her floral, miserable, very same face.

"It was the twenty-eighth. Remember, her palm? Twenty-eight."

I hadn't made the connection until then, though I was hesitant to believe in a fate that extreme. There was plenty that could've been done, plenty we missed. And besides, it had been done *to* her, her death.

"Makes me want to light myself on fire," she said. "All those orange peels I thought I was reading, horoscopes, pumpkin seeds, stars—*Manifest YOU. Fulfillment IS*. I feel like I caused it, like this was the consequence of my guessing, so God could show me: *See, girl, you never know what's coming*." Then she looked at me, accusingly. "Didn't you get tired of me? Why didn't you say so?"

I thought about midheaven, though the phrase had morphed in meaning to me. It had been repeating on a reel in my head for weeks, especially when the sky was clear or the water in a puddle held perfectly still. I kept thinking: Baby A has reached whatever heaven she was pulling for, while Baby C and I are stranded here, alone, at the halfway point.

I scooted across the floor to my sister. "Nothing is your fault, and there was nothing for us to guess. That future stuff is just fun. God doesn't punish you for fun."

She turned her body to face me completely, both of us cross-legged. "It wasn't just fun, though. I believed it. I really thought I had a window into what might happen. Do you know how much money I've spent on this shit? The magazines and things? *I* could have bought Gull those hearing aids. *I* could have . . ."

She was trying so hard to blame herself. We still didn't know a thing about what had really happened. The casket in the wake room had been empty. Our sister was still on the coroner's table, the police were still asking their questions, and the only sister I had left was trying to figure out a way for it to be her fault, just to riddle out some sense.

I patted the carpet floor. "Some things just can't be imagined for being so horrible."

Before walking out of our room, I looked back at my sister, who hadn't moved. Maybe we stayed like that, both of us, forever; her stoic with fear, wondering what she'd done wrong, and me sad but still leaving.

Between the day the initial news broke and the emergence of the whole story, the town filled in the blanks with conjecture, already choosing sides. They'd shown at her wake, dry-cleaned their suits and skirts in preparation for her funeral, all the while whispering that our sister must have lured Pete Martelli in, that such a promising young boy's life had been ruined. They said *seduced*. They said *suicide*. They said *You heard what those boys did at the boat dock*. They threw our sister's memory on the fire of hot gossip.

According to the police, the whole mess began with texts from our cell phone. Later, I pinned down the first exchange of messages between Pete and Baby A. It was the day the pH spiked, the day I told her that Pete hadn't called me back. Pete said in his official statement that Baby A, masquerading as me, started asking him to do little things like pick up extra cough syrup at the corner store, bring her thread for sewing, meet her on the ninth hole every few nights, which had been her spot with Rich Goodson. Pete would idle up quietly on his Jet Ski and creep across the dock onto the green. There, Pete told the police, is where they'd fool around. She'd ask him to steal her a new tire for our truck, and then to maybe get his hands on a couple of old irons his dad wasn't using anymore, and because he'd done all that, didn't he have a gun? A small one, just a varmint rifle. Did he know how to use it? And didn't his daddy have a deer lease not too far outside town? There they could be alone, huh? And didn't he have acres and acres? Nobody would hear a shot for miles. And anyhow, it was hunting property, and that wouldn't be so strange.

Sheriff said that's where they found her. Pete had come into the station early in the morning with Julie's hand at his collar, having dragged him in, and their father, we found out during the trial, was back at their house on Casa Grande, trying to bleach the blood out of Pete's boots. Pete told the officers he knew where the Manatee's girl was, directed them from the back of a cruiser with Julie by his side the twenty minutes out to his daddy's deer lease. Initially, they'd thought Pete was showing them where she was hiding out, until Pete started unbuttoning his shirt, his jeans, down to his boxers, then waded waist-deep into the algae crust and reached down, feeling around until he got a grip and started walking backward, pulling something. The sheriff said it wasn't until he saw her bright feet, Peachy Keen—pink toenails, that he really confronted the idea that she might be dead. She'd been in the sack dress made of our mother's clothes, purple glitter smeared across her face with the wetness of pond water. It dawned on me then that the shapeless form of her dress must have been an investment in my imitation. That she'd told Julie she intended to wear the outfit she designated for me on purpose. We heard Julie got physically sick at the sight, then lay down in the back of the squad car, sobbing.

The sheriff blurted, stunned, "Sweet Christ, son. What happened?"

And Pete, still holding Baby A by the feet, responded flatly: "She asked me to."

"We'd like if we could get you in a room with him and set up a tape. See if you can get some truth out of him." Officer Fenoli and I sat across from each other at the clubhouse dining table, while another officer and the sheriff lingered by the wayside. Gram, Baby C, and Aunt Rachel flanked me in chairs.

"You don't think he's telling the truth?" Gram interjected. She held a half-burned Marlboro in her fingers, bringing it to and away from her lips compulsively. Turns out she'd had a stash of cigarettes in her closet all that while, and dove headfirst into chain-smoking the morning of the wake.

The sheriff huffed, annoyed by the smoke, as he stared into the wall behind us. Officer Fenoli's eyes never left our faces. "We know your granddaughter was asking . . . what she was asking around town, yes. But even if she was right on that edge, this young man pushed her off, and he's had plenty to say so far. We're just hoping he might tell you more."

The women of my family and I squirmed in our seats, wringing our hands, chewing the linings of our cheeks. Officer Fenoli asked if there was anything we'd like to share. Gram said, "No." Then, after a few moments, she added, "She was in a bad way."

I glared into the side of Gram's face as she let smoke ease out her mouth to cloud the officers' faces. Although it was true that Baby A had been in a bad way, it seemed a whole lot like blaming her to offer this up. When they'd told us Baby A's toxicology report came back clean, save for low levels of alcohol, Gram was so stunned that she had them run it again. I was starting to think she wanted to blame my sister. I was afraid Gram was going to turn on Baby C and me next.

We answered the rest of the officers' questions as the wooden dining chairs dug into our legs, then Gram walked the officers out and Aunt Rachel went into the laundry room to cry in private. A few patrons dotted the driving range, swinging clubs above empty tees.

"Why do I feel like I did something wrong?" Baby C asked quietly.

"If anybody is in the wrong, it's me."

She knew I was right. She said nothing.

Aunt Rachel wandered back into the room, still choked up, and stood over us, her fingers wrapped around the headrests of our chairs. "How could this have happened? She had to have said something. What did we miss?"

Baby C cleared her throat. "Baby A was talking to *you* more than anyone. You tell us."

Aunt Rachel pulled back as if Baby C had swiped at her.

"Around here," Baby C said, "she just locked herself in our room while she destroyed all Mom's clothes, which *you* gave her. Yours was the house she was talking in." None of us had ever called our mother "Mom," and Baby C had never taken this tone with anyone other than Q Johnson, those few nights before. I was just as prepared for Aunt Rachel to burst into tears again as I was for her to sober up, sit down, and say something worth hearing. It was quiet awhile. Aunt Rachel stared at the scratched tabletop, and we stared at Aunt Rachel.

"All she said," she began slowly, still staring off, "was he was older. I was afraid to ask questions because I knew she needed someone to talk to, and I didn't want her to clam up. She was already having to meet with the reverend."

I wanted to scream *She should've been talking to us!*

"Are you surprised?" Baby C asked coldly.

Aunt Rachel stunned herself again. "What?"

"Are you surprised?"

Our aunt shuffled her feet and mumbled, "She had plans for next week, next month, next year. Of course I'm surprised. She didn't seem sad or moody. If anything, she'd seemed more excited lately. Almost calm. She wasn't hurting herself or anybody else. She seemed . . . fine."

At the last bit, Baby C and I bristled. Our sister had been hurting others—us—and she hadn't been fine.

"Did she have plans with you?" There was real disdain for our aunt in Baby C's voice, which I understood. Aunt Rachel's overt display of grief was clearly irritating her, and I was ashamed to admit that I felt the same. Nobody could have felt Baby A's loss more than us, her deserted fractals.

Aunt Rachel was deflated at this, the incessant questions, but Baby C and I had endured this with police for the last few days. "Not specifically, but I expected her—"

Baby C sighed so loudly, it cut our aunt off. "Why did you give her all of our mother's clothes?"

Aunt Rachel let her arms flap frustratedly against her sides. "She told me y'all wanted them for a project."

"Exactly. She was a liar. So why are we driving ourselves crazy over the last few moments of a liar?"

I pushed her knee. "Hey. That's not fair."

"No. *This* isn't fair. This shit she dragged us into."

"Your sister didn't pull the trigger, young lady."

Baby C slammed her hands on the tabletop. "But she went with him to pick out the fucking gun. How are we supposed to understand that? What's the use in trying to figure this out?" The bags under her eyes were purple—none of us had been sleeping, but Baby C especially. She spent most nights on the phone with her telepsychic, weeping, arguing. I shuddered to imagine how much money she was spending. And I realized—I hoped, anyway— that most of her uncharacteristic rage was exhaustion.

Baby C pushed herself away from the table and began walking down the golf course. I followed, neither of us looking behind at our aunt, who was sobbing again at the table, and neither of us looking for Gram.

We ended up on the dock, sitting, staring at the water as if it were any old day. I wanted to say, *She went looking for this trouble, all on her own.* But I wouldn't have meant it. What I'd really have meant was, *It's my fault—all of it—for bringing him into our lives.* But I said nothing.

I thought of Pete. What the officers would want me to ask him. If he'd be shackled in a jail jumpsuit and handcuffed. I imagined him, still, sitting at the kitchen island, eating. Then I imagined him dragging my very own body out of a pond, and that body having my sister's spirit in it. This big, irreparable mess—it couldn't possibly be a misunderstanding. I felt Pete's touch behind the Shrimp Shack. I felt his breath on my sternum. Without realizing, I'd stood up on the dock and begun stripping my clothes off, like a snake shedding its skin. Baby C couldn't have known why I was doing this, but she did it, too, stepping out of the loose, dirty clothes we'd worn for days. We took off our bras and panties. I would've ripped my hair out if it'd been that easy.

I didn't kneel on the dock edge to dive into the water. Instead, I sat on my bare butt against splintering wood and eased in like it was going to be really cold. Then I swam with broad strokes down the bayou, conscious of my sister following behind. We moved slowly, taking deep breaths, until we got to the Upchurch dock across the way. I pulled myself onto the dock and lay flat, spread-eagled, aware of my bared pubic hair and breasts but careless about them. Baby C did the same, lying down opposite me so the bases of our feet touched like we had been cut out of paper to create a mirror image. The sun was forceful, drying our bodies, burning our fair skin. I'm not sure how long we lay there. I heard Jason scream "Girls!" out toward the water. We stayed still as his voice echoed beyond us.

After a while I asked, "Do you want to be alone?"

"Yes and no."

I sat up, and so did she. We stared at each other fully without shame. Our parts were outlined and shaded and filled to the same tee. It had never felt like this to look at either of my sisters before. Looking at Baby C then, thinking about Baby A, our congruence seemed undefeatable. Like we'd done something wrong to deserve this.

I moved closer to Baby C as I put my left hand to the back of my head, where our sister had been shot, pressing the base of my palm against the thickest, biggest bone my body could grow, trying to feel for a hole. I stared at Baby C, pressing harder, more angrily into my head. Then I screamed in a way that had become monotonous for us both, screaming so steadily that my sister began to scream with me, too, creating a seismic wave to reach our other sister wherever she was—really was, not her body in the coroner's office or her rumor in the mouth of our town. We waited for a scream back, looking at the horizon as if we would be able to see it in gradient rings, like the illustrations in textbooks that diagram the sonar calls of bats.

On the dock, Baby C put her own palm to the base of her head, too, and pressed down. I'd still been pressing, discovering as I pressed that I was in fact trying to manifest or create a hole.

Baby C was pressing curiously, both of us still screaming flatly, almost like tenors in a choir. We droned on, screaming and pressing, until my sister finally began to get angry, frustrated that she, too, could not get the hole to appear in her skull. Then her scream sharpened, and mine did, too, until we were piercing the cloudless sky with our sheer will and slamming our hands into the bases of our skulls, asking God to show us how to die.

Naturally, we'd begun to cry somewhere in there. When we agreed to be depleted, with just a swift look between us, Baby C and I stopped screaming, slowed our crying, and focused separately on sections of the bayou's surface that hadn't rippled a bit.

After a slice of stillness, of balancing our chests with breath again, I asked, "Why didn't we know?"

"Maybe she didn't let us. Do you know how to do that? How to shut us out?"

I shook my head, hand on my stomach. "No."

As the sun blistered and slipped lower along the water's surface, we began to shiver.

Ultimately, we knew we couldn't be sprawled there nakedly for much longer. It was miraculous that no fishing boats had whizzed by.

We walked up to the Upchurch house naked, swiping towels from the laundry room before hustling upstairs to pull on Jason's old shirts and athletic shorts. All was as fractured as we'd left it. Aunt Rachel had found her way back, slicing carrots in the kitchen.

Baby C and I fell asleep with Gull nestled between us on the living room carpet. I tried to think myself to sleep. All my focus seemed to allow was repeated playing of the homily a few weeks before when Reverend Olivia had said, "If you ever go to the Holy Lands and they offer to take you to the farm of the prodigal son, don't go. It's not a real place." And everybody in the congregation laughed. It *was*, though. In that moment on the floor with the siblings I had left, I felt like I was on that farm, standing bereft at the mouth of a driveway, watching my love wait for someone to come home.

[ENTER] FRONT PORCH CHORUS

We shouldn't say a thing. It wouldn't be right. Or appropriate. We have no idea—no cosmic clue—what those Binderups are going through. But, between us, I heard that [ ] and [ ] were at the [ ], or at least [ ] saw them there. She said she heard [ ] say, "[ ]," but we couldn't get her to swear to it. And people are bringing back up those things Rachel Ronsino, now Upchurch, and those girls' mother used to get up to, playing tricks with boys. Of course, Isadora never would accept that Murphy was trouble, and now turns out trouble trickled down. [ ] ran into the girls' father, you remember, the [ ] boy, when he left here and ended in Dayton or Virginia Beach or I don't remember where. Said Murphy wouldn't let him stay, though we'd guessed as much. Those girls always toying with boys. Course, we're not saying it's their—her—fault, we're just saying [ ] saw [ ] and [ ] in the days before, and we know how [ ] is, has always been. Maybe it *is* always about mothers.

SAY SOMETHING PETE

Gull had started wetting the bed again and not telling us about it until morning, when we smelled it on him at breakfast. We knew, Baby C and I, that most nights Gull would stand outside our bedroom door for five, ten, twenty minutes, wobbling on sleepy legs, wanting to come inside for comfort but unsure how to ask, wanting us to open the door suddenly to scoop him up, welcome him into our idiosyncratic sadness. We didn't know what to say to Gull. We couldn't explain the vacancy, and we didn't want him to feel welcomed into such grief because we were afraid he'd get comfortable. We saw his feet beneath the doorjamb. We let him stand there, each night, neither of us letting him in.

The driving range had stayed open, but the course was closed, and our patrons, though they understood, got antsy, calling to ask to book a tee time in advance for "whenever y'all are ready." Jason said the usual afternoon eighteen-hole crowd had started milling about local bars, perusing lunch specials, walking confidently into neighboring country clubs, just to wince away like limping pups when told the price. Mr. Seeglow had begun busing up groceries, unannounced. He'd knock on the clubhouse door, one of us would open it, and he'd cart in brimming paper sacks. None of us had to say anything, and that was a gift greater than food.

In the clubhouse Baby C and Gram and I sat around, limbs on tables, pungent in our must and Gram's smoke. We didn't say much except to purge what pushed against our mouths like bile.

"It feels like we're supposed to say, 'She was the best of us.' "

"I just want her back. I want her back back back."

"Someone called me by name at Seeglow's."

"Wasn't this, some kind of *this*, always coming?"

And it was. It had to be. One of us was always going to go first, which was always going to be the only way they started calling us by our names. It felt like the last thing I wanted to be: Baby B Binderup, stuck in the middle, with her face and half her name. Around town, they looked at us like they wished we'd go away already.

That night it was just me and Gram in the kitchen, scrubbing burned bits off the cast iron, when she paused, the water still running, and said without looking at me, "With your mama, there wasn't any blood at all, besides the birth stuff. We were just as shocked as she was."

"Shocked? At her dying?"

"Yeah," Gram said as she thrust her hands back under the hot water.

I put on a plain blue dress and sandals to talk to Pete, like the detectives asked. By then, we'd covered all the mirrors in the house or outright removed them from the walls. Each time Baby C and I passed one, we retched or sobbed or stood there and reeled. No matter how I tried, I couldn't convince myself that the girl in the mirror was just me; it glowed like her and posed like her, and even when I cried, it crumpled like my sister always had.

I was surprisingly placid, or maybe just numb, the day it was arranged that I'd speak to Pete. I didn't wear any makeup or do anything to my hair. I needed him to see me and know me, to know that I didn't think he was stupid; he had known it was her. For some reason, he needed someone to need him in an unfathomable, unreturnable way. My sister set up her own trap and let Pete waltz into it with her.

I walked into the state building, down a hallway, another hallway, into a room inside a room.

Pete and I weren't separated by anything but a steely standard-width table. I was sweating profusely. He sat there, cuffed at the ankles and wrists, in a beige linen outfit that resembled hospital scrubs. He was just as sharp at the eye corners, uncrusted with cry-gunk or the flakes that gather after a good sleep. His cheeks were covered in stubble, with considerably large bald patches. I hadn't noticed before, but the space between his eyebrows was entirely bridged by thick hair, as if someone had pasted pine needles crudely to his forehead.

The air was thick with the knowledge that we were being watched and recorded, which neither of us seemed particularly impeded by. Pete was not as ashamed or self-loathing as I wanted him to be. He looked at me fully, as if nothing were wrong, as if my face were not encapsulating all he'd obliterated. I stared at my palms; hers had told us this would occur. Why hadn't I seen the great big slash through it all?

"Your freckle is darker," he said, pointing to the spot on his neck where each of my sisters and I had an identical mark. "There."

I folded both blameful hands in my lap, squeezing them pale. "Say something real, Pete."

"Saw y'all at the festival. You did really good. Should've won."

"Say something else."

He looked puzzled for a moment, then took a breath. "What's there to say? I thought you needed me."

"I don't believe you thought she was me. Not for a second. You knew, Pete. You knew."

At this, his face contorted, and he leaned in. "I don't understand—I figured you'd be . . . relieved. I didn't seek her out—I mean, she started texting me on her own, first talking about *why haven't I called*, and then asking to meet up. She wore your clothes. She talked like you. Smiled like you." They're *our* clothes, I wanted to scream. That's our *mother*'s smile. "But I heard it, just as you walked in—the officer called you Baby B. And my lawyer, he does, too, when we talk about you. They can tell. Now that it's just the two of you, you and Baby C being so different and all. Isn't that what you wanted? You said it, in the clubhouse, remember?"

I couldn't help the involuntary, cratering sob-gasp that escaped me. In an instant I was hyperventilating, my head between both legs, snot and tears dripping against the concrete floor. Officers swarmed me, touched my forehead, asked me questions. I begged them to go away.

"It was like a perfect deer waltzed up and *asked* me to—well, you know. I was happy to do it for her. She needed my help."

I was still hunched over, leaking. "You were *happy*?"

He got quiet, almost gentle. "It was the damnedest thing. There were the smallest signs, I suppose I should've picked up on them, but I was too distracted by how . . . well, sad she was. Just in the way you seemed to be. I wasn't trying to understand it. I was just trying to help."

"But why? Did she say why?"

He fidgeted with his fingers but never looked away from my face. "I didn't take her seriously until a few nights before—"

"You took her seriously enough to screw around with her on the ninth hole."

"It was the damnedest thing," he repeated. "She was just like you. It was just like you."

I thought about the Shrimp Shack. I wanted to fucking evaporate. "I don't believe you."

He blinked, stupidly.

"At the festival, when we were onstage, what was I wearing?"

"I wasn't looking at your outfit. I was listening to your voice."

"She didn't tell you what outfit she'd be in?"

He shook his head.

Lies.

"Which voice was mine?"

Pete scrunched his eyes closed. "The deeper one, the middle. Consistent."

"And what was that voice wearing?"

"Hell, Baby. I don't know. Everything was happening at once."

"She wore that stupid babydoll dress on purpose. To look simple and small like me. But her voice was the highest one. Hers was the one that rose above." I shook my head. "I can't even look at myself, Pete. I hate my own face."

"It'll go away."

"No, it won't go away!"

"It doesn't matter who I thought it was or what she, or you, were wearing. She didn't waver for a second, B, not even toward the end. Whoever it was, they wanted out. That's all I knew. It's what she wanted. Really."

"You have no fucking clue what *she* wanted. What *I* want. Why are you this way? Thinking you know what's best for other people. What gives you the right?"

His face and voice hardened. "She asked me every day until I said yes. Seven times, she asked me. That's why I stopped coming around the clubhouse—couldn't stand to look her . . . you . . . in the face and say no anymore. Felt like all I was doing was hurting her by saying no. I just didn't want it to hurt anymore. And I knew how to do it so it *really* wouldn't hurt. She felt nothing."

"But I felt everything! I feel it. Everything!" I was clutching the collar of my dress, bunching the fabric in hand as my heart raced. "And I don't know why she did it, but I know what she wanted; she wanted you to want her enough to say no. No, she wanted you to want *me* enough to know it was her. To have been paying attention. Never in a million years could she have thought, even if she did go with you to pick a shotgun off your sick father's wall of 'em, that you were sadistic enough, detached enough, to pull the trigger."

He began to ramble. "But she did. She mentioned that article in the paper from when I was a kid, getting the first big doe of the season. Said it made her feel confident in me. We ate ice cream sandwiches in the clubhouse kitchen, and she said, 'Shhh, my sisters are asleep'—"

"Why would you care that much about me? We were just a summer thing. You were supposed to know that. Why?"

Pete stilled his hands, an indecipherable look on his face. "I just hate to see a beautiful thing in pain."

I stood on fatigued legs, looked past the reflective glass, and motioned to whoever was watching to unlatch the door. Had I brought this on my sister? Even then, in the concrete room, Pete was earnest, tender. His face was still as symmetrical and bright as it'd been before. I prayed and prayed that he'd be disfigured and disheveled, but he wasn't and would never be.

As I waited for the door to open, I realized that if there was blame for me, then there was blame for Gram. Blame for Murphy, for leaving us all alone. The town, for being the place. Baby A, for having my face. Me, for having hers. Pete, for picking out a gun and lifting it up. Gram, for bringing home Gull. It wasn't only Pete who'd be persecuted for this; we'd persecute ourselves and each other for Baby A's death, forever.

The door opened, and as I walked out, Pete started to call my name. "Bay——"

FRACTURES

The sheriff warned us it'd take months for the trial date to come around. Until then, Pete was released to his parents on six-figure bond, barred from coming within a hundred feet of us. Baby C and I stayed at and around the course. Jason hadn't left the clubhouse in weeks, taking over the most demanding of chores, though Baby C and I had craved the distraction. Sitting at the desk to look the town in the face was worse than sweating days away in the sun; at least then we could be held by the heat. Being comfortable—cooled by air-conditioning, eating warm food, wearing clean clothes—felt sinful. Made me, at least, want to tear the comforts forcefully off; the cutting teeth pulled from my head, the food that filled me forced from my belly. The confusion of what our sister had done bred a specifically vengeful kind of self-loathing in Baby C and me.

Patrons began to pat our shoulders or rub our heads, grab for us in well-intended but flat ways. They no longer summoned us casually over with a "Hey, girls" to ask for blister patches or a bag of potato chips. Instead, men who'd known us our whole lives called us "ma'am" or, after all that time, by our Baby B, Baby C God-given names. It was sad. They didn't know how to know us anymore.

They patronized Gull in the ways they always had, speaking loudly, moving their lips widely. Gram got to remain Isadora, the Manatee, the most beautiful woman in town, with an added layer of sorrow. At church, even though she hadn't made us go with her anymore, Gram said they'd pull the offering plate past her. "Guess I'm not allowed to tithe. And Reverend Olivia," Gram said, "preaches every sermon right to me."

The real fracture was between Baby C and me. What was broken for us was the "we" through which we regarded and told the stories of our lives. When *we* went to the boat dock that one time. When *we* were seven. When *we* stole those glitters from the store. The "we" was broken because looking into the past still held all three of us. As we grew and were just the two of us, our presents and our futures didn't have our sister in them. It felt like walking with blindfolds on. Without talking about it explicitly, Baby C and I tried on other things. We'd say, "my sister Baby C and I," or "my twin sister and I," though nothing felt right. We hated ourselves for all the time we spent wishing the bond between us away, because we could never be our truest selves without each other—all three of us. And we hated Baby A, too, for taking this away from us, which was the worst of all.

Gull walked into the clubhouse one afternoon with oranges tumbling around inside the basket of his T-shirt. He rolled the rounds into an empty bowl on the table and picked the perfect one, ate it noiselessly over a placemat like an ashamed bird. When I noticed he was being extra careful to keep the peel intact, it dawned on me what he was doing, and I braced myself.

Gull sucked the citrus from his fingers and walked the doily of an orange peel over to Baby C, who was sitting on the clubhouse floor over a magazine, staring at a dramatic editorial page of models straddling pins in a retro bowling alley, tongues out. Gull flopped the peel down on top of her opened page. It took her a few beats to finally look up. Without a word, Baby C stood, kissed Gull on the top of his head, and walked out of the clubhouse onto the course. There'd be no fortunes from her anymore. Gull picked up the peel and began to walk after her but stopped near a stray golf cart and sat in the dirt. He tore the peel into small pieces and began to toss them measuredly, as if feeding an invisible flock.

I walked out of the clubhouse softly and sat beside Gull, my legs in a sore tangle.

The pieces of peel took the place of *love-me-not* petals as he tossed them away, not wishing, already resigned to the amount of love he'd allotted for himself. In a few moments he'd torn the peel as small as it'd go. Citrusy, sticky bits decorated my ankles. One nestled into my sock.

"I tried to imagine her heaven," Gull said, his gaze fixed on the orange confetti. He moved a hand toward my folded legs in a fist and set his knotted fingers against me. He'd recently stopped signing as he spoke, so kids would have less to make fun of him for. "You know how Gram said heaven is whatever you want it to be, and hers would have a lazy river and a lot of golden retriever puppies and endless guacamole? I tried to imagine *hers*—"

He paused, afraid he was imposing in trying to understand Baby A's deepest wants and loves, what she kept in her cave-heart, a place Gull knew that Baby C and I had thought we'd known, before all of us at once realized we'd never even approached its entry. I nodded: *Go on.*

"I thought it might have pink blankets and a nice burning candle. Then treats she liked, like popcorn and those frozen graham crackers with chocolate and toffee on top. And God was real big, outside in a big chair, waiting to decide whether or not she could come into her heaven." He paused again, careful to gather the right words. "But when I tried to put them together in a room, they wouldn't go. It was like I had all the parts, but when I tried to make it a picture, my brain went blank."

He looked at me as if I would know how to unblock this scenario in his mind, as if somewhere in this conundrum was the Big

Answer. My throat wanted for words, wanted to force them out and have them be right, be salve to Gull's wound, propel him up and away in the right direction, but there was nothing inside me that shimmered like that, nothing beyond feeling self-absorbed and perverse. I put my hand around his fist. Gull started to cry quietly, folding inward, like a beetle into its shell. He toppled against my legs and cried in his curl. We stayed that way for years.

Newspapers had begun to pile up at the mouth of our driveway. Since the paper kid didn't like to make the trek to our clubhouse door, they were stacked in little gatherings, like a sickness spreading toward our house. For us, there was nothing to know. Not the weather or sports scores, especially not reporting on my sister's death. Some papers called it *accidental slaying* and others called it *assisted suicide* and we could never decide as a family which was more wrong. As the trial neared, most outlets labeled it *murder*. People kept news clippings, like it was an event to scrapbook. The papers couldn't get their hands on any photo of just her, or if they had, nobody could confirm it was really *just* her, and that was a screwup none of them could afford.

One evening stuck me in its dull clutches so tightly I thought I might finally claw my own skin off to escape it all. I realized I was ferociously, violently sick of driving past those damned newspapers, so I walked down the driveway with a golf ball bucket and collected sixteen newspapers bundled in plastic. As I walked back toward the clubhouse, I thought hard about where to go from there. A few yards before the driveway curved into our parking lot to make me visible from the clubhouse, I dumped the bucket out and sat in the gravel. First I yanked off the plastic sleeves and crumpled them in the bucket. Then I sorted the papers by city— Baby C's subscriptions came from all over—then ordered them from oldest to newest, dug through to the only section that mattered, and pulled the folded pages out. This took me a while, yet tempered my rage, which eventually settled into a kind of disgust for myself that I'd begun learning to live within. I canned the rest and left the bucket by the road, walking into the clubhouse with a handful of limp, rot-stenched pages. Baby C was in the kitchen, helping Gram chop up a head of iceberg lettuce. I said "Here" as I handed her the stack of backlogged horoscopes. "They're from oldest to newest, bottom up."

She and Gram stopped chopping. Gram watched Baby C's face as closely as I did while my sister fluttered the pages like a fan; a tool, not something to read. Instantly, I was embarrassed. Gram seemed unsure, looking urgently between my sister and me, still holding a knife. Baby C pulled the oldest page from beneath the stack, and after scanning it a moment, read aloud: " 'For Gemini, shared knowledge is the gateway to romance. And in Aries—devilishly clever and altogether cool—has Gemini met their mental match. As Gemini tries to untangle the Aries logic, so Aries will attempt to tap into Gemini's deepest withholdings. With a Gemini and Aries pair, love has no choice but to make sense of itself.' "

She looked up from the paper at me, placing the excised leaflet on top of the rest. " 'Love has no choice but to make sense of itself,' " she echoed with a sourness—nothing mean, just something that had spoiled in the days it took someone down at the *Sacramento Bee* to write those words and me, the only sister left, to deliver them to her. Baby C looked away from me as if there was no conversation to be had, back to cutting the lettuce.

I burst into tears before registering the devastation. I cried hard and loud as the three of us stood there, shocked by my delivery, her reaction, and my reaction to her reaction.

"You're a bitch." The words came out of my mouth. I didn't know I meant them. My eyes were so full I couldn't see what either Baby C or Gram were doing. Somebody hugged me, put their head in the crook of my neck. I felt how gray and thin that hair was, that it wasn't the head I needed there. "I hate you," I screamed. The grip around me tightened as I repeated the lie. "I hate you I hate you you bitch I hate you."

By the time I calmed, coaxing away hiccups and trying to steady myself, the place where Baby C had stood cutting lettuce was empty and the stack of astrology pages was set neatly, flatly on the top of the trash piled in an uncovered bin. I looked at Gram, bereft. "She hates me, too," I said.

"No, no," Gram shushed me. "You girls don't hate nobody."

And we were like that for a while, me and Baby C. There were days we truly did hate each other. We felt grief and anger and stillness at such a volume that no other noise could break through. Often I found her in the clubhouse at night, on the phone with her psychic, weeping. We caught ourselves staring all the time, at patrons, our palms, the walls. We didn't say much for the next few months. The only person I brought my head above water to worry about was Gull, but he seemed to understand the silence. Sometimes I thought he might've known why Baby A did what she did, just didn't have the heart to tell us.

The grief kept Baby C from speaking up, but self-loathing had intensified her occasional sicknesses in unforeseeable ways. In November, I'd had to take her to the emergency clinic because she couldn't stop vomiting, and I couldn't ignore it any longer. It had started in the morning and was relentless until finally, she fainted. Gram was gone that day, helping Harriet hunt down some very specific altar guild materials, so I called Jason in from the golf course, where he was helping a customer ground his swing, to watch Gull. Baby C and I stayed overnight at the ER. Even the doctor wouldn't look at us like people—she stared at Baby C's chart the whole time, talking into the paper as a nurse prodded my sister with IVs, droning on about all she didn't know.

On the way home the next morning, Baby C was curled in the passenger seat, lips dried out so bad that one of the cracks had begun bleeding. The doctor had given her heaps of anti-nausea and knock-you-out medicine, momentary fixes. I knew that she'd been thinking nothing could cure her, not this far gone, and I knew she was grateful to have a physical manifestation for confronting this grief, however living-hell it was. I felt her pangs in my stomach, too. As we sat in the doctor's small, thinly curtained office, I'd pulled my knees up in the dinky steel chair, rocking in small pulses with the pain Baby C was railing against. On the papered table, she was sobbing.

I made sure to take the smooth toll road as long as I could, even without a toll pass, because I didn't want to rattle Baby C's stomach on the heat-cracked feeder roads. She began to speak so softly, her voice nearly blended with the radio murmur. "Do you really hate me?" she asked, already convinced. "B, do you?"

"Of course not. Why would you say that?" Yet I had said exactly that to her, loud and on loop, that day with the newspapers and the lettuce.

"I hate me," she said, curling both legs further into her shaking chest. "I hate the disgusting girl inside me. I want to make her so sick she starves. She's the same ridiculous, pitiful creature every day. I look at her, and I hate—I want to dig her out and chuck her across the yard. I want to drown her."

The pastures we passed were dotted with pairs of egrets balanced atop cows, like a pointillist painting. I was devastated for us.

She spoke up a bit. "You hate you, too, don't you?"

"So much."

"How could we not?" The town was passing us slowly in wakeful blue tones. "Is that why you said that to me? Because you hate you."

"Probably," I said, trying to think that far back through such a thickness. Even though it was only a few months prior, it felt like time hadn't moved at all, which somehow made it harder to re-member. I didn't know why I'd said that, but my thoughts clung to our other sister—our dead sister—and all the whys she'd left for us to sort out. "Did she hate herself?" I asked. "Was that it?"

This was the first time Baby C and I had really spoken since I'd said I hated her with such belief. I loathed myself for making this, driving her home from the hospital, the resumption of our dialogue. We still slept in the same room and wore each other's clothes, but none of it had any words.

I could hear Baby C's teeth clatter against her kneecaps as the toll road ended and our truck tires shook against broken chunks of tar. I asked her and the road, "Do you think we'll ever be okay again?"

Baby C shifted in her seat and uncurled, sitting up against sun-aged leather as cracked as her lips. She looked at the dashboard and then at the side of my face. "I feel fractured forever."

"Do you think that's how it should be? When a sister dies."

"How could God mean for this to be how it feels?" Baby C said, almost angry, but courageous, questioning our God, wherever they were, up in the sky or at the bottom of our bayou. Maybe they were waiting this whole thing out. Maybe they'd reveal themselves to us in a dream and pull us out of the murk. I pictured our God sitting on top of the clubhouse with wide paper wings, a leg dan-gling languorously above the back door, chin propped up by their hand as they watched us fill water buckets and point patrons in the right direction. As we swerved onto the course's gravel driveway, the neighbor's chickens scattering toward the trees like repelled magnets, it felt like we could never truly drive home again. This place was just a clubhouse we lived in with our brother and Gram and an empty bed between us that Gull said he'd wanted to sleep in but never could. There was no God on our clubhouse roof. There was no God at the bottom of our bayou.

[ENTER] FRONT PORCH CHORUS

———

Down here God is the honeysuckle. God is the alliteration. God is fried catfish skin. God is missing the train. God is the link between animals and animals. God is the acre. We believe in God. He comes on over to dinner. God is the old roof that holds. God is luck. God is war. God is warm soup on a warm day in a warm belly. God is the hole in one on Pine Needle Walkway. God is humming and singing and speaking all at the same time. We had a nightmare that God has Murphy Binderup's face. We wonder if she's up there with God, angry at us. We wonder if her little girl is up there, too—we can't really know which way she went. Still, we think maybe all of heaven watches us, and we want them to know we did our best with what we got. Really, they look just alike, and really, it is becoming easier to tell, but only now.

MY BODY HER BODY

Things became more complicated as the trial approached. It was set for January, the coldest time we got around the coast. The county district attorney and the sheriff kept in touch with us almost too much at the beginning. Gram had to ask them to only call with essentials; she'd begun getting panicky when the phone rang, unable to talk to patrons inquiring about open tee times. The initial rumor had been that Pete was going to plead insanity, though eventually we found that the plea would be "not guilty" with a heavy push on the idea that there was an element of consent, which we didn't know what to do with in our minds. The district attorney reluctantly asked if we'd be comfortable with her offering Pete a deal. We'd just stared at her across a conference room table, not knowing what that would really mean. "Doesn't matter," I said. "The bastard would never take it." And I was right. It didn't matter what the DA offered the Martelli family; they insisted on a trial.

Somehow worse was the talk around town. Everything was, naturally, our fault. Gram got called names when she went to the store or the bank. The papers and reporters stopped phoning to hear our side of things. Baby C and I never left the clubhouse, not for church or the corner store. Aunt Rachel was getting grief, too. Mostly from the women her age, wanting to talk about Murphy's tie to it all. "I dealt with this ignorance before," she said. "Now, at least, there's someone to blame."

The sheriff called just after Thanksgiving. Jason had been working hard at the course during the day, frequenting dance halls and bars that didn't check IDs after dark. He was at the Spinout one night, many beers deep, when Rich Goodson's twin brother Cart shot off his dumb mouth about how Baby A was just a slut, that she'd slept with his brother so easy, it wouldn't make sense for Pete to just *do* this. It had to be Baby A's "ways." Really, she was just a slut with a good body (a great body), and greater men than Pete sure couldn't resist, and who could tell the Manatee's girls apart anyway—which was as far as Jason let him get before slugging Cart square in the jaw. "That's my family!" Jason shouted.

"They're not your blood," Cart scoffed. "Jason, the crazy whore asked me to blow her brains out, too. Now what? What are we *really* supposed to think 'bout her?"

Jason swept Cart's legs out from underneath him with a kick and started to knock him in the side of the head. The doorman and a few riled-up customers pinned Jason and Cart until the police showed up and took both boys in, equally bloodied and bruised, surging with drunken pride and prideful rage. Jason said Uncle Henry bailed him out without a word, just drove him home and let him sleep. Cart threatened to make a big deal of it, but the deputies who drove him to the station had long been disgusted by Pete's apathy about his crime, how listlessly the town was mystified by it. They persuaded Cart to shut up and nurse the couple punches he'd brought upon himself. And while he was at it, Cart and his brother would be wise to stay away from our family. We heard the Goodson twins sold their trailer a few months later and enlisted.

I'd been hearing Baby A's voice for months. As the weather got colder, it became more frequent and penetrating, like someone was pressing pause, yanking me out of life and stuffing me into a fever dream, then just as quickly depositing me, frazzled and reeling, back into a life that felt empty and wrong and very much a trick.

In the middle of tasks or thoughts or training a new caddy at the course, a gangly high school boy, Baby A would overpower me. *Look at his freckles and pimples! They're like a map of disgusting stars.* I'd go to empty out rain buckets or rake bunkers, and she'd say, *Jump in the water for me. Hold your breath. There's treasure at the bottom I've left you. Or maybe! I'm at the bottom, B. Come find me at the bottom.* And she'd almost convince me. I'd step toward the edge with whatever in my hand and lean over, but something always broke the trance. When she tried to get me in the bayou, the umber film spotted with pine needles and trash reminded me we'd already found my sister. There was no mystery in that water anymore. It was of necessity that we swam, to calm Gull and get quickly across town.

Sometimes when I gazed at Baby C, our sister would rush my temples. *Look at that! You look like that, you gorgeous girl. My eyes! I knew I'd left 'em somewhere, Baby. How perfect they sit inside our sister's head. Get 'em out for me, B. Our sister has stolen my eyes.* And I'd want to. I entertained reaching over the bowls of mashed potatoes that separated us at the dinner table to scoop out the same glassy blues I housed in my own head. I could tell sometimes that Baby C was looking at me this way, too, as if stalking a deer in woods, at once admiring the seamless life of the creature while just as intently imagining it decorating a den wall.

These were hateful moments for us. Our sister's great big haunt. She was good at it, too. Almost better than she'd been at taunting us when she was entirely living and standing next to us, whispering her wants into our blushed ears. In this awful way Baby A was constantly present in us and around us. I'd wished it were sweeter, the way she loomed, but it was almost unbearable.

In weak moments I could feel Pete, too. His breath at my neck, his knee slowly wedging itself between my legs as we leaned against the Shrimp Shack. These torture-moments pushed themselves in front of my everyday thoughts. Texts he sent, things he said. Moments he'd gazed at me like he knew me—I was still convinced that he did. Around Longshadow people lamented the veterinarian career he'd have had, the animal lives he'd have saved. They spoke as if it was he who had been robbed of something, not my sister, who lay next to our mother beneath cold, broken ground. Mostly when Pete forced his memory upon me, it was the moment when he helped me pull broken glass from Gull's hand. I tried to stay in that moment and search for a clue, moving my mind's eye as wide as it would go. I navigated the memory like a video game, trying to see around all sides, zoom in on his face as he clutched the tweezers and Gull's sweet hand. If he'd wanted to hurt our family, why hadn't he just wedged the glass deeper and run, or why hadn't he hit me, spit on me, hated me to my face? I couldn't reconcile what had felt like a moment of extreme tenderness, regard for our family's lives and bodies, with the open back of my sister's soft head. Was it evil inside him, or had he truly been persuaded? Did that have to mean he wasn't evil, and did any of this mean I was supposed to understand?

I'd begun to let myself feel hostile toward Baby A. That she'd allowed herself, our connection, her animal steadfastness, to become a game of roulette. There was meanness in what she'd done, real calculated horror. The pretending, kissing a guy I'd kissed, luring him in with a mockery of me. She really had been hateful. I understood on its face the desire to be seen and to be saved. But, even knowing her boldness, seeing the scene vividly in my head—her kneeling, letting the seconds tick by, not stopping it, not revealing herself—I couldn't comprehend in my heart how it ended as it had. Had she wanted to get away from us that badly? Or had she underestimated the worst that Pete was capable of? All I could picture anytime I sat still for more than a few minutes or caught my rippled reflection in the bayou's face was Pete, anchoring a shotgun at his shoulder, Baby A's hair clouding her face in wisps. I wanted to pull her out of the picture and scream in her face. I wanted to turn the gun on Pete and shove it into his chest. I was so angry I was afraid to sit still.

As often as I had these moments of rage, I felt rushes of appreciation and immense love for Baby A. Some days I used her shampoo in the shower. Some days I wore her sweat-stained shoes. It was never an attempt to *be* her. It was more an effort to carry her with me in sensory ways. When I smelled my sister in my hair, I could exhale. When I walked on top of her feet like a child learning to dance, I was safe. Some days I smiled hugely just to have had her.

My body was her body was a place she moved and lived forever. Even now she was gone, her face still looked out at the town through me, her voice still shimmered when I opened my mouth. It was a flood on top of a flood.

Anyway, they tore us apart at the trial. Slandering my sister's mental state, boasting Pete's good family and collegiate accolades on the backs of our dead mother and hippie golf course. We looked pathetic next to what held Pete's family up.

We'd known we would.

IT ENDS WITH JULIE

There were plenty of people on our side of the courtroom—rustic, homegrown people who'd been brought up alongside our mother or frequented the course. There were the rebellious people who didn't want to see a pretty boy with money get away with something awful. These kinds of people dragged their own sorrows into the courtroom. Some of the people in the courtroom were just angry because a boy had killed a girl, and that was unnatural. Those people didn't see Baby A as anything beyond pinkness and breasts. They looked at us with pity, which is what they thought we wanted. It was mostly older people behind us, people who'd given things a good bit of thought. Behind Pete were people we'd thought were our friends in school; beautiful young people who made the town proud by going to universities and playing in minor leagues. A prominent side of the Martelli family came in from Dallas for the trial and sat on the wooden benches in business dress, leather shoes. The people on Pete's side were madder than we were—fueled by thoughts of injustice and fantasies of what Pete could have achieved, the good-looking babies he could have made. They looked at us with anger. We were just tired and sad. The only thing to be angry about was the way they slandered our girl. What would happen to Pete, I knew, was on God.

Gull sat between Baby C and Aunt Rachel in the courtroom, not understanding much but ever-present. They brought in an ASL interpreter from the city, but Gull spent more time looking at his feet than he did those speaking hands.

Baby C had not been designated as a possible witness, so she was allowed to attend the trial while Gram and I had to stay away because the defense had us down as people they were going to call, and if they decided not to, the district attorney assured us she would. So Gram and I sat on a bench outside the courtroom, hours at a time, with her taking intermittent smoke breaks and me wandering around the building to remind myself I was alive. Officer Fenoli kept an eye on us, brought us deli sandwiches and black coffees. Sometimes he'd sit in silence with us. Harriet did the same, though most days she was inside the courtroom, eager for gossip fodder.

Gram didn't dress up much on the day of her testimony. None of us wanted to feel pretty, which might have been the only thing we agreed on. Baby C and I wore loose dresses, let our hair air-dry on the car rides to the courthouse while wind muffled our ears. Gram wore a matching linen set in a light-pink shade that Baby A had always teased made her look like a lesbian. Gram sat in the grand wooden cubby beside the judge with firmness, kicking her Birkenstocks against the legs of her chair—I couldn't see her doing this as I sat in the lobby outside the closed doors, and I couldn't hear it, I just knew it was her way. Baby C said Gram seemed held by the cubby, encapsulated, like a baby bird in a nest. I knew this was what they wanted her to feel, and I knew the safety of the cubby was a lie. Pete's rigid attorney, with his professionally colored hair, leisured up toward Gram with a folder in hand that he seldom referenced. His questions were pedantic, repetitive, pulling information from her that the newspapers had been printing for months, all in all a numbing twenty-five-minute ramble, until he cleared his throat, locked eyes with Gram, and said, "Mrs. Binderup, don't you feel this is your fault?"

Aunt Rachel said that was when God themselves appeared, right there, glowing and floating in the middle of the courthouse to yank the Great Big Rug out from under them, taking with it every breathable particle in the room and any peace or self-assurance my gram had left in her. The lawyer kept his resolve, staring Gram down. Even though the room had stilled, Baby C's body moved quickly as she stood with force and began to scream. Her words staggered to reach me in the hallway, where I heard them clearly. "It's his fault!" she screamed. "My gram is good, and so are we. It's him. Pete! Look at me! Look what you ruined, Pete. Look at me!"

The gavel, of course, rattled in a furious stampede. Uproar in the room took force, but God bless my sister, who didn't sit or resist, who stood to stare into the vacant soul of a boy I'd let taste every part of me with his gaping, selfish mouth. I'd been ashamed to be alive until Baby C did that. It was as if she'd taken me by the chin and pointed my gaze in the right direction. Even after all that hollering, Aunt Rachel said Pete hadn't flinched, staring forward as Baby C kept screaming and Gull bolted from the bench toward Gram, sobbing at all the commotion. The district attorney caught Gull mid-bolt and hugged him to her legs.

Time didn't start up again until Gram, still on the stand, began to cough violently, covering the microphone with her hand. The judge handed her a tissue, and the DA went to help her up, but she coughed with such force that she couldn't walk. The bailiff grabbed a wheelchair and took Gram to a side room, where an oxygen tank was waiting. There was a recess. As I was being called from the hall into the side room with Gram, Pete's family trickled into the hallway, inconvenienced by all this Binderup-dying around them.

I hadn't gotten to look at Pete, but I imagined him vacant, shrunken, shriveled even. Pale and subdued. I hated myself for imagining him, but I did it all the time. I wished he would just evaporate. I wished he would die, without pain or stimulation, just vanish. He wasn't doing anybody any good, and he wasn't living on this time he'd stolen, anyway.

The rest of the trial was draining. They showed pictures that weren't theirs to show and printed out catalogs of our texts, calls, even a few of Baby A's high school essays about identity and dreams. Teachers who'd had both Pete and Baby A testified; they called my sister "unnerving" and "intent" in the same breath as calling Pete "unforgettable." What they called "unnerving" was the multiplication of her face, going three different directions, in the hall. It was her existence, not her, that they struggled with. The lawyers kept on. They talked about "irresistible impulses." They said that Baby A had talked about someone killing her—had asked Pete to—with such ease that he was confused, dear jury; his idea of wrongness was warped by her body, her wanting.

I thought of great beauties like Helen of Troy and Lady Anne being blamed for their loveliness, and the men who burned worlds for themselves, saying they just couldn't help it, she's so beautiful. Hadn't the town raised us with winks? Weren't we supposed to be what they wanted? Baby A had thought Pete wanted me, so she became me—I would never, could never, comprehend it.

Julie took the stand. She played the dutiful sister very well, wearing fake eyeglasses with plain glass lenses, a silk bow clipped above her bouncy ponytail, which curled up at the ends. As she sat in the raised, gated wooden seat, Baby C said Julie didn't look like the girl we knew.

Her testimony began with stupid questions, establishing her relationship to "the defendant" and her relationship to "the deceased." As I envisioned Julie's performance, I thought about one of our high school sleepovers. We were safely stashed in her bedroom, surrounded by magazines, with the contents of a makeup bag scattered across the rug. Baby C had twisted her wet hair up in one of Julie's T-shirts atop her head. Julie had been begging our sister to read her palm, so Baby C paused to set the scene, putting clumps of black mascara on only her lower eyelashes, clipping clothespins to her earlobes, though our ears were all pierced. Baby A and I went first to familiarize Julie with the process, assuring her there was no blood offering required, no pledging of one's soul to the devil. Baby C traced our palms with tickles as we, her forever sisters, giggled but nodded seriously at the prophecy she dictated. We'd gasp and coo, reach to tug the wooden clips at the sides of Baby C's head. Finally, Julie sat with her legs folded across from Baby C, palm laid upward and trembling a bit from all the soda we'd drunk.

Baby C began tracing an unpolished fingernail along the creases in Julie's palm. "Now, there are five lines: marriage, money, head, heart, and life. Your heart line is long but thin; this means you have a lot of love but aren't sure how to show it. Money will stay consistent; abundant." Baby A and I snickered. Baby C reached behind her, slapped our knees, and kept on. "Your life line is fairly stretched, with a few interruptions which could be very good things—" She paused to look dramatically at Julie. The mascara beneath her eyes was beginning to run in the hot room, creating a deep shadow. "Or very bad." We laughed harder.

"What about marriage?" Julie pleaded. We understood; it was what we'd wanted to know, too. Whether we'd marry the baseball boy or meet someone from out of town, if *we'd* be the person from out of town someday.

Baby C simply put a finger to her lips. "Your head is a bit crooked; see there?" She pointed to a deep squiggle in the line. Julie pressed her face closer, squinting to see for herself. "As for marriage, there'll be two."

Julie rolled her eyes at this but kept her hand steady.

"One a man and one a—"

The room seemed to freeze. We were dangling with Baby C as the play-performance washed away from her face, and she seemed to be earnestly worried, looking at Julie as if she needed permission to speak.

"What? A zebra, a Toyota Camry? What is it?" Baby A said with zeal, laughing.

Julie was nodding, smiling, nudging Baby C forward. "A what?"

"A woman."

Julie's face contorted. "That's ridiculous," she said, her voice rising. "Why would you say that? What kind of bullshit is this? Why would you say that, you freak?" She yanked her hand away and crawled onto her bed, away from us, as if there was something to escape.

Baby C's face gentled at Julie's reaction. "I'm just saying what's in your palm. And you'll be happy. Look, the rest of the marriage is happy."

"You made that up, you bitch." Julie's words had real venom. She turned her back to Baby C and spoke exclusively to Baby A and me. "Why would she say something like that? She's a jealous freak."

Baby C didn't shrink at this, and neither did I. Baby A puffed her chest out a bit. "Hey. It's just a game. Relax. And it's fine, we don't care."

"There's nothing to care about. I'm not gay, bitches."

I piped up. "Julie, it's okay. Let's just play something else. There's another *Cosmopolitan* quiz to take."

"You know," Julie said to Baby C, who was still sitting on the floor, her hair slowly unraveling from the twist of Julie's T-shirt. "I think you should probably go home."

Baby A had started to interject when Julie interrupted. "You can stay," she said. "And you," she added, looking at me.

"If she goes, we go."

Julie put her hands on her hips, sitting with her back pressed adamantly into the headboard as if it were her throne. "Fine. Get the fuck out, then."

So we got the fuck out. As we left Julie's house, I dipped into the kitchen and asked Mrs. Martelli for some gallon ziplock baggies. She handed them over, not asking why we were leaving in the middle of a sleepover, not offering to drive us home. Mrs. Martelli's scowl had been trained on us since childhood, for no reason we could ever discern, though I'd always imagined it made her feel weak, not being able to tell us apart. That's what I'd considered her anyway, all of them who couldn't tell: weak.

We'd known about Julie in our own ways, Baby A's more concrete than ours, considering Julie tried to feel her up each time we slept over. Julie *insisted* Baby A was the only one small enough to share the bed with her. We hadn't cared. And we hadn't held it against Baby C for saying this aloud.

That night Julie kicked us out, we stripped to our underwear on the Martellis' dock, shoved our cell phone, magazine quizzes, and spare clothes into the baggies to tote across the bayou in our wide-swooping arms. We shone in the dark.

We were perfect back then because we were together. We were secure, even swimming in the midnight, because we knew which way was home.

"She was depressed," Julie said, now, on the stand.

"And how is it that you know this?" the defense attorney asked.

"She moped around. Avoided everybody except the reverend, who she was forced to talk to. Told me all the time that she was planning on running away. The only thing she had to look forward to was the festival. I knew when it was over, she was going to have a mental breakdown."

"But she spent weeks planning this . . . scenario with your brother?"

"I guess."

"What do you make of that?"

"I don't know."

"Miss Martelli, could you tell the Binderup sisters apart?"

"Yes."

"And could your brother?"

"Probably not. It's a difficult task—was."

"What sense can you make of Baby A Binderup pretending to be her sister? Why do you think she did this only with your brother, and not other men?"

Julie shrugged. "Baby A was dramatic. She liked to stir the pot. Clearly, she said something to confuse my brother, or to convince him to do this awful thing. He wasn't in his right mind." When she said this, Baby C said Julie looked right at her. "They have that effect on people."

The district attorney traded spots with the defense attorney, holding a bundle of papers to the side of her hip like a baby. "Miss Martelli, is it true you turned your brother in to the police?"

Julie stiffened. "I brought him to the station, yes."

"Because he came home that morning and confessed to you that he knew where Baby A was?"

"I asked him where *he'd* been. He said, 'At the lease.' I told him Baby A had run off, and our dad was out looking for her on our boat. Then Pete told me, 'It's no use.' And he wouldn't say anything else for a long time."

"Where, in fact, was your father?"

Julie went silent, bouncing her heel against the floor.

"Miss Martelli, I'll ask you again: Where was your father?"

"He was cleaning Pete's boots in the garage."

"Pete's bloody boots, yes?"

"I wasn't there. I didn't know."

"But you know now that, based on your father's written statement and the forensic evidence, that it was human blood on those boots, the blood of your best friend Baby A Binderup."

"She wasn't my best friend."

"Then why did you turn your brother in?"

Julie's voice deepened with frustration. "She was *missing*. I just thought he knew where she was, not that he'd—"

"Killed her? Didn't you see her mangled body? Didn't you vomit and nearly faint at the crime scene?"

"Objection!" Pete's lawyer erupted.

"I—I wouldn't have . . ."

"You wouldn't have brought your brother to the police if you'd known he was guilty? Would you have helped him cover it up, like your father?"

"Objection! Badgering."

The judge, in an unenthused tone, said, "Sustained."

"Miss Martelli, do you look back on that day with any regret about your own actions?"

Julie's voice caught in her throat. Baby C said she blinked a couple of times, hard.

"Nothing I could've done to Pete would have changed anything. Baby A was sad. And I couldn't have changed that, either."

I knew she'd never speak to us again. Couldn't, for the sake of her family. "It was unlike her," Baby C said. "Very flat. Like she's given up. Or she's just as tired as we are by it all."

"She can't be tired like us. We're the ones who've lost," I said.

Baby C tilted her head. "I'm surprised she took him to the police."
I nodded; I was, too.

Pete's hired Houston suit wasted no time launching into a tactical
speech, trying to make the jury see a human worth pity in the boy
who lifted a gun confidently, unabashedly, to the back of my head
her head, kissed her on the ninth hole, kissed me beside the Shrimp
Shack, said he'd kill her, yes he'd kill me because it was just too sad
to watch and he thought I was pretty, so he'd do what nobody else
would do, then drove us out to his daddy's land and had me kneel
beside algae and murk as the frog-song renegaded around our
heads, screaming *Don't do it don't take her Pete Pete Pete no* but he
who had such focus kept that shotgun nose wet against her neck and
pulled a confident trigger as if he were shoving his tongue down my
throat for the very last time and killed my sister in a swoop so fell it
was revolting, how he met the silence behind the shot and surely her
gasp or maybe just her loud, confident last breath; then Pete weighed
our body down with dumbbells stolen from the high school weight
room and pushed, letting tepid water engulf our girl. My mind raced
in the hallway, Gull sitting in my lap with his fingers submerged
in a plastic cup of Play-Doh he was too old to be fiddling with.

Jason came into the hallway in the middle of Pete's testimony,
disgusted, to fill in the gaps for me, because it had become clear that
neither the defense nor the prosecution was going to call me. "She
was vibrant in the day, but at night she was emptied. I just thought
she was going through something," Pete said. "Sometimes all she
could talk about was the Bluegrass Festival, then other times all she
talked about was how sad she was, how hopeless her life seemed. I
was naive, I suppose. But she—they—were like that, sir. Erratic."

"Were there any obvious distinguishing marks that only
Baby B had?"

"I wouldn't know, sir."

"Are you saying that you were not intimate with Baby B Binderup, Mr. Martelli?"

"No, but it was always . . . fast. I never paid close attention."

"So you were indeed intimate with *both* Baby B Binderup and her identical sister, Baby A, is that correct?"

"It seems that way, yes, sir."

"And there was nothing unique to either woman? They were entirely the same?"

"Yes, sir."

Your freckle is darker, he'd said in the police station. *There.* He'd known it. I knew.

"Could you see how a trick such as this could drive any young man crazy? No more than twenty-three, still stuck in the clutches of desire, not even old enough to rent a car." Of course the jury was instructed to disregard that comment, though they could never unhear it.

"Lastly, Mr. Martelli, was Baby B Binderup the kind of girl who might ask you to assist in her suicide?"

"I believed she was, yes."

"And do you still believe this, Mr. Martelli?"

Pete paused a moment, then regurgitated a sickening rehearsed line. "I believe that I never really knew her at all."

Suddenly Baby C burst out of the courtroom to vomit across the parquet lobby floor. Her shoes slid ahead of her as she slipped against the spill and fell to the floor, crying and coughing up flecks of sour bile, trying to get the taste of Pete's lies out of her mouth. Jason and I gathered her up by the armpits. A bystander handed us a roll of paper towels and I took Baby C, crying uncontrollably, into the ladies' room to rinse her off as best we could in the sink.

Baby A was the one I didn't know anymore. But Pete—Pete knew me. He did. He had to. My sister was the mystery. All the times she snuck out the window in a nightgown, and not one of us woke to ask her where she was going. I pictured her on the ninth hole with Pete, yards away from our bedroom, kissing him where I'd kissed him, going all the way, then walking back into our bedroom, passing me to get to her bed, knowing what she'd just done, then being able to sleep peacefully. Truly, what had she thought would happen? That Pete would put the gun's cold nose to her neck and say *Nah, never mind?* That he'd give her a ride back to the house, shotgun still in the car? She'd giggle her way to our room and wake me, recount all the deceit, and say, *See, B, he knew it wasn't you. All along. He knows you.* Or maybe it really had been what she wanted, to die. I couldn't stomach the thought. It made no sense, not with how much I needed her here, and how intrinsically she'd known that.

After Baby C was cleaned up, we left the courthouse to sit in the bed of Jason's truck. Baby C lay down flat, allowing the sun to wash over her, taking deep, paced breaths. I lay down beside her, our bodies concealed from the media huddle on the courthouse steps and anybody who'd come looking for us. I draped Gram's heavy down coat across us to subdue the January breeze's bone chill. As we lay there in silence, reeling, I realized that it wasn't Pete I'd wanted, not really. It was the things he had: opportunity, means, talent, support. I'd wanted him to take me with him, not so we could be together but so I could have somewhere to go. Maybe Baby A recognized this in Pete, too: a way out.

Gram and Aunt Rachel were the only ones to stay for the closing statements, when Pete's lawyer said this was a crime not of passion but of *com*passion. Said Pete was just putting Baby A out of her misery, like she'd asked; and wasn't this boy studying to be a vet, being trained in that very trade of mercy? The courtroom reportedly shuddered as he compared my sister to a disease-ridden dog panting into oblivion, suggesting that there was mercy or peace in her death, as if parts of her weren't shotgun-blasted into Pete's daddy's pond and across the pallid summer grass.

Though the DA had already given her closing statement, the judge let her respond to this. She stood in her coordinated navy-blue skirt suit and said, "Such a tasteless suggestion about a young woman who was murdered with a rifle the defendant *planned* to use is not only defamatory but disparaging to her legacy. Young girls, emotional or misguided in whatever way, are not creatures to be relieved of life by merciful male discretion. Baby A Binderup was not an animal for Peter Martelli to study, diagnose, or treat. She was a person who spoke radically, yes, yet with hope that Peter would know mercy, and would know not to follow through with the evil Peter claims she asked him to perform. Ladies and gentlemen of the jury, there was no compassion in this crime. There was murder and a young man with a gun who thought he had the right to take something that wasn't his or anybody else's."

At the dismissal Pete's family raced out to hide miles and miles away at their deer lease—the place where all this dying had gone on.

Gram and Aunt Rachel got a big bucket of gumbo on the way home, not from the Shrimp Shack, and we ate it out of the container with plastic spoons in front of the clubhouse TV, watching episode after episode of *Jeopardy!*, none of us wagering any answers. Gull sat in my lap and picked out the okra. The bugs outside zzzed against the screen door as if to say we weren't alone.

Stray golf balls strewn across the course grew legs and walked themselves politely back to the ball machine. The truck revved its own engine. The moon rolled around the sky like a marble, back and forth. We saw none of this because trees were in the way. Or we saw none of this because we saw none of it. We were beginning to allow things to *be*, too wounded by all the fragments of happening we didn't understand. I just couldn't wrap my head around any of it, not Pete or my sister. In those two days after the trial ended and the jury was out, all I did was wonder what Pete had been thinking. That night, in my dreams, I knelt with hands out over the bayou, waiting for epiphany or a prophet to whiz up on a fishing boat. I stayed in that dream the whole night long, waiting, starving, and never really woke up.

Anyhow, the jury found Pete guilty of murder in the first degree, with deliberate premeditation and extreme atrocity or cruelty.

[ENTER] FRONT PORCH CHORUS

Somebody plays "Now the Day Is Over" on the church organ with the red doors wide open because, though the organist is playing, they've just treated the carpets. Tow trucks and school-teachers drive up and down Handover Street to save people. Oranges, strawberries, and pecans are sold on the roadside. Middle school kids walk out of gas stations with beef sticks and Dr Peppers, litter the plastic and tin in yards they walk past toward the VFW Hall, where they're going to watch a fistfight between two boys over a foul ball during PE. The pH in the bayou is still too high. In fact, it'll never go back to the way it was. Seeglow's has a sale on for paper towels and chicken thighs. Across town, every backyard is smoking with barbecue coals, and kids roller-skate up cobbled-together ramps. It is ninety-six degrees out, and it feels it. We stand in the yard to watch our children on those ramps, close enough to the back gate to flip the burgers or the corncobs or the flank steaks or the kebabs or the onions or the potatoes or the pork. See—we didn't stay the way we were. The day the Binderup girl died, it felt like we'd left the back gate open and woke to find she'd wandered out. And the day Pete Martelli went to jail felt no different. Our faces are made honest in this light. We can't say we love her because we don't, but we love our children, who she makes us think of. The whole place has felt all this while as if we've been in the audience at the community playhouse, come to watch a revival of *Annie Get Your Gun*, our child some chorus member, the red curtains hung very still with excitable whispers and commotion just beyond them, all the crowd quiet, on our best behavior and waiting, and waiting like this.

ISLAND BRIDGE

Patrons persisted in taking oranges from our tree, but it had started to feel as though they were stealing. They'd walk around the holes, gentle toward us as we paced about like fragile ghosts, then they'd follow through the same old backswings and sink their teeth into an orange as they sauntered to the next hole. They ate the rind. They wiped the sweat from their foreheads with the peels. They stowed stacks of fruit in their club bags. They used their polo shirts as baskets to hold the surplus. We didn't talk about it, but we shared a rising anger.

On a particularly stifling afternoon, one of Gull's favorite patrons passed a small orange to him, wordlessly. Gull took the round in his hands and unhinged his baby jaw, rolled his baby eyes into the back of his baby head, and screeched into the hereafter. He screeched and screeched. The patron supposed, in a panic, that Gull was frustrated that he couldn't open the orange, so he took the fruit and began to peel. Screeching, Gull snatched the orange back and squeezed it violently in his hands, which dripped with juice as Gull threw the fragments at a nearby ball. He then sank his hands into the man's golf bag to pull out the oranges he'd stowed to take home. Gull threw the fruits like hacky sacks, without aim, forcing them away. Gram saw this happen, and so did I, but we knew Gull needed that moment to be his and only his, so we watched. After he'd silenced the course with his screeching and throwing, Gull stopped screeching and walked away, hiding in a favored wooded spot behind the clubhouse until dinner. Most of the patrons didn't play through their next holes. They picked up their golf balls where they lay and left, quietly, out of confused respect for us as we rattled around so publicly inside that humid globe of hell.

We'd put off packing up our bedroom, limping past her belongings, shoving them under her bed, when eventually Gram showed up with liquor store boxes and Gull was stood in the corner of our room with a tape gun, ready to seal the cardboard shut. We had a donations pile and a storage pile. Gram urged us to be sparing in what we gave away because we might regret it later, but she didn't understand just how much of Baby A's we had. In things we had in tercets, like dresses and blouses or heavy coats, we donated one, usually the most tattered. We threw away her hairbrush, toothbrush, lip liner, and mangled bobby pins. We threw away the notes in her bedside table drawer, the Zippo Rich had given her. We threw away her childhood glasses and her retainer. Baby C kept the letterman jacket our sister had bought for three dollars at the thrift store, and I chose to keep her scuffed cowboy boots, not that we'd wear either.

The shriek of Gull's tape gun resounded in rhythmic repetition, and by the end we had three yard-work trash bags and four boxes filled. We dragged the bags to the curb and drove the boxes to the Catholic consignment shop. I wondered if the town would be able to tell whose clothes were on the racks. It seemed like one more thing to be on the lookout for; her clothes on other people, her flip-flops on their feet.

The evenings became pedantic. We folded laundry, watched television, tried to make soups from what we had in the pantry. Often Baby C and I found ourselves manically cleaning things with dishrags and harsh sprays. One night, with nothing else to do, we united forces to scrub the kitchen tiles with old toothbrushes on our hands and knees, hair pulled into messy lumps on top of our heads. We didn't have music on, like we would've a year before. And we didn't have the heart to chat in the useless, light ways we once had. Baby C sat back on her heels a moment and exhaled. I took this as a sign to get something off my chest.

"What would you do if I left?" I asked, still scrubbing the grout.

"I suppose we'd get along. Not much we could do to stop you, is there?"

"Sure there is. If you said no, then I'd stay."

She tilted her head and looked flatly at me. "You know we wouldn't do that."

"*You* wouldn't, but Gram sure might."

"Not now," she said. "Not anymore."

We let it get quiet again, Baby C still sitting on her heels, staring at the kitchen cabinets. "Would you miss it here?"

"Probably sometimes, like at holidays or tournament weekends. But it's starting to feel too small."

"You mean it's starting to feel like it's suffocating you?"

"Yeah. Would you come with me?"

"Somebody's gotta run this place and look after Gull."

"Gull will grow up," I said.

"He will?" she asked, seeming to mean it.

"Running this place isn't your dream," I reasoned. "The town would just build another golf course, or someone would buy it."

"Maybe it *is* my dream." Her voice became firm, edged with irritation. I put down the dull toothbrush and sat cross-legged to give her my full attention.

"How is that your dream?"

"My dream is for everything to be okay and for our people to not be so sad anymore. My dream is to want to be here. I used to imagine I'd never leave, and I liked that life I saw. Now I feel like the place is running us out like witches, and I want them to screw off and let me be okay staying." Tears started to pool in her eyes. "Why don't they want us anymore?" She asked with such sad confusion, it physically pulled in my gut. "We didn't do anything wrong, and it's like they can't stand to be near us."

"They're ignorant," I said.

"No. I think they're afraid. Of whatever it is we radiate. They'll never celebrate us, B. Not if we have weddings or babies or make big money. We're just scraps of our sister's disaster." She paused a moment to look up, then looked back at the tile.

"I guess I just wish I was strong enough to run away like you," she said, which stung, though she hadn't meant it as a slight. It stung because I was ashamed of myself for wanting nothing more than to desert them, to never come back. And worse, there was real glittering envy in my sister's voice. "If you went somewhere else, would you talk about us?"

"Of course."

"Would you talk about her?"

"I can't talk about us without talking about her."

She lingered on that and picked up her toothbrush, flitting it around the soapy bucket of water. "Do you feel like she's really gone, yet?"

"No."

"Me either. It's kind of fucked up."

"Yeah."

Then, in wordless tandem, we resumed our tile scrubbing, ever so often taking deep breaths or cracking stiff bones in our knees because we'd been postured by grief just like that, kneeling and bewildered, for months.

We had to wait for sixty-two days after the verdict for sentencing. February and March were cold and wet, full of canceled tee times, flooded roadways, flooded buildings. We stayed home, bundled up, unpretty and unprovoked. Gull stopped telling us what his friends talked about at lunch when he got home off the bus. We figured this was because their jokes became meaner and clearer to Gull.

"Are you going to make a statement?" Gram asked us across the dinner table. The district attorney had told her that impact statements help get longer sentences.

I wasn't sure I could give Pete any more of me, my attention or voice, so I shook my head. Gram looked to Baby C, who was spearing single corn kernels onto a prong of her fork. "I think I will," she said.

That night, lying on our beds, I asked Baby C what she'd say to the judge. She paused for a long while before saying, "I think I might just read the paper."

I rolled over to face her with a puzzled look, partially because she was farther from me than she'd ever been. We'd taken Baby A's bed out of the room and moved it into the toolshed, pushed Baby C's and my beds farther apart to make sense of the space. "I don't know why," she said. "That's just what feels right to do."

"Reports on the trial?" I asked.

"No," she said. "Just the paper."

Baby C and I wore the white lace dresses we'd gotten for Easter a few years back, which still fit. We wore the same shoes and socks, and put our hair in half ponytails. We stood in front of the bathroom mirror as we'd done the morning of the festival, ensuring that we were seamless, seismic echoes.

It felt surreal to walk inside the courtroom and to sit beside Gram and Baby C. We shook and sweated with nerves. Gram, consumed with anxiety, allowed us to hold her hands. The bailiff led Pete into the room through a side door, wrists shackled to his waist. In the white county jail jumpsuit with dirt rubbed along the ankles, Pete became the vision of what I'd known he was, the vision I was unable to create for myself, as all my memories held him in eternal summer light with bright teeth, almost beautiful. At the sight of him, I started to cry quiet tears of relief; the evil had finally shown itself.

As I cried, I tried to focus on the district attorney's heels, padded with bandages that peeked up from inside her shoes, intermittently wiping the water from my face.

The watchfulness of the crowd was heavy; neighbors, builders, next-town-overers with their eyes at the backs of our heads, whispering about our matching outfits, begging for a scene. Even though it was Pete who was guilty, I think we knew that good people who didn't know much better would hate us from that day on for taking their hometown star-boy away.

Gram cleared her raspy throat as she adjusted the microphone at the lectern, facing the judge. Said she'd forgive Pete someday, maybe, but not today or anytime soon. Said she didn't take joy in standing up there to ask for somebody else's baby to get locked up, but he'd taken hers in the worst way, so that's just what she'd have to do. I wondered if Murphy was on her mind.

Baby C walked up with that day's edition of the *Galveston Daily News* in her hand.

She'd flipped through the paper with a pen on the two-minute drive over. Her voice was a trill like the gentlest bug; I wished she'd have screamed. " 'It's Pisces season, March babies. In a time of uncertainty, dreams are more viable. Though all around have lost their heads, you are in a self-contained fog of personal aspiration. Be serene. Soon the naysayers and fearmongers will tire and the waters will part. Maintain the fish consciousness, "whatever," and know that what is yours will come to you. Gently lead.' "

Baby C closed the paper and turned her brave head toward the defense table, her back to the judge. "Pete," she began. "My sister was my barometer. She tested waters first before we got in, and now Baby B, Gull, and I are without. We don't believe you didn't know what you were doing, or who you were doing it to. I hope you are never fortunate again, and that the universe's grace toward you disappears today. Your honor"—she faced the judge—"these people can't even look at my sister and me anymore. We won't have lives if he ever gets out. We'll be haunted. Thank you."

The courtroom exhaled, shifted in their seats, and cracked their weary bones. A few minutes later, the judge cleared her throat and sentenced Peter Martelli to thirty to forty-five years at the Texas State Penitentiary in Huntsville, with the possibility of parole after twenty.

Aunt Rachel's fists balled up at her side, and Jason put his arms around his mother's shoulders, steering her toward the courtroom exit. I couldn't comprehend what twenty years, thirty years, forty-five meant; our sister's hourglass had shattered at nineteen with a life full enough to span a century. I shook the thoughts away, watched the bailiff lead a stoic Pete from the room as his mother wailed, clutching at the air as he receded. She turned wickedly toward us as we stood in a small collection in the aisle. "You!" she screamed, pointing at the group of us.

Aunt Rachel broke free of Jason's grip and moved in front of Baby C, me, and Gram, her arms outstretched to cover the breadth of us. I could see curses and venom pressing against Aunt Rachel's lips, all the awful things she wanted to make Mrs. Martelli see her son had done, but she just kept her arms across us, staring forcibly, holding Mrs. Martelli's gaze until the woman dropped her eyes and the men of the Martelli family put their arms around Pete's mother to pull her from the room. Our emotions told us they were awful, evil people. But when I looked at them, trying to see, I didn't know what they were. Maybe there wasn't a core that united them like the one that united us. Maybe they were just circling each other's orbits, wounding each other, tethered by overwhelming obligation. It scared me that Pete's family could love him so much—or whatever it was that compelled them—that they couldn't see the hole he had blown into the world, into my sister's head. Mr. Martelli, awful as he'd been on his own, had scrubbed my sister's blood from his son's shoes without even asking Pete what'd happened, out of pure instinct. He was fined a couple thousand dollars for obstruction, which amounted to nothing, and went to the police anyway. I decided that day that I would never have children.

We made it to the parking lot and stood numbly between the truck and Gram's car, Gull crouched down in the gravel, sifting through for smooth pebbles to skip across the bayou later. He hadn't been saying much, but he'd been helping. He helped with our bedroom and he helped Gram around the course, helped the volunteer Boy Scouts mark the scoreboard right on tournament weekends, and he helped with supper and cleaning up after. That seemed to be how he was speaking with us. Watching him sift through gravel with his bare, baby hands, I felt sorry we couldn't give him more than this loss-filled childhood. I wasn't convinced what was left for him was enough. The best of us was Jason, crouched next to Gull, aiding in the search.

Aunt Rachel and Uncle Henry asked if they could take us out to lunch. "No, honey," Gram exhaled. "We'd better not."

"You're right." Aunt Rachel was instantly disappointed in herself for suggesting we go anywhere but home, and especially that we spend this time with *them*. "We'll pick up chips and salsa on the way, then. At least let us make y'all dinner."

Gull looked up, hopefully. All any of us seemed to want to eat was Aunt Rachel's cooking. The soups we made from the pantry, the eggs we scrambled on the stove, any food cooked at the clubhouse, tasted wrong, so every couple of nights she'd bring over a lasagna or enchiladas that we'd eat straight out of the pan. We couldn't bear during the trial to go over to the Upchurch house on Casa Grande. Even though there were rumors that the Martellis were set to move to Dallas, nothing was concrete, and after the revelation that Pete was to serve his time just two hours away, we were sick, knowing they'd probably stay indefinitely.

Gram agreed to let Aunt Rachel pick up chips and salsa, agreeing also, albeit silently, to let the Upchurches sleep on the couch, take over the course chores, pop in on us whenever they wanted for the rest of ever. They were all the family we had, and they were in this with us, just as sad and devoid of understanding. As people passed us in the parking lot, the looks we got were a mix of pity and fear, like they were afraid what ailed us was contagious, like they could catch grief like a cold. Maybe it was that simple. Maybe that was why they'd rejected us all the while; we carried in us the grief of missing our mother, always had.

Baby C slipped her hand into mine, intertwined our fingers, and pulled me gently toward her. We still wore the matching white dresses, but I'd pulled my hair elastic out, and she held her shoes in her opposite hand. "We're going for a swim," she declared. They'd all been looking at us as they talked about food, staring at our void. When Baby C said this, Gram nodded. Aunt Rachel squirmed a bit, clearly with something to say that she pushed away. I moved toward Aunt Rachel with a hug, and she held me like she was holding her best friend again. At least, that's how I chose to see it. Gull poked at Baby C's bare toe with a pebble. "But the pH?" he said in earnest, and for the first time in weeks, we all laughed.

Instead of driving to the boat dock or stopping at the boat launch beside the church, Baby C drove our truck down the entirety of I-45 until it ended—Exit 1—at the seawall in Galveston, where no one would find us. She parked in the Walmart lot, the only Walmart for fifty miles that sold the right cleaner for our clubs and sod for the course. We'd made the drive once every few months, never thinking to swim these waters because we'd had our own. Baby C had thrown a mismatch of bikini components in the back seat before leaving for the courthouse that morning in some sort of premeditation. As we changed strategically inside the truck, my sister seemed almost happy. A weight had lifted from her shoulders that was still heavy on mine. Or maybe that was what I wanted to think—that the way I suffered was worse than anyone else's, that it was all mine. Fishermen stood along the shore, casting lines and reeling in nothing, casting big arcs of line out again. There were lifeguards at the beach; we'd have to decide just where we were going to stop, so they didn't whiz out on Jet Skis, trying to save us. As Baby C surveyed the water, we leaned against a guard stand.

"What now?" I asked.

She shaded her eyes with a hand, calculating distances in her head. "I guess now you run away like you want."

I looked out at the water, trying to see what she could see; the limits of this space, just how far we could go before they decided we'd crossed something. "I think I'll wait awhile."

"What for? If it's the right time, then it'll never come."

She began walking through the sand, so I followed. "What do you mean?"

"You either leave, or you stay. There's nothing to wait on anymore."

"It doesn't work like that," I said, trying to keep my voice down. "I could go whenever I want."

"That's what I'm saying. You won't want to."

"Maybe."

The world around us splashed.

"I asked my psychic if I'd find love again. She said, 'Not there.'"

"Then why would you want to stay?"

"I don't want love again. Not for a long time."

One of the fishermen yanked a catfish swiftly onto the sand and knelt over it, took pliers from his belt band, and twisted the hook from the catfish's mouth. The man put the fish in a nearby icebox. I realized I hadn't really watched anyone catch a fish before; I'd found myself half expecting the man to cut the fish's throat. After closing the icebox with his booted foot, the man rebaited the hook and cast his line back into the murky water, stood perfectly still, waiting.

"Do you hate yourself for fucking him?" Baby C asked.

I whipped my head away from the fisherman to face her. She was almost smiling. No—she was unafraid, and it settled in the lines of her face like joy. The veneer of caution that'd kept her timid had shattered with the sentencing, it seemed. I must've looked at her like she'd slapped me. Void of energy or ability to reckon in the ways she wanted, I reached down into the sand and pitched the biggest rock I found perfectly, beautifully, over the fishermen's casts. The plunk shattered the serenity their lines were depending upon. They looked back at me briefly and muttered a communal nothing.

"They want us to explain it," she said. "They think we know what she was thinking."

We took a moment to think about the place we'd grown up, how it had treated us and how it no longer felt like home. The novelty of "belonging" had evaporated for me. So had the kinship with our patrons, and any safety I'd felt in living on the golf course.

"It's not supposed to be the same place without her," I said. "It's completely changed."

"It doesn't feel like they changed with it."

"They have," I said. "Maybe they don't feel like they can say it to us."

"Maybe they'll name the festival after her."

We scoffed, trying to picture it in our minds. We assumed the town would need time to get past the trauma of the trial, losing Pete, to reaccept us into their fold.

"When you think of her, do you picture her alive?"

I shook my head *no*, but I knew that wasn't true. Baby A sparked inside of everything I did and saw and wanted and was and became. "I have to think of her riding around town," Baby C said, "on the longest errand."

We walked to the edge of the sand, then farther, until the water was just above our navels. I stretched my arms over my head, rolling at the rotator cuff, preparing to pull myself through time like a dog army-crawling across carpet. "Let's just go as far as we can," Baby C said. The truck keys dangled from her bikini top, clipped around the strap. I was already thinking about the drive home, passing over the island bridge, breaking through other towns to get closer and closer to ours. So my sister and I swam for as long as we could. Then we swam back. And before we dried off with towels in the Walmart lot, it began to pour, ponds of warm, heavy rain. Instead of a flash flood, this rain would stretch across the next two days. Flood the golf course. Flood dirt roads and highways. Flood the bayou so high that old tires and lost golf clubs washed onto the eighth hole. As we rode in our rickety truck through the downpour, a near-opaque sheet obfuscating our view, I trusted that Baby C would steer us through it. I knew that if I was behind the wheel, I could get us through it, too. But looking out the window, unable to see the exit signs or landmarks, headed home simply by feel, I became amazed that water evaporates. That one day, all this rain can flood the highway so badly that people pull over and turn their hazards on, sit on the shoulders for hours, and the next, it's gone somewhere, supposedly lifted up and dissipated. And we know, amazingly, the water will come back again as rain, heavy and bewildering, and will eventually leave in just the same natural way.

ACKNOWLEDGMENTS

Infinite gratitude and admiration are owed to my agent, Elizabeth Pratt, whose fierce belief in the heart of this story propelled me through—hers are the shoulders this novel stands upon. I am equally indebted to my editor, Edie Astley, who has loved these characters from the beginning, and hemmed in these pages with elegance. Thank you to the teams at Park & Fine, Trellis, and HarperCollins for lending their resources, support, and wisdom.

I have received immense and selfless investment from the faculty and staff of various public educational institutions, including and especially Christine Butterworth-McDermott and John McDermott, Jill McCorkle, Eduardo C. Corral, Dorianne Laux, Joseph Millar, Barbara Bennet, Faith Rice-Mills, Megan Thompson, and Hayley Booth.

Heartfelt thanks to my friends, early readers, and ardent champions Jenna Smith, Amber Cloud, Hannah Tumlinson, Abbey Bernier, Michaela Booker, Jessica Simmons, and Rachel Hiles.

To the writers who lift me up with their luminous work and fellowship—Melanie Tafejian, Ariel Kaplowitz Hahn, Josh Tvrdy, Mackensie Pless, Jessica Dionne, Alex Webster, Jaclyn Grimm, Laura Rosenthal, Emily Townsend, and Lauren Jeter—it is an honor to work beside you.

This book is for my parents, Paige and Jay Hill. It is the privilege of my life to be their child, to have been raised with love and imagination at the center of my world. And to my brothers Otto and Jackson; the most fun I have ever had has been with them, stalking through woods in pursuit of critters or each other.

The love of my husband, Zachary, who supports me completely, and our darling dog, Bark Ruffalo, who curled warmly by my side as I wrote most of these words, anchored me throughout the writing process.

A final thank-you to readers of this book; I cherish you.

ABOUT THE AUTHOR

TENNESSEE HILL holds an MFA from North Carolina State University. Her work has been featured in *Poetry* magazine, *Best New Poets*, *Southern Humanities Review*, *Adroit Journal*, *Arkansas International*, and elsewhere. She is a native of South Texas, where she still lives and teaches with her husband and their dog.